POWER OF THE CROWN

POWER OF THE CROWN

SPACE DARLINGS SERIES
VOL. III

B. L. DANIELS

authorHOUSE®

AuthorHouse™
1663 Liberty Drive
Bloomington, IN 47403
www.authorhouse.com
Phone: 1-800-839-8640

First published by AuthorHouse   09/13/2011

ISBN: 978-1-4670-2846-2 (sc)
ISBN: 978-1-4670-2845-5 (hc)
ISBN: 978-1-4670-2844-8 (ebk)

Library of Congress Control Number: 2011916196

Printed in the United States of America

Dedication

This book is dedicated to friends and family who have encouraged and aided me in reaching the point of publishing my writings. Along my way there have been and are special people who stand out. Alva Underwood is one such person. She is a special friend who helped me take my first steps in writing the Space Darling Series. David Michael Fanshier, my son, is my computer guru, proof reader, and positive cheerleader. Shawn Fanshier read, proofed and critiqued my first novel and made suggestions. My mother Harriet Daniels encouraged me many years ago to keep on writing. In her honor I chose to use my maiden name (B. L. Daniels) for this series. My friend, fellow traveler, and college roommate Virginia Kraft is still in my corner cheering me onward. My husband Donald Phillips, who is my idea and sounding board, is always helpful and positive.

Prologue

"That was quite a party, Lori," said Gladriel as she undressed. Her beautiful almond toned body was trim and well structured. She ran her fingers through her black silky hair after she slipped into a rose leisure romper and put her uniform through the cleanser. She looked at blonde vivacious Lori, her best friend and partner in Space Exploration, who was still wearing the gray uniform of the Space Military.

"I'll say. I never expected the Blatherians to be so rowdy. I didn't think they drank much, other than water. 'Wow' they were putting away the fruit juice," said Lori as she removed her jacket and straightened her knit top. Her fair skin and Nordic features were visible in her 6'2" frame. She checked her image in the mirror and shook her golden hair.

"So tomorrow we leave. Wally is quite a fellow," said Lt. Colonel Gladriel.

"He was so wrapped up in hugging you with his eight arms; even his wife had to help him get untangled. I think he forgot he's going to see more of us before we all get back to Glather. I'm sure he took a lock of your hair, Glady."

"I know he did. Look here," she pointed at her scalp revealing an irregular cut of her black softly curling hair. "He cut it off."

"Wonder why he'd do such a thing?"

"Did he ask for anything from you?"

"Yep, I gave him a kiss. He blushed. Then he turned a reddish purple color. After which I gave him my time piece."

"You gave him your own watch?"

"He gave it to his wife as a going away present. I think it made her feel better to think of the time we spent in her and Wally's world."

"What do you mean, 'going away' present?"

"He's going with us to meet Sheffield's and your family on Acuman and then back to Glather."

"Now, more than ever, I wonder why he wants a lock of my hair."

"I have no idea, Glady. Maybe he forgot we were going away from Blather with him. Maybe he drank too much fruit juice. You wait and see. You ask him. Are you packed and ready for tomorrow? I've packed my clothes and Sheffield's too. He's having a crew member take it over to our ship. Oh, for your info, Redford will be in charge. Fergus will be the pilot."

"Fergus is piloting our star cruiser?" She instantly thought how he had found her on Gloriel and saved her from being killed by Bwhari, her father, before he knew he was her father. She was still adjusting to this startling discovery. She really owed a great deal to Fergus. She smiled as she thought of Fergus in his work clothes and unshaven face. He always looked like a rough and dirty old cowboy.

"He's been reinstated, in a way. He is now our personal pilot and protector. He is so proud he saved you. You won't recognize him. He's in an Academy uniform. He's cleaned up and shaved too. This is according to Redford."

"That is unbelievable. Well, I'm impressed." She finished loading items into her luggage and set it outside the door to join the other two for pickup and delivery.

"Do you want to sleep here tonight or on our ship?" asked Colonel Lori.

"I'm going to eat supper and sleep on our ship. Redford is preparing my favorite dinner tonight. So I'll eat with Fergus and Wally, why don't you join us?"

"I'd like to be two people tonight. I'm on duty and standby as Admiral Sheffield's aide-de-camp. No doubt we'll have a private dinner and sleep here. I'll see you in the morning. I'll let Redford know when we're coming. I'm sure Sheffield will have a bundle of things to do. I'm supposed to keep him informed of any problems."

"Okay, I'll tell you good night and head over," she said as she kissed and hugged Lori goodnight. "See you tomorrow." She hurried out to take the flyer to *The Empolo*.

Lori sat down. She smiled as she picked up her median tea and her techno-diary of Gladriel and her first assignment. It seemed so long ago. She turned it on and let herself slip into the work.

Chapter 1

The first thing she remembered from her first official day on their own star cruiser was the ship's silvery tones flooding the ship as it spoke. "Welcome, Spacer Lori, I am your ship. I am designed to collect and store any and all data. I provide for entertainment and mental stimulation, meals, sanitation, ships' guidance and engineering? So, my job is routine, though demanding. I'm merely a ship." His voice had taken on a martyred tone as he finished.

She shook her golden locks and laughed as she turned to face the chromium surface which masked only one percent of his circuitry. "You are more than a ship. I have thought of a name for you—Redford. How do you like the name?"

"It is an exceptionally good name. Thank you, Spacer Lori."

"You may call me Lori and my partner is named Gladriel or Glady."

"These are wonderful names too. I regret this is not an exciting assignment. All you women have to do is find and dismantle a THRAX unit. Central Glather expects nothing out of the ordinary. For countless centuries nothing unusual has been reported from this sector. I had hoped for more." His voice sounded melodramatic as if he was a woman on stage tragically throwing her head back and touching her forehead with the back of her right hand saying dramatically. "Oh, the stigma of it all. How will I cope with the knowledge this operation was 'unimpressive? I won't be able to hold up my circuits."

"I'll be happy to erase your memory when we return, if you still fear the stigma will be too great for you to bear," countered Lori. She was enjoying Redford. He wasn't like some of the 'stuffy overall' ship brains she'd worked with before. She was glad she'd tried a few new ideas in programming.

Before Redford could respond, Gladriel, the third member of the party, spoke up. "I'd be happy to erase your memory, anytime. In fact, I think we could manage the whole trip without your aid."

His circuits blazed in furious activity, yet Redford's voice serenely responded. "I never said anything about wanting to be shut down or wiped clean. I am quite capable of withstanding any ridicule." A tone of confidence blended with his now softened voice as he addressed Gladriel. "And I thought you enjoyed my company even more than my advice."

Gladriel laughed, "Not necessarily, Redford, not necessarily." Only to herself would she admit she was finding him interesting. Still she had difficulty dealing with some of his humanlike qualities. Especially irksome were the wolf whistles and sly remarks.

"Now, my sweet ladies, it is time to sleep, perchance to dream," he said as a way of reminding them it was time to enter their cocoons."

Gladriel smiled at his words. She had caught the old Shakespearian remark. Lori must have added some literary files. Perhaps, too many things had been added to Redford. She was particularly unhappy with the whistles she heard when she stepped out of the cleansing chamber. Lori never seemed to have it happen to her or at least she'd never mentioned it. Gladriel wondered how Lori had programmed him and made a mental note to ask, as soon as they were out of range of Redford's snooping sensors.

"Do you have further instructions?" he asked.

Lori looked at Gladriel who shook her head no. "Redford, we are ready. Did you remember to double check the calculations on fuel consumption?"

"I can assure you everything has been checked, packed, stored and numbered as ordered."

"Well done, Redford. Have you reconsidered joining us in person?" teased Lori.

For a moment Gladriel feared he might have found a way. She could imagine his constant barrage of altruisms and gossipy chatter.

A touch of sorrow and longing echoed in his voice, "Alas, I must remain where I am, even though I might enjoy the change of scenery." He paused briefly before continuing. "I have tasks to perform. You will earn all the glory, while I serve. Although there is no sacrifice too great for me to make, I can assure you I'll continue working while you ladies sleep."

The two young Spacers shook their heads in comical bemusement at his answer. He certainly enjoyed his dramatic martyrdom.

Slowly two slabs with deep beds fully extended into the chamber. Lori looked nervously around. There was nothing requiring her attention. Lori, an extrovert, paid no attention to Gladriel who was shyly unsealing her single-pieced mouse gray colored uniform. Lori simply ripped hers off and flung it aside revealing her nude full figured golden body. She was quite tall over 6'2" and her muscles were toned. Her beautiful deep blue eyes highlighted a Nordic influence on her face. Her nose was narrow and not overly large and her wide forehead ended in a thick covering of golden hair which was hanging in soft waves over her upper torso. She glanced over at Gladriel who was now nude and trying to cover her body. It was then Lori heard a wolf whistle split the air. It must be Redford. She shook her head no. Redford had not complied with her orders and hadn't stopped his bad behavior.

Gladriel, meanwhile, was fighting back angry words and tried to steady the shake of her hands as she took her helmet from its chamber. She tried to twist her ebony black hair into a bun and cover it with her helmet. Her brown eyes were moist with tears and the corners of her mouth showed tension. The whistle, as well as her own tenseness, at the thought of entering the cocoon sleeper showed in her voice. She climbed onto the slab and jammed the helmet tighter on her head and adjusted the visor. She was ready. Impatiently she called to Lori, "Are

3

you ready?" She had avoided looking in Lori's direction. On Phisman no one saw another nude. Such an act would be an invasion of privacy.

Lori glanced in Glady's direction and noted her almond color and fidgeting. "I'm ready. Redford, you may tuck us in for our nap," ordered Lori.

"I shall gently cradle you in the arms of love," he answered.

Gladriel, forgetting her shyness, turned, flipped up her visor and yelled at Lori, "This has gone too far! Couldn't you have programmed a compu-ship which would tend to business? This one sounds like a hot potato wanting butter."

"Relax, Gladdy, Redford was only teasing. Once we're in orbit, he'll be all business," she said soothingly. She mumbled, hoping Redford could hear her, "He better be."

"Ok, Lori, I'm ready," Gladriel said with a touch of doubt showing in her voice.

"Give me a few more minutes, Redford. My hair doesn't want to stay in this tiny bonnet," said Lori as she clutched at two elusive golden strands. "I always feel I'm being sealed in a glass tomb when I get into a cocoon. Why couldn't it have more room?" She peered up at the waiting cover never quite sure it would hold her statuesque body.

Gladriel laughed, "There's plenty of room in mine. I'm only 5'7", not a six foot something golden giant. Stop you fidgeting." Although she didn't dare to look at Lori, she said reassuringly, "Your hair is fine. We're ready now, Redford."

"Very well," his voice dropped several levels in pitch as the chamber filled. "I shall awaken you when breakfast is served. Sleep well."

As each awaited her cocoon, many thoughts reeled through their minds. Uppermost was their concern of doing a good job.

Trying to hide her inner fears of being in a tight place, Lori called cheerily to Gladriel. "Even though I hate this part, I'm so excited I can hardly wait. My mind is whirling. I love the feel of adventure and action." Lori arranged her body precisely on the slab, as it conformed to her body lines. She waited for the chime which indicated she was aligned.

Several seconds passed before Gladriel answered. "I'm trying not to think about it. Remember Redmond told us, 'all you have to do is wait.' Then he told us, 'Relax, trust me.'" She quoted him sarcastically.

When both were positioned correctly, a chime sounded. Wide metal straps slipped across their shoulders and upper torso and their thighs. They were secured and immobile in their respective chambers. Two clear body covers lowered from the ceiling and settled over them. The chamber grew silent. A bluish mist rushed to fill the entire contoured cylinders. Silently it wrapped around their young bodies drawing them into a wintry sleep. Gladriel's dark eyelashes fluttered fitfully. Finally she lost the struggle and succumbed to sleep.

Lori was more reluctant to give way to slumber. Her black eyelashes were like captured butterflies. They fluttered and beat against her cheeks. Once she opened her eyes and measured the limits of her crystal prison. Soon she surrendered.

Chapter 2

A number of jumps later, as well as several weeks' passage, Redford settled *The EmPolo* into orbit around a class M planet. He carried out a series of orders as programmed. Then he turned his attention to his charges. Soon the ship was restored to proper oxygen and temperature levels.

While Redford busied himself exchanging tidbits of gossip and news from various channels, one part of him kept constant surveillance on the two cocoons. Shortly both chambers showed signs of internal change, indicating the women's wintry rest was reversing properly. A visual check showed the clearing of the blue mist and a gradual return of color to the two who still slumbered. The wintry look faded from arms and legs. Lori's golden complexion became richer, Gladriel's toasty olive tones returned. The awakening continued.

At the end of the third hour, Redford awakened Gladriel with a sweet gentle whisper, "Good morning, sweet Gladriel."

Cautiously she opened her eyes and found herself staring into the last fading series of lights which played almost musically over her inert body. She blinked and sought to move. Her arms were still bound by the straps. She relaxed and closed her eyes momentarily. Roused once more by Redford's second call she tried to reply, however, her mouth was dry. All she could manage was a faint croak.

"Don't try to talk now, Gladriel. You are a bit dehydrated. I have released the straps, and you may sit up. I must caution you to sit up slowly and carefully."

It was impossible for her to ask him the questions which had rushed across her mind as she awoke. Instead she inched her torso into a sitting position. Across from her she could see a slowly awakening Lori stretch free of her straps. Gladriel got to her feet and found Redford was correct. She was a bit unsteady. She leaned for support against the slab.

"Gladriel, you will find liquid refreshment waiting for you on the servo-tray. Please sip it slowly." He turned his attention to rousing Lori who was still groggy. Soon he had her up and on her feet too.

"Ladies, your apparel awaits and your breakfast is ready. I would advise you to tend to this as soon as possible. There is much to do," warned Redford in his most motherly voice.

Lori smiled at his concern, how unlike a computer he was. In fact, he had personality. While the women finished sipping their juice, Redford routinely informed them all was well. *The EmPolo* was in orbit and he was awaiting their command.

After dressing in coveralls and heavy slippers they were ready to eat. The juice had restored flexibility to dry throats and Lori was awake enough to tease Gladriel and Redford.

This teasing didn't sit well with Glady. It wasn't until after she had eaten she spoke to Lori. "Lori, I want to apologize for my lack of courtesy. My sleep has left me with an unsettled feeling as though something was wrong. I don't know why. It's a nagging feeling. It's as if I put the wrong shoe on each foot and each somehow still managed to fit. Speaking of which, Redford, my left ear is sore. Could I have been pinched in my chamber?"

"No, Gladriel, you were well within the limits and tolerance of the contour."

"Are you all right, Glady?" queried Lori.

Gladriel cupped her hand over her ear and held it for a second, and then shrugged. "I suppose so. We need an update and a little assurance this trip isn't a dud. You know some missions have been dry runs."

"Glady, why would you say it's a dud? You helped me research the information on the missing THRAX unit. Relax. Like the ancient saying goes, 'Nothing ventured, nothing gained.' This is going to be as easy as taking our frosty naps. Now relax and stay positive."

"If I may have your attention, ladies, my report is ready." Since there was no response to the contrary, he continued, "We are orbiting a class M planet with an atmosphere almost identical to old Earth's atmosphere. It's definitely breathable. The planet has . . ." His voice droned on for several minutes. Abruptly he stopped. "Ladies, I feel I don't have your full attention. Shall I repeat my report?" he asked curtly.

"Oh, no, Redford, we have confidence in your skills. We're sure you have checked everything. Besides, if there were anything unusual you'd have told us," said Lori as she spoke with confidence and authority which seemed to pacify him. After all, she thought, he is partially my creation and I know what he can do.

"I think he's put us in orbit so he can reestablish communications with the other compu-ships. You know how 'lonesome' he gets," taunted Gladriel.

"I do not!" Redford sharply responded.

"Cut it out, both of you. You're like little children. Glady, Redford is efficient and does an excellent job. So, please, Gladriel let him do it. I don't know why you woke up grumpier than an old dog. You must have slept with some lousy nightmares to be acting like this. Remember, you put information into his system the same as I did. So, let him do his job. Now, Redford, do not respond to her verbal jibes. You are sensitive. On top of this Redford I want you to stop baiting Gladriel. Consider this an order. No more wolf whistles or hoots, or whatever sound you can come up with to tease her. Do you understand me?"

"Yes, Sir, heard and obeyed."

Gladriel looked at Lori for a moment. So she did hear those sounds after all. At least the knowledge was reassuring.

"Are you all right, Glady?"

"I'm fine, thank you. Redford, give me a report on the planet's surface." She smiled as she waited.

"Broad areas of the planet are covered with thick blankets of clouds. It is composed of three large continents and a number of large islands. The land is covered with vast forested areas.

One continent is largely a humid jungle. Another continent, which is partially visible now, shows a registry of life and a variety of terrain and climate and vegetation. My systems indicate this planet life is quite active. Also I have picked up residual traces of radiation, of the type common to THRAX units. My initial survey has been verified by two specific scanning's of the planet. This convinces me the unit is on the equatorial continent. Any of four locations could hold the missing unit. However, I have selected the most likely target. It is close to the other areas. The second most likely target seems to be fractionized, coming from a settlement. The life form reading does not indicate massive population although it registers humanoid. To avoid encounters with the alien life form, I have selected a small clearing within the proper distance as regulated by the Council. As further precautions I have checked your blood for immunization needs and you are both okay."

Redford continued, "If all goes well, the first location should be the site. Therefore the mission could be a mere fraction of an hours work. Once you locate and dismantled the unit, load it on your flyer *The Flynn* and return here. I believe a dawn descent will be the most favorable and should be unobserved. I have prepared maps for each of you. They show the areas of population and the four major spots of concentrated radiation. You will land around 10 miles from the nearest settlement. Do you require further information?"

"Sounds good to me, Redford," said Lori as she stroked his gleaming chrome surface.

"Stop it, Lori," Gladriel said with disgust. "You act as though he were a pet. He's only a machine."

"To some he's a machine, to others he's more," laughed Lori. She pulled her field equipment out of the storage bin. "I need to get dressed, Glady. Got to get into my new outfit" said Lori as she went to her bedroom storage chamber.

"What outfit?"

"Wait a few minutes and I'll be out." She laughed gaily.

"What can she be doing? Do you know, Redford?"

"I can't really say. Bedrooms are off limits to me and my grid. It's the privacy thing. Do you have everything packed and ready to go, Gladriel?"

"I sure do." She sat down and waited for Lori. Suddenly she thought of their first meeting. It had occurred during her first year at the Academy, when she was fifteen. Through some strange twist of fate they had been assigned to the same wing group. Surprisingly to everyone, they were able to understand and enjoy the company and personality of the other. Previously they had each been loners. Now they were a balanced duo. They were capable of chasing and catching the others thoughts. Gladriel thought about the nights they had laughed over some small mischief or idea until morning arrived.

Glady thought of their different personalities in particular. Lori was actively vocal. She almost always questioned the instructors on what they were teaching. She wanted to know the why of everything. Nothing was ever static to her. Gladriel, on the other hand, was quiet. She listened intently, categorized things and assimilated information. She spoke only when it was required of her. Mentally she laughed as she remembered how Margline, their flight instructor and wing commander had called them "a team of contrasts." Gladriel thought of the differences in appearance. Lori was golden honey to her own permanent summer tan. Temperamentally they were different too. Yes, she had to admit they were definitely opposites. Lori was filled with beaming optimism while Gladriel hovered on the darker side of reality. Yet, they had found themselves able to communicate on a level never possible to either one before.

When they met it was as if each had finally found the missing piece of her own jigsaw puzzle. At first neither had been sure the friendship would be solid enough to build on. They soon discovered it was firm from the beginning.

"World to Glady, what are you smiling about, Gladriel?" asked Lori as she entered the room wearing a startling outfit. "How do you like it, Glady? I have one for you too. These are unique uniforms. The cloth is impervious to sharp objects or projectiles, it is light weight yet keeps the body cool when hot and warm when cold. The jacket flares over the hips allowing for a belt which has loops for all kinds of things. The boots are to protect us while traveling over rough or dangerous terrain are impervious to rain. I know they are tall. Mine go over the knee. Yours aren't as long; however, I think these black boots look sharp and feel comfortable. Go get dressed, Glady. I hope you like the outfit. There is also a skin suit which should add comfort and use as an outfit if necessary. You'll notice the outfit is in the Academy gray and the hat is regulation for dress. I checked these through Margline and she thought the material and ideas were great. So I splurged. Happy birthday, Happy New Year, Happy everything!"

Gladriel was astonished. The outfit looked great on Lori still she wasn't sure it was the right thing for her. "Lori, I d—"

"Now, try it on. I know it will fit."

"How do you know this?"

"I took a hologram of you and sent it to the tailor. So please, try it on?"

"Oh, okay. Now if it looks bad you have to let me know." She disappeared into her bedroom and shortly returned. She was beaming when she came out. "Lori, I never thought I'd look this good in a uniform and the boots are stunning and ever so comfortable. This outfit is perfect." She ran over to Lori and hugged her. "Thanks so much." She hugged her again.

Lori spoke up, "I hope this turns out to be the best and quickest mission of our senior year."

"We were almost late getting it to the Academic Department. We chose the simple and most dangerous task of dismantling a THRAX unit."

Lori told Glady, "It'll be a snap."

"But, Lori, it requires six more months of additional training." The course made it seem it was an easy senior test, although they'd never heard of anyone who'd dismantled a THRAX. Redford reassured them later it was possible.

Lori chuckled softly when she thought of the mild ribbing a couple of the other cadets had given them over their 'easy adventure.' In a way she feared it would be too easy. Personally she hoped there would be some challenge, however, 'easy' was fine for a regulation graduation exercise.

During the five weeks following graduation most of the new junior officers had left by two's and three's. It was almost a year before they had finished outfitting *The EmPolo* and its flyer. During this time Lori had worked constantly to update and improve Redford's programming. Together they had carefully planned each step of the mission, spending hours researching the unit's dispersal and the methods of dismantling. Now Gladriel wondered why she should feel uneasy. It had to be a form of stage fright or first mission jitters, she thought.

A distinct noise drew Gladriel's attention back to the present. She saw Lori packing some items in her jacket pockets. Then she saw her strap on a blaster.

"Where did you find the weapon, Lori?"

"These are government issue for hazardous voyages." Lori handed Gladriel her weapon and some emergency rations and a beamer for night time use. Then she picked up two canteens filled with water and two packets containing water purification tablets. She handed a packet and a canteen to Glady, "Drink plenty of water before we leave the ship. Do we have the camping gear ready, Redford?"

"It's already in *The Flynn* as are the protection beams, which I hope you won't need. I've also included three scanners, one for each of you and a larger unit for the camp site. I've checked the list of supplies twice and sent you each an extra outfit of clothing, in case you need it."

They got onto *The Flynn*. Lori took the con. Her mind refreshed the facts about the THRAX. A number of these had been inserted on scout flyers, as well, as on colony ships. Their purpose was to explore the galaxy and collect data, and then relay it back to the home base. Unfortunately in the last century it was discovered the units could become lethal and unstable. A number had already imploded. Destruction could be avoided only by dismantling the unit. She thought, 'It'll be a quick easy job and home again and a real space assignment.'

"Check list, Glady?"

"Done, we are ready to leave *The EmPolo*." She sat down and buckled up. "All set."

12

As Lori adjusted a mini-scanner to check the surface for any sources of radiant energy she turned the volume down on the voice channel. She streamed the recorder feeding information into the small computer. On their first swing around the planet, Lori checked the immediate area of the proposed landing site. It was clean.

Lori's work was interrupted when she heard Gladriel speaking anxiously to Redford.

"Redford, one of the gauges is malfunctioning."

Lori turned to Gladriel, "Give it a good thump it often helps."

Glady made a fist and hit it hard. "It worked. Thanks, Lori."

Lori turned back to her console.

"Can you still hear us, Redford?" asked Glady.

"Somewhat, unfortunately I have some surface interference. It is gone now. One last reminder: Remember to check in on time. I'll worry if you don't."

"We can handle it, Redford. We're big enough to be on our own," Gladriel gave a sigh of relief as she switched off the intercom.

Lori maneuvered *The Flynn* through the dense upper cloud layer and was amazed at the selected site. "Look, Glady this is an area of deep underbrush and almost impenetrable jungle."

"Let's check out the next landing site," suggested Gladriel.

The flyer approach took them over a mountainous area fronted by a large yellow capped mountain. This area was totally barren and quite forbidding. It loomed over the brackish swamp land which lay to the west of it. A steep cliff separated the flat upper land from the denser jungle below. Holding to the rim of the cliff, Lori guided *The Flynn* to a small clearing below the cliffs and south and west of the yellow topped mountain and the swamp. She slowly descended and hovered over the area while Lori scanned the immediate area. Lori gently settled the ship onto the grass.

"Isn't this interesting? Think of it Glady, we may possible be the first non-humans to touch this planet. Doesn't it send chills up and down your spine?" rattled Lori in a storm of words.

"It's exciting to be sure. Have you finish scanning the vicinity? I must give Redford a call." Gladriel was impatient with Lori's excessively enthusiastic attitude and the loss of contact with Redford.

Lori opened the doorway and lowered the ramp. She took two steps and paused then flashed the life-form identi-unit left and right. She carefully covered the deep green vegetation of the jungle which faced her. There were no signs of animal life. Suddenly a hissing rattle came from her left. She turned. It was difficult to distinguish one plant from another. She aimed her scanner. It was then the movement of a tall willowy green sapling caught her eye. As she watched it, it extended finger-like lacy soft green fronds which were spreading over a slate gray boulder. Gently the fronds caressed the rock. Again the hissing rattle filed the air.

Lori's excitement was too great to be contained when she saw what was happening. She hollered, "Glady! Get out here! You've got to see this."

Gladriel swiveled away from her controls. "Have you finished checking the area?"

"This is an order, you have to come out here and see this now! Checking can wait. A green fern like tree is eating a gray rock, right before my eyes. Hurry!"

"Lori, this is no time for jokes. Get back to work."

"Spacer Gladriel report here immediately. It's an order," screamed Lori.

Reluctantly Glady pulled away from her work and walked to the doorway. "Have you lost your mind? I have things to do."

"Glady, look over there," said Lori as she pointed at the quivering green plant which held the rock in its embrace.

"Oh, my, it really is eating the boulder. Are you getting vids of it?"

"Of course I am. Remember seeing is better than a recorded oral report."

"Lori, we can't leave *The Flynn* until we know more about this thing."

"I don't really want to blast it and I'm afraid it could dissolve the ship or damage it. I certainly don't want to harm it. What do you suggest, Glady?"

"Let's hold off from destroying it. I'm curious too. It's finished. That was amazingly fast."

They watched as it majestically stood upright and grandly swept its fronds around itself before gliding away.

Gladriel was stunned. "Did I see what I thought I saw? She looked to Lori for confirmation.

"It is amazing. How can a plant walk?" Lori asked. Lori studied the plant as it moved into the jungle. She learned nothing more from observation. Neither had expected anything like this.

Lori fretted, "How do we explain this? It looks like a plant or something similar to plants in coloring and foliage. Its behavior is not like a plant I've ever heard of or seen. My multi-unit life reading says plant. Their planet's lines of evolution must be unique. Contact Redford, Glady. He may have an idea or two."

"I've been trying to do more research before we saw this creature. I'm sorry I was so rude, Lori. You were right. I had to see it to believe it." Glady tried once more contacting to Redford, instead static hummed on the line. "It looks like we're on our own. I feel it. Do we need to explore this area more thoroughly?" she asked a subdued Lori.

"I was for moving out, now . . ." Lori turned and walked back into the flyer. Gladriel followed close behind her. Lori shut the door.

Chapter 3

They finished up their written records and put on their blasters and sheathed their machetes.

"Do we have any plant spray, Lori?"

"No. I don't think anyone thought of moving plants." She laughed.

"Well, it is time for us to go out and meet the planet. We've left messages for Redford and orders for the flyer to elevate itself once we leave the area and report back to Redford. Hopefully he can send it back again to find us."

"The part about the ship leaving worries me, Glady. It can hover; however, we shouldn't go too far the first trip out. Honestly I think we're in the wrong spot. It doesn't feel or look right. I'd like to try another location. Let's explore here."

"Okay. I'll order the ship to hover high enough to protect it and shelter us later."

Once down they opened the hatch and descended. The view of the edge of the jungle chilled them. Beyond the edges of the multi-unit's scanner field stood three more willowy things. Each had its fronds folded around itself, yet appeared to be swaying slowly in a nonexistent breeze. The sudden rush of movement from the largest plant caught both their attention. With an umbrella-like movement its fronds formed themselves into a huge green blossom four times as big as the stalk. The creature advanced toward the ship. When it reached the bottom edge of the ramp it stopped.

"OH," gasped Gladriel and took a step back.

Lori pushed past her and moved quickly down the ramp. She stopped within a foot of the plant.

The umbrella blossom held for a moment, and then it relaxed, letting the fronds droop from its crown. From their mass of leaves one feathery frond slowly edged forward and touched Lori. Gently it explored the contours of her body. After a bit of time it wrapped several feathery appendages around her arm and sought to pull her closer. She didn't yield. Another frond reached forward to stroke her hair.

Slowly Lori reached out and touched the branches which hung limply before her. The plant retraced its fronds tightly around its trunk and retreated to its companions at the jungle's edge.

"What made you touch it, Lori?"

"I don't know. Curiosity was probably my reason."

"It could have killed you as you stood there. I was frightened for you. Standing behind you like I was I couldn't have gotten a shot in to save you. It wasn't a smart move, Lori."

"Please don't lecture me, Gladriel. No harm was done. Say did you manage to any message from Redford when you called him?"

"How did you know I called again?

"I heard you mumbling something. So I figured you were communicating our situation."

"Well, my wrist communicator doesn't work any better than the console. All I got was static. He never reported any communication problems due to natural forces on this planet. Did you find anything to account for the plant life on your tapes?

"No, I didn't. I should have listened more to Redford when he gave us his report. I guess I was too excited about the trip to really listen."

"I felt the same excitement." No reproach came from Glady. They both had been caught up in the excitement of their first mission to demand more information from Redford. Fortunately their first encounter with an alien world thus far, had not led to any injury.

"The outfits are now changing colors to blend in with the terrain. This advantage should help. Now I need some tonal for my face so we don't shine out in the green world. Is yours handy, Gladriel?"

Glady dug around in her pocket and pulled out a tube and handed it to Lori.

When Lori was finished adding the mixture on her face she put some tonal on Glady's face. Then she unhooked her gloves from her belt and slipped her hands inside her gloves.

Glady handed her a machete and a copy of the map Redford had prepared for their trek.

They moved away from the flyer setting a course for the first red dot Redford had marked on their maps. Their entry into the dense jungle led them close to the three plants which appeared to be sleeping. The women hurried past.

As they pushed deeper into the forested area they found themselves confronted by huge palm-like structures and dense heavy trunks which often barred their way. They worked around these; unfortunately they were forced to slice their way through lush thick underbrush. Periodically Lori stopped to check for signs of animal live, while Gladriel recorded a visual of their movement.

Several hours into their journey Gladriel recorded her first oral report.

> "Day 1: 8-01. We have left *The Flynn* and are traveling in a southwesterly direction. It is difficult because the underbrush is so thick we have to cut our way through. This continent, as Redford said in initial discovery is covered with a variety of tropical plant forms, particularly tall primeval plants which resemble palms and ferns. Their color is a basic green, though the shades appear to vary with the specie. The tree-like trunks are foliated with short stubby outcroppings from base to crown. The sunlight penetrates deep enough into the thick jungle to produce heat and light enough to feed the masses of low growing plants."

She paused to take a drink of water then reminded Lori to do the same.

Lori paused and checked her map. They were making good time. "Glady, let's set up more guidance buttons so we can return to the flyer along this same trail if we have to return sooner. I know it will close in a couple of days; still it could be useful too. I marked up to here. Can you do the rest of the way while you narrate and record?"

"I sure can, Lori. Do you want to narrate while I hack through the jungle?"

"You're doing a good job. I'll trade places with you the next break, okay?"

Glady nodded and turned on the recorder.

"An occasional ball-like structure with orange fringed petals can be seen hanging from tall palms. Perhaps it's a blossom or a parasite. At this point we have not met any aggressive specie other than a willowy sapling which digested a boulder as we watched. In a personal contact with Lori, it was not aggressive, although it did posture aggression as it advanced to meet us. At least it was my interpretation. I taped the encounter for further study by the bio department. Generally the plants are deep Kelly-green or lime green with touches of red or orange near the tops.

As a note of interest, we have not seen nor heard any animal life. We may be unable to reach our first designated campsite as scheduled because the jungle is so dense. We are forced to travel slowly.

She put away her recorders and joined Lori who was investigating an area of sparse plant growth. From beneath a tangle of spikes and tangled roots Lori pulled something out of the ground.

Lori looked up at Gladriel then spoke, "I have definite proof of human habitation, at least one time human habitation." She handed Gladriel the femur she held and dragged several more bones from their shallow grave. "It can't have happened long ago. No more than a few weeks in this climate. My readings indicate they are the bones of human females." She handed Glady the femur she held and dragged several more bones from their shallow grave.

Gladriel took her spectrometer from her pack and further scanned the bones. "This large section is a pelvic girdle and the femur is from a young adolescent female under fifteen. The skull you're now holding is from a woman of about twenty-five."

"I wonder what happed. Curious, isn't it? Both are women. We had better be extremely cautious," said Lori as she studied her map. "There's a large settlement not far from here on the secondary grid. Perhaps the two are related."

"Redford told us the population was humanoid; these bones say definitely human. Something is wrong."

"You aren't suggesting we go to the settlement are you, Glady?"

"No, we shouldn't go there. Besides, its ten miles further than our initial destination. We've taken tapes of my readings and your bone fragments, there's nothing more we can do here."

"Yes," Lori said and then added, "We'd better move on while being more cautious. You might be right about this senior test being tougher than I thought." Lori now was taking their task more seriously. "Gladriel, something is definitely wrong here. Somehow this planet isn't quite right. I don't think it's where we're supposed to be."

They took up their struggle through the dense jungle again. Lori led. She cut a passage through the increasingly thick leaves and branches. Gladriel followed. From time-to-time Lori was sure she saw a walking plant or two, sadly the thick vegetation did not afford any clear view through the shadow blocked jungle. Within the next hour Lori was forced to stop twice because Gladriel could not keep up the pace. The second time they stopped, Lori watched as Glady paused and kicked at a large lump of dirt. It rolled over with a kick from the toe of her boot. At first Lori thought Gladriel was tired. Then she saw her pick up a stick or limb protruding from the underbrush. She realized Glady was searching for bones. When Gladriel lagged behind a third time, Lori stopped, went back where Glady was and hacked out a small area where they could sit down. She handed Glady a food bar. "What's bothering you, Glady?"

"Those bones weren't in any grave and the site wasn't even marked. It appears as if the women were dumped there. Why do you suppose they were left on the edge of a clearing?"

"There could be any number of possibilities I can think of," said Lori. "First they may have been on a journey and were killed by highwaymen. Second they could have been some sacrifice to some unknown deity. Thirdly they could be runaways who became ill and simply died here or got caught and killed. We may never know. At this point in our travels we don't have the time or supplies to find out. Set it aside and let's go on. Remember we have a mission," Lori gave Glady a good long hub. "Let's get moving, okay?"

"Lori, I think the mission may be more than we can handle. I don't remember hearing or reading of any records of human habitation here. Surely Redford would have said something. Speaking of Redford I've called him two more times since we found the bones. He doesn't respond. I'm still recording and sending, though we may not know if he receives these. I don't think both his equipment and ours could be malfunctioning," she grumbled.

This planet may be difficult to reach because of the THRAX unit being so close. It could be anything. Perhaps there's metal in the ground. Whatever it is he is trying to contact us. I can guarantee this. I don't have any more answers than you do. I have questions, sitting here isn't going to get them answered. Cheer up. Think of this as an adventure."

"You and your damned optimism, make me sick. We have problems and you want me to ignore them. Our problems began on *The Empolo*. We didn't listen carefully to Redford's reports. I suspect, if we had, we might expect fewer surprises."

"Perhaps we would, Glady, and again, perhaps not. We don't have the time or the expertise to discuss this properly. We still have a few hours of daylight left. Let's go on." Lori stood and stretched. She pulled Gladriel to her feet. "How about having a bit more to eat? I have a few pieces of dried fruit in my pack." She dug into her pack and pulled out two long strips of dried fruit and handed one to Glady. They ate the strips and drank plenty of water before setting off again.

Their trek continued until dusk forced them to camp. By this time most of Lori's natural cheerfulness had returned. She swept the area clear of vegetation while Gladriel taped new plants and worked on her log. Next she set up the perimeter field which would shield the camp from any unexpected visitors. When finished she watched while Gladriel took a bearing on their and Redford's location. They discovered they were five miles closer to the first site. Gladriel tried to contact Redford, who should have been passing overhead at the time. She received no response. The strain of the day and the loss of contact place a drain upon her mind.

Lori walked over and touched Gladriel's shoulder. She felt the tightness of her muscles. Lori massaged Glady's neck and back. "Think, Glady, maybe he can hear us, even though we can't hear him. Did you get anything this time?"

"No, I didn't," growled Gladriel, as she replaced her communicator.

"Most likely he's covering us. Let's hope he can monitor us anyway. Don't worry. Relax."

"You tell me not to worry, to relax. You can't mean it. He never mentioned those green walking rock eaters, the human bones and this almost impenetrable jungle. Were any of this on the scanners?" Before Lori could answer Glady continued. No! And what's more—this 'snap' is beginning to be a big 'stretch.'"

Lori kept rubbing her neck and shoulders and sought to reassure her. She could hear fatigue coated with fear and anger building in Gladriel's voice. "I don't know the answers. I can only tell you what I do know. It could be a malfunction in our equipment or maybe radiation shielding on this planet. His final instruction was to call in to him. We did. Tomorrow things will be different. If he's malfunctioning he could have himself repaired by then. He's a sophisticated machine capable of doing anything. In fact, it's his strength."

"I don't doubt you believe he's smart, if he is then why hasn't he corrected the situation by now?"

"I don't honestly know. I'll guarantee you he is trying right now. He is quite competent."

"I know this fact," said Gladriel. "I know you don't know any more than I do and I don't mean to push you." Gladriel turned her eyes upward, "You know, Lori, I miss the rascal's voice. Right now I'd settle for a chauvinistic joke, if only to hear his speak.

Lori laughter and their tension eased. "I could, in a pinch tell you one."

"No, thank you."

"I programmed in a couple of joke packs for variety. He seems to like those. Since Redford is known to eaves drop he's probably learned dozens more. I wonder how many he knows. Don't you enjoy his voice when he wants to be charming of when he's giving information? It almost sends shivers and good bumps over me. I doubt any other ship has a sentient compu-ship with a male ego. Perhaps I've stumbled onto something new."

"Stumbled is right. Where did he get the whining voice?" Lori shrugged she didn't know. Gladriel continued, "This discussion is leading nowhere, as far as our present situation is concerned." It was then Gladriel noted Lori had shaken out both sleepers and had dug out the food concentrates. "Thanks for breaking trail today. The combination of the vegetation and those bones disturbed me. I'm so exhausted I really want to sleep. Should one of us set up and guard?"

"The perimeters should keep anything out. Say, Glady, aren't you going to eat?" Lori held out a package to Gladriel. "I'm starved. Redford told us to eat regularly. Now take this and eat."

Gladriel took the package reluctantly. She watched as Lori tore hers open and took a big bite from the chewable bar. Lori chewed noisily for some time.

Gladriel laughed. "You're eating of a food bar makes me think you're devouring a roast. Why did you chew it? It can be swallowed with a lot less trouble.

"I know, however, I'm pretending I'm eating a five-course meal." Lori replied cheerily, putting the other half in her mouth.

Gladriel bit into her food bar and grimaced. She tried to swallow a big bite. "Yuck! A pellet is a pellet is a pellet. I can't make believe."

"It's filling," Lori said and swallowed her last food bar bite.

Night shadows swiftly replace the fading mottled glow of sunset. In the twilight the women settled their sleepers. Gladriel twisted around to get comfortable and pulled her sleeper over her head and soon dozed off. Lori sat hunched in hers one end was draped over her shoulders and the other was pulled around her waist. She peered out into the gathering night at the jungle which lay mysteriously beyond the safety perimeters which glowed dimly around the camp. She could see nothing, yet she felt something or someone was observing the camp. She looked into the darkening sky and watched the approach of stars made visible in the moonless night. Giving a shrug of her shoulders, she pulled out an illuminated game cube from her personal belt and began a game of solitary. Sometime later she joined her companion in sleep.

Chapter 4

Dawn broke the dark night, but not the silence surrounding the camp. Had they been awake they might have seen the silent green sentries fade from the edge of the clearing and disappear into the jungle. Lazy banners of red and orange streamed across the sky and drifted south. Their passage marked the full rising of the sun.

Gladriel awoke instantly. After spending a restless night dreaming of dancing skeletons and walking monsters, she was staring into a patch of pale blue sky edged in white clouds. She couldn't comprehend her location for a moment. To her right was a grey lump which breathed rhythmically. It was Lori. Somehow she had managed to roll into a pile of equipment during the night. Gladriel smiled. The fact it was daylight made her feel alert and ready. She brushed away the fading remnants of her dreams and stood up. Once up and moving, she felt calmer and happier than she had last night. Now she felt able to cope with the fact there were humans on the planet. Today she could handle it. Shrugging off the last of her troubled thoughts, she set about preparing Median tea, Lori's and her favorite drink.

While the tea steeped she went to awaken Lori. Now she discovered Lori laying half in and half out her sleeper. One booted leg was exposed while her head was tightly held under the top of the sleeper. Gladriel bent to touch Lori's shoulder when the game cube caught her attention. She picked it up, gave it a half twist clockwise, and then rotated the counter a full turn backwards, and placed it where it had lain. Moving to the other side of Lori, she reached over and thumped her on the covered top of her head.

"Is it time to get up?" Lori asked through a yawn.

"Yes, it's full daylight time now. We should have been moving before now. Get up sleepy-head.

Lori stretched, yawned again, and untangled her legs from the sleeper. I smell Median tea. You must be feeling better."

"Somewhat, still the warmth of the tea is so nice in the morning. It may make up for whatever we'll encounter today. We have water enough for two days. We could look for a stream." She looked at the half wakened Lori, a golden Aphrodite basking in the morning sunlight in a beam of radiance from a hole in the tree coverage. A halo framed her head. Gladriel smiled.

"What?" Lori asked.

"Nothing new" I was admiring a beautiful picture. Your hair is like molten gold in the sun. Are you ready for today?"

"I'm ready for anything," Lori said and she walked around the perimeter stretching her arms overhead and doing knee bends and lunges. She was awake now and the jungle seemed to come alive.

A soft breeze rustled playfully among the upper branches while the crisp sounds of moving leaves and chattering intrigued the women. Once Lori was sure she'd heard a distinct noise. Quickly the sound disappeared and she began to doubt she'd heard anything.

The two women squatted before the prism, sipping their red tea and chewing on concentrated wafers. It took them less than two minutes to finish their breakfast and pack up their equipment. They were cautious. Before removing the perimeters they took a long look at the area.

"Did you hear anything, Glady?"

"I thought I did; now I'm not sure."

"It's probably the breeze through the leaves.

"You are such a damned optimist, Lori." Gladriel took out her disruptor and held it ready. Lori switched off the perimeter, collected the poles into a bundle and folded the tent into a compact square and placed these all in her bag.

They shouldered their packs. Before they had gone far, Gladriel was urging Lori to walk faster. From behind them came loud cries, each one distinct and even closer. The earth shook. There was no denying the voices now. The women hurried even more. It was almost upon them when they turned.

"Blasts of Hades!" shouted Lori as she pulled out her blaster.

"Watch out, Lori!" screamed Glady.

The creature towered over them by more than ten feet. It resembled a plant in coloring and had leafy green fronds which looked like wings. It swarmed with undulating pencil-thin tendrils. Some formed the pads serving as feet. Perched precariously on top was a fuzzy yellow and orange ball which resembled a smaller porcupine plant they had seen fleeing them yesterday. The massive creature clutched a small sapling to its midsection. The shrill loud screams emanated from the captured plant which thrashed wildly.

Only for a moment were they stunned. Gladriel decided it was better to get out of its path and shouted. "Run, Lori. Two directions will confuse it!"

Lori grabbed hold of Gladriel's arm and pulled her out of the thick underbrush. "That could even be more dangerous. Take positions left and right still stay in the clearing as much as you can."

"It's not slowing!" screamed Glady.

"We'll have to kill it. Shoot for its head."

"It doesn't have a head!"

"Go for the fuzzy ball!" ordered Lori as she concentrated on shooting off a leg and foot.

Gladriel aimed for the top knot and fired three short rapid bursts into the fuzzy crown, neatly separating it from the trunk. Shortly the top knot tumbled to the ground.

The creature, now devoid of two limbs and the top knot stumbled and released the sapling which tottered rapidly into the jungle and collapsed.

The creature rebuilt its limbs from more small tendrils and charged again.

Gladriel fired a series of shots vertically as the creature neared her.

Lori fired horizontally cutting off the new foot and a leg.

Gladriel fired a second series of vertical shots which cut the remaining portion of the creature into two sections which fell apart like a peeled banana. Mustard colored liquid burst outward and collected into a number of lemony pools about the creature. Two more shots reduced it to charred remains.

Satisfied it was dead Gladriel joined Lori who knelt over the quivering sapling. Gently Lori stroked its fronds. She turned each one over to see if it had suffered more damage. The plant palpitated as if it was breathing.

Glady knelt beside the creature and ran her medical scanner over it. There were no patterns for the creature, although what she could read did correspond closely to the scan Lori had taken of the small trees near the flyer yesterday.

A twig snapped. Glady jumped. "Lori, let's get out of here. Where there's one there may be more."

"No, Not until I rescan this plant. I need to make an adjustment or two." She adjusted several settings and then pointed it at the sapling. "After all, I many never get another chance to collect such fascinating data." Lori scanned the full length of the main trunk. Her readings were confusing. She placed her hand, palm down, on the spot where she hoped the creature's brain might be, if it had one. The trembling ceased. Amazed she felt a temperature change in her hand. The plant had grown warmer.

It was then Glady heard another sound. It wasn't from the trail they had freshly cut. She spun around.

"Don't shoot!" Lori shouted as Gladriel brought her disruptor to waist level.

Shuffling into the clearing were two creatures identical to those at the flyer. They advance with waving fronds. The downed sapling uttered a rattling burp, and the fronds lowered their branches slightly and advanced even faster.

"Lori, get away from the creature!" screamed Gladriel as she moved to cover her.

Lori was on her feet and moved over to Gladriel's side. Both women stepped back from the little sapling, yet held their weapons ready.

A sound like captured bees in a jar emanated from the injured plant; this seemed to reassure the two who had glided to its side. Each extended fronds which the downed sapling grasped. The two pulled the smaller one to its feet. Now all three turned to face the women, and advanced.

As the plants advanced the women retreated. Almost at the jungle's edge Lori touched Gladriel's arm. "Don't fire. They didn't harm us yesterday. I don't think they will now. Stand still," Lori ordered.

Gladriel moved back reflexively and tugged at Lori's left arm. "Lori, these can't be the same ones! Get back here!"

"How do you know?"

"I don't know, and you don't know if they are either."

Lori had noted the creatures stopped moving while she and Gladriel were talking, and continued when they stopped. This spoke of intelligence or curiosity. Lori grasped Gladriel and held her still. "We have to find out sooner or later. If they were going to hurt us, they'd have done it the first time."

By now the plants were so close they could touch the women. Gingerly, as though doubtful of contact, a frond stretched forth and touched Gladriel's hair and face. Its touch was cool smooth and light. Its questioning leaves explored her head, chest and arms. Satisfied it turned to Lori and repeated its actions. Finished, it extended a frond to its companion and hummed. The second creature repeated the touching, and then lingered over the face and hair. While these two investigated the smaller plant hummed steadily

Once satisfied, the plants swayed around and moved across the clearing, taking the young plant with them. Silently they disappeared into the thick jungle.

Gladriel released a pent up sigh. Lori swallowed several times to moisten her dry mouth before speaking. "I wonder what it was all about."

"Beats me," said Gladriel as she retrieved their packs.

"What have we gotten into? Margline's report led us to believe this planet was relatively free of living creatures. I don't remember any information on these creatures on Redford's scanner tapes," mused Lori who seemed to be talking to no one in particular.

"I think we were overly eager. We could have been suckered in too. If you recall, Margline kept hinting the assignment wasn't right for us.

"Oh, I took it as her way of making sure we'd take it. Are you suggesting we weren't told the whole truth about this planet? It could be a part of our training?"

"Oh, I don't know what I'm suggesting, Lori. Let's log these events and move on.

Chapter 5

They made good progress for a time. Each took turns hacking a trail through the dense underbrush. Their spirits lifted. From a distance, across a shallow stream where they had stopped to rest, they saw another creature, only smaller, than the one they'd killed. It did not appear to notice them. When it moved on they went to the water's edge. Lori took a sample and ran tests.

Gladriel anxious to wash up had taken a cloth from her bag to begin the process when Lori informed her there were traces of caustic chemicals in the water and some radiation.

Lori ran some more tests. "Glady, it is undrinkable and unsafe for skin contact."

"In simple words, I can't drink or take a bath in it. What good is it?"

Lori smiled and shrugged her shoulders. "No good to or for us. This isn't a safe planet or at least not this portion."

Glady took another reading on their location. "We're approximately three miles from site one."

"Then we'd better camp for the night and finish tomorrow," said Lori. "Let's find a spot not close to a 'waterhole' for the vegetable community. We still have a couple of hours of light."

They continued on for another half hour and found a small clearing where they set up camp. In the day light left to them, they collect and recorded various plants and rocks. Lori handled the vegetation and Gladriel tested for minerals and soil fertility.

When it became too dark to continue, they retreated inside the perimeters and activated them. Routinely they ate their evening rations took a few sips of water and curled up in their sleepers. Evening wrapped the night with a blazing display of stars. The women lay on their backs, gazing heavenward, and enjoying the spectacular show.

"Lori" said Gladriel as she broke the magic spell of silence.

"Yes?"

"I've been thinking."

"About what?"

"Several things have come to mind. One: Why didn't Redford warn us about the denseness of the vegetation? Two: Why did Margline tell us the planet was uninhabited, when it was? Three: Do you think Redford can hear the reports I'm sending? Four—"

"Hold on, Glady. Redford's viewers might not have shown either of the creatures or the humans. He told us there were humanoid beings here. Plants do not register as creatures. Remember we are having trouble with our scanner. So it may not be his problem; it's ours. You're right about Margline. She did not tell us about humans or creatures. Thinking back this doesn't seem to be the planet she described for us to retrieve a THRAX unit. There is the strong possibility there is one here. We may know more tomorrow. We need to check the coordinates when we get back to the ship. This is your job."

"Lori, there are many questions and few answers."

"True, do you want to turn back now?"

"Not now. We'll soon be finished. Besides, I'm not a quitter. If we have to go a few more days here, we can. So far, we've been able to handle the situations we've met. If we keep going, we might learn more about this planet and have some good stuff to take back. Agreed?"

"I'm with you all the way," answered Lori as she smiled up at the sky. She knew Gladriel was a scrapper when she met her. This verified her first impression.

She continued to watch the stars for some time before she heard the sound, like someone slipping over rocks in their bare feet. She listened intently, straining to catch it all. Softly she called to Gladriel, "Listen, Glady."

"Hum—"

"We have visitors." She heard Gladriel rouse. "Don't move Glady. Look to your right."

Silhouetted above them were three green plants.

"Guardians?" asked Glady.

"They're either guardians or guards. Good night Glady." Lori rolled over and pulled the sleeper to her chin. She wondered if the creatures, or others like them, had stood around their camp last night. She heard the slow steady breathing of her companion and allowed sleep to settle into her own mind and body.

Chapter 6

The intercom rang. Lori picked up the receiver, "Colonel Lori speaking."

"I'm going to be a bit late. Can you see to my luggage?"

"Already done and sent. Gladriel's over there now. I'm going to go with you, whenever it works out. Have you eaten?"

"No."

"May I order in dinner and snacks for you and the staff?"

"That will be great. I'll see you as soon as I can."

"Is there anything else?"

"No. I'll call you if I need anything else, Colonel Lori."

She thought, 'It must be something serious.' She ordered meals and beverages for the staff plus snacks. She also ordered her dinner and drinks. While she waited she brewed some more tea and waited. Dinner wasn't long in coming. She ate then set her pot of Median tea beside her on the table along with her cup and picked up her techno-diary and continued to read of Gladriel and her first mission.

*   *   *

In the afternoon they arrived in the immediate area of the first site. Suddenly the terrain changed and the jungle thinned out. The ground cover was replaced by shoulder high globular plants. The women recognized them, having passed through a small patch earlier in the day.

"Have you noticed the area around each is stripped clean? It's bare dirt. I judge the patch extends for several acres. Would

34

you think these might be voracious eaters, judging by what we saw yesterday?" Gladriel asked as the two of them stood on a rise looking out across the patch.

"They don't appear active, at the moment. Let's investigate one. We could—"

"Lori, record the data."

"Glady, think of the value-"

"We don't have the time to give each unknown we meet a thorough investigation. If we did we'd be here for centuries. Let's find the THRAX and dismantle the unit and head out of here." Gladriel felt uneasy again. Although the globes were passive, she saw slight movements among the leaves. This indicated to her the plants were quite aware of the women's passage among them. "Besides, we don't have extra supplies for dallying along the way. I sure don't want to try eating any of the things we've seen. Even the water is tainted." She ran her hand around the collar of her skin suit. "I feel as if I were in a giant sauna."

"Be thankful there are no insects," said Lori as she wiped her sweating forehead. "I find this surprising."

They continued forward through the patch. Each monitored their progress by their hand held scanners. They hoped they would soon locate the unit for the reading was strong.

Lori stopped, "Did you hear anything?"

From their positions half way up the small hill they could see the jungle's edge for several yards. A medium sized globe near Lori shuddered and retracted its leave into itself.

"Did you touch it?" asked Gladriel.

"No, I don't think so." Lori turned to survey their route through the patch. "Look," she said as she pointed. Each plant they had passed by was drawn into a tight green bulb. Their path was clearly mapped by bright green bulbs.

Gladriel's scanner chimed softly twice indicating it had detected metal. "There, Lori, look to your left. It could be the unit?"

"It might be—" Lori grabbed Gladriel's arm and pulled her down behind a large closed bulb.

A short stocky young blonde man, of eighteen or twenty years emerged from the forest. He wore a simple richly embroidered tunic. He wasn't armed, as far as they could see. Once he stopped and stamped the toe of his left sandal on the ground, probably to remove a pebble. They noted his confident stride as he carefully worked his way to the mound on their right.

They watched him in silence. He was unaware of them. They noticed he avoided the plants which held their green petals in an open lotus position. He appeared to be looking for something. He stopped frequently to stare at a hand held drawing checking it for something.

Ten yards into the patch he stopped. Directly facing him was a plant taller than he. Its pods were partially open exposing an orange interior. Within, cilia beat and swayed rhythmically. He stared at it. He slowly circled it. Three wiry filaments from a nearby plant whipped out lashing at his ankles. He screamed. Before either woman could rise or run to his aid he slapped himself free of the tentacles. They watched as he darted toward the mount in the center of the patch. A second plant struck him hitting him waist high. He screamed and fell.

In seconds the women were at his side. They raked the area with disruptor fire. Plants turned themselves inside out when they were hit. The plant which had slashed at the man withered under their fire.

In the confusion, the man crawled into the mound.

The women cut their fire when they heard him shout. They looked up He was standing in a doorway. They began to approach him; however, he frantically waved them back. When he yelled again they realized they couldn't understand what he was saying.

"Is he speaking ancient Sol" We learned forms of it in Basic linguistic!" exclaimed Lori.

The man stopped his frantic actions and stood watching them. When he made no further motions, Lori suggested they retreat. They promptly did so. They only went to the edge of the forest. He turned and entered the mound. In a few minutes he appeared carrying a long rod with a hook on one end. He went to each plant they had killed and probed among the burnt vegetation.

When he spoke to them again they were able to understand him. "Go away! This is forbidden territory to women!" He ignored Lori's questions about his wounds and continued looking among the burnt vegetation.

One nearby plant opened. Lori raised her disruptor to fire.

"Stop!" he screamed. "Get away. These flaggets are forbidden to you."

"Are you all right?" Lori asked.

"Yes, you shouldn't have killed so many."

"They were attacking you," countered Glady.

"They were not. They reacted because women were present. Now go away. Leave this area."

The women stood their ground. Lori watched him, while Gladriel replaced her disruptor on her belt and scanned the huge vine encased mound. Because they did not move he ignored them and continued his search.

Each inspection brought him closer to them. Lori began looking at the plants near her. Almost all had curled up. She watched one too large to cover its interior. Some of its leaves had unrolled. By now the man was close. It may have sensed him for it whipped out filaments toward him.

Lori acted quickly and fired, searing its outer edges. When the smoke died away she could see the crown-shaped boney ring inside untouched by the beam. She stepped forward to examine it.

The young man shoved her aside so quickly and unexpectedly she lost her balance and fell.

"Don't touch! I told you this area is forbidden to women. Leave now and I won't report you."

Lori stood up and brushed off the dirt from her clothes. "I wasn't going to touch it. Besides, the thing's dead and can't harm us now."

She watched him insert the hooked end of the rod into the charred remains and lift out the crown. What the women had believed was dead glowed bright red as it came out of the plant. Once the crown was free he turned toward the women.

"Lord Ameral will be angry. You women have trespassed." For the first time he looked at them. "I don't know either of you. What village are you from?"

"I'm Lori and this is Glady. What is your name?"

"I'm Jeames. How did you happen to be here? Have you been cast out?"

"Cast out? I don't understand this. Please explain what you mean by 'cast out'?" Lori was sure Glady was recording their conversation.

"Come," he ordered, "we must leave this area. I have a crown now. So I am a man. Come."

Still curious, they followed him. Holding the rod level before them he led them to the jungle's edge where he pointed to a grassy hammock. "Prepare me a place to sit." When neither moved, he commanded again, "Prepare me a place."

"I don't know what he wants, Lori, you keep him busy and I'll check the mound." Gladriel turned and walked away.

"What did you say, you with the dark hair?"

"She said for me to help you," Lori spoke up and smiled.

"Then do as I command."

Lori looked around wondering what she was expected to do. She finally trampled a small area and sat down. Deliberately turning her back on Gladriel she sat down on the flattened place and patted it. "Sit, I'd like to know more about you. Sit, please."

"Where does the other woman go?"

"Oh, don't worry, she'll be all right. Please," said Lori as she reached for his hand.

"I shall want her later. Don't touch my crown!"

"I can assure you I won't. It is yours."

He jerked the rod up and away from her and in doing so caused the crown to slide down the rod and onto his hand. Almost instantaneously a change came over him. He filled out and straightened to his full height. After a moment he cast aside the rod and placed the shimmering crown on his head. His pale green eyes dilated; he breathed shallowly. He looked down at Lori. Slowly he lowered himself to the place she had indicated. Lori watched him. She was fascinated by the rapid changes in him.

When Gladriel was sure his attention was fully on Lori she moved back into the patch toward the mound. She felt confident Lori could handle the young man.

Now he faced her and sat comfortably on the ground. Lori watched him as he leaned back on his elbow and began stroking her boot. "Who are you? What village do to you belong to?" he voice was mellow and husky. She didn't answer him instead she smiled. "I would be sorry to learn you are condemned. Maybe you were sent to me." He rubbed his hand knowingly on her inner thigh.

Lori made no effort to remove his hand. In fact, she thought it felt nice, warm and comforting even through her uniform. He was close enough she could detect a musky odor and it excited her. She lay back on the ground beside him stirring the air. Briefly she wondered why she was enjoying this interaction with a stranger.

She asked, "Where do you live, Jeames? How did you come to be here?"

"That is a strange question to ask. I have never seen a woman who would not know. I like you," He leaned closer to her touching her breast. "You know I must prove myself. I did not dream I would get a crown and a woman so easily. The council did not tell me this."

"Oh, you mean the ring on your head."

"Yes," he touched the plant corona gently. "I shall accept you as my woman and one day I shall be a Lord." He leaned over her even closer this time to touch her flushed cheek with the finger he had rubbed against the crown. Then he traced her chin and mouth, "A fine beautiful woman. Never have I heard of a Lord getting both a crown and a woman at the same time, still Lord Ameral says customs must change." His fingers continued their march down her throat to trace the outlines of her breasts.

Lori took his hand to control it. "What's this about a woman and a council?" Somehow she was losing control and her train of thought. A voice in her ear kept urging her to ask questions.

She wanted no part of questioning him. All she really wanted to do was to kiss and fondle him.

"Do not worry. Today I will become a man I have taken my first flagget and soon I shall take you as my first woman." He reached up and squeezed the rim of the crown and looked at her. He took it off and placed it so it circled her right breast. "When you become my woman," he said fingering the crown's velvet skin. "I will be deemed fit to rule, for I know we will have a son. It is the law." He paused, frowned slightly as a new thought intruded. "Do you belong to another man?"

She nodded her head no.

Then you are a free woman and I claim you. You will have a place of honor for as long as you serve me well." He picked up the crown and put it on his head. He leaned over and kissed her while holding the inner ring of the crown. It suddenly adhered to his head.

He knelt beside her and slowly undid her outfit baring her body. His kisses became more fervent. He pulled her to him and then laid her down. Softly and gently he touched her right breast and felt it fill his hand. He bent over and kissed it, and then sucked it firmly and she hardened. His right hand took her left breast and squeezed it gently while he continued to suck her right breast. Then he licked it with his tongue and flicked the end of her nipple, while continuing to massage and roll the nipple of the left breast.

Now she was arching her body toward him. Lori's breathing was more shallow and rapid. She wrapped her arms around his neck and pulled him closer. She kissed him deeply and let her tongue find its way into his mouth. She felt him harden and knew he wanted her as badly as she wanted him. Still they skirted on the edges of total passion.

He removed his robe and inserted his legs between her legs. He rubbed her body in soft circles and then harder around her nipples. Then he kissed her and she arched her body toward his and he kissed and then sucked each breast and let his tongue play with right breast and felt it hardened. Her hand reached to his manhood and he moved her hand away,

He wasn't ready yet. Jeames pulled his chest away from her and lifted her hips so these rested on his upper thighs. He pulled her to a sitting position and felt his passion build until he climaxed as he took his first pleasure with a woman. They never uncoupled. Then he lay back and she began to please herself as she moved in rhythm with him. Her body rocked him rhythmically.

Pleasure poured through her and she ignored the questions beating into her ear. Instead she wrapped her legs under him and pulled him tighter and she rode him to the heights of passion. Then she rolled slightly to one side and he was on top of her. She almost purred in delight. She felt an overwhelming desire to remain with him forever. They were unaware of anything except their passion.

As they built to a grand mutual passion Gladriel returned. Screaming and cursing she ran to them and pulled Jeames off Lori. Roughly she pushed him a few feet away. His crown fell from his head. He was too dazed to catch it.

In a rage she stepped on the crown, crushing it. For a moment she felt a weakness in her loins and a great desire for Jeames.

She rushed to Lori's side. "Lori," she shook her, "Lori, wake up." Out of the corners of her eyes she saw Jeames struggle to his knees. "Stop where you are, fellow." She booted him back to the ground where he lay quietly. "Make sure you stay where you are."

Lori was beginning to lose her dazed look. Gladriel shook her, and then slapped her cheeks gently.

"I'm okay, Glady."

"Sure seam up. Lover, over there, did a number on you." Gladriel squatted on her haunches waiting for Lori to regain her senses and fasten her suit. "Want to tell me what happened?"

"I don't know. He was talking about crowns, lords, women and things I didn't understand. I could only think about how much I wanted him. I still want him. I have never wanted anyone more in my life."

During the time they were talking, Jeames was regaining his composure. His movements caught Gladriel's attention. She turned to watch him. He looked around him, and then he ran his hands through the grass and sniffed them several times.

"Looking for this?" Gladriel asked. She stood up and pointed to the pieces of the crown slowly turning brown.

"My crown!" he screamed as he reached toward a piece of his crown, she lunged forward and grabbed his wrist, spinning him around. She bent his arm back up against his shoulder blade.

"Let me go! It's mine!" He yelled "Get your hands off me. You're only a woman."

Gladriel shoved him away from her. "Let's talk. Why are you here?"

He wouldn't look at her. When she kicked at his sandaled foot he sneered, "I don't answer women's questions."

Gladriel drew her disruptor and leveled it at him. "I suggest you answer my questions and fast."

Sensing how dangerous this woman was he swallowed and spoke. "I came to get a crown and I did. Now you destroyed it. This is my year. I was chosen. I didn't know there would be women here."

"Why would you want a crown so much you'd brave those horrid plants?"

Lori, still struggling to regain her senses, noted the terror in Jeames' voice as Gladriel tried to force answers from him. She saw Jeames was reluctant to answer questions from so violent and angry a woman. Even though Lori still felt spent she knew she should take over. She walked over to Gladriel and touched her arm gently to let her know she wanted to question the boy. Lori smiled at Jeames and sat down beside him. Her quiet and gentle manner disarmed him and he allowed her to elicit a number of answers. She touched his hand and held it.

Jeames told her his world had three settlements, all within a short distance of one another. The farthermost one was a ten day walk. Each of these villages contained a small number of men and several hundred women and children. Men in the villages were scarce. Since the men were set apart from the rest of society, they were the leaders and rulers. Once a man became a leader he established a household. But, in order to be a leader, a man must secure a crown. Then he must sire children and a son. Then he would be treated with respect and loved by those he ruled. Too, a crown established he was a Lord. And, as a Lord he was a protector, a ruler of women and a fertilizer. After many years the villages had prospered and increased in numbers. Soon, perhaps, even in Jeames' lifetime a new village would be established. He spoke of his dream of being declared a council member if such happened. The population of his settlement had been increasing steadily since before he had been sent to secure a crown. He wanted desperately to be chosen by the council to start a new village.

"What is a Council on your world, Jeames?

He lifted her hand to his lips and kissed it. Then he went on to explain, "The council is a group of several Lords once guided by the Rex. Recently it was led by Lord Ameral. The laws established were the laws for all the villages. The Rex, a kind man of advance years, still had the final authority. He did not live in Jeames' village but Lord Ameral frequently did. For several minutes, Jeames went on about the virtues and position of Lord Ameral. He truly admired the man."

Jeames willingly told about the initiation ceremony. He was being tested into the Fellowship of the Lords by Lord Ameral and his men. "It is the rule when a young man reaches his eighteenth season he would begin the testing. The culmination of the trials would occur sometime before he reached twenty seasons. Today Jeames had finished his trial.

Jeames grew excited as he explained when he returned with a crown he would be anointed Lord Jeames. In time ten available women would remain with him in his own household. They would be subject to his commands for their lifetimes. In addition, over the following seasons he, as a Lord, could add to his household a number of women each year until he reached an optimum number of one hundred.

Lori checked to see if the recorder was collecting properly for she knew without a doubt she and Gladriel had stumbled into an antiquated society requiring more study. Next she guided Jeames' remarks to the crowns.

"If not miss used and used properly," he said, "the crown will last for many seasons. Some say for perhaps a Lord's lifetime. I do not know of any Lord's crown lasting beyond a dozen seasons. The more mature the crown, the better the chances are for its longevity. No one knows why the crowns are so powerful, or how they function. Fortunately they give many powers to a man. Possession of the crown improves a Lord's ability to father many children. I hope to do the same. Those, who are not Lords, do not live many years.

Today Lord Ameral led me to this location and told me I had two days to find and secure two mature crowns. I have been blessed because I found such a mature crown. Now I will need to try again," he said bitterly as he looked at Gladriel." I cannot go to the meeting place and finish the ceremony nor will I become a Lord without it. In fact, if I do not secure the two I will be killed. You," he pointed at Glady, "have committed a sacrilege. You crushed my crown and interrupted fertilization." He sneered at her, "Lord Ameral will condemn you to death. I shall tell him what you did!"

"She didn't know of your culture and did not mean to interfere. Please forgive her," begged Lori."

"Gladriel, we need to help him get two crowns since you destroyed the one. I have never seen you in such a rage. If I didn't know you as well as I do I would say it was a jealous rage. Could it have been jealousy?"

"Don't be a fool, Lori. I suppose we can help him get two."

The patches are forbidden to women, only men are allowed to pick a crown," warned Jeames.

"Well, Lori" Gladriel shrugged and stood up. "What Jeames said was interesting. I don't believe his story for one minute." She was intently studying the horizon when sounds of a scuffle caught her attention. She turned in time to see Lori was pressing a hypo against' Jeames' right leg. Shortly he was asleep.

"I'm going to get some crowns." Lori picked up the hook and wandered into the patch. Shortly she returned with two. One big one with rainbow colors and one smaller one more subdued in color. She placed them both on Jeames' chest. I wish we could take him with us. Now he needs to prove his worth to this society. Let's keep an eye on him until he wakes up.

"Say, Glady what did you find in the mound?"

"It turned out to be a shuttle ship. I could recognize it although all the instruments and seats have been removed. I think someone took everything out. There's no THRAX unit there."

"Then we'll have to check out location two. Once he awakes and leaves."

Once he awoke and began his trek to where the men waited, the women followed him. They were surprised to find an actual path which they used to follow him. Once at the encampment of seven armed men, they settled into the shadows.

One tall over six foot mature blond man with broad shoulders and deep set eyes wore rugged clothing, leg wraps and a waist band which held a large knife rose to meet Jeames. The other men, when they saw Jeames, rose and gathered around him. They inspected the crowns and were careful not to touch either one. Each man patted Jeames on the shoulders offering congratulations. The one who had greeted him first took the hook and thrust the handle into the ground. They feasted and drank.

Jeames told of meeting a golden goddess who had encouraged him to select these particular crowns, promising Jeames he could fertilize her. He told them of the powerful weapons she carried and how he'd stopped her from destroying the patch.

The men laughed, while the bit blonde man studied the young man intently and asked several questions. The men toasted Jeames and ate heartily as did he. Then one of the men asked Jeames to model the big crown. Jeames obliged. He lifted the crown from the hook and set in on his head. The crown exuded its aroma. Suddenly the men stopped their laughter and stood swaying. Jeames was unaware of what was happening. Tugging at the leaf rope he'd used to secure the crown it bruised it further and it released more aroma and pheromones into the air. All stopped talking and a low moaning began. They circled him and tightened it until he was almost held up by the group. They began to tear his clothes from his body. They were going to rape him in their frenzy.

Suddenly the big husky blond grasped Jeames from behind and forced his arms tightly to his sides and pulled him from the circle.

"Stop!"

The men stepped back as both the man and Jeames' were sharing the Crown's pheromones.

"Is not this the lad, the young man who has won a crown? Is this not a new Lord—a fertilizer?"

"He's so young, Lord Ameral," said one man.

"Why couldn't one of us use his crown? Mine is not so fresh or as large," whined one older man.

"Yes, what about a new one for me, father?" asked Pall, the youngest member of the group and Lord Ameral's son.

"Jeames was now unconscious and had slid into a small heap in the center of the living circle. Ameral pulled his knife, bent over the lad, and grasped his hair. Ameral gave a quick jerk to the limp body and brought the boy to a kneeling position.

"What are you doing" asked a burly man with the scared cheek.

"My son deserves a new good crown." So saying Lord Ameral severed Jeames' throat with one stroke. Blood spurted forth, drenching many of the Lords. "You are now baptized to my cause. Now swear my son took the crowns from the flaggets and I shall see each of you receives a new crown." He released Jeames' hair and shoved the body to one side. The crown fell from his head. Pall grabbed it before it struck the ground.

Ameral stepped over the body "Swear by this knife, or I shall see none of you ever get another crown and the one you have now is taken from you."

The men knelt, each touching Ameral's knife. One asked, having some shred of conscience and courage asked, "Lord Ameral, why did you kill the boy? He had passed all the tests?"

"He was telling old women's tales. Who would believe a story about a golden goddess as big as I am?"

"That's true." said the whiner. All except one agreed, he lowered his head and remained quiet. No man wanted to dispute Ameral's words for they did not want to be accused of believing women's stories or stripped of power and position or killed.

Lori and Glady were stunned. Anger rose in Lori and she reached for her disruptor. Gladriel caught her arm and whispered, "No, Lori, I know what you feel. Remember we can't reveal ourselves. To kill these men will not do any good for Jeames. Besides, we'd be interrupting what might be a ritual for this society."

"He killed Jeames," Lori choked.

"Yes, I saw him do it, but, Lori, we can't interfere. We have a job to do. Best we retreat and set up camp. Let's rest here until they leave."

They heard pieces of conversation, "Who do you think the Council will select to replace the old Rex?

"I don't know. I do know Ameral really wants the title."

"That young lad reminds me of my son who died two seasons ago."

"I remember him, he was a good lad. I didn't go on his initiation trip. How . . ."

"What are we going to do with this one?" growled one man.

"Leave him. The jungle breeds death," said Pall.

The body was dragged to the clearing's edge after stripping it of all clothing and usable items. The men returned to the fire and had a couple more drinks before Ameral joined them.

The women slipped back into the partially forested area where they set up camp against the trunk of a large tree like plant. Gladriel tugged her sleeper from her pack and settled it comfortably around their shoulders. Lori snuggled closer, laying her head on Glady's shoulder. She sobbed quietly. For a long time they each dealt with their own thoughts and demons. Somehow before morning they settled their issues and slept.

Chapter 7

"We're not getting anywhere," said Gladriel. "We might as well check our maps and get on to the next location." She palmed the small area map, checked the coordinates of their location and then consulted her recorder. A distinct blink at H-7 put the reading within the confines of the settlement some eight miles away in a southwesterly direction.

"We can reach there by nightfall," said Lori as she leaned over her friend's shoulder to read the map. "Maybe we can locate the unit during the night. I'm wondering how they could keep it from blowing up this planet."

"I'd rather think of finding it soon. I really hope it's easy to find when we get to the settlement."

"Probably it's a decoration. Maybe it's a statue in the square or in a Lord's home."

"Let's hope for the square. Well, wherever it is they're only a breath away from dust."

"Maybe they found a way to disrupt its functions so drastically when they removed it they altered it. Central's only known now for 200 years THRAX units can disrupt. It's only been 50 years since Biddle discovered how to stop the destruction. Could these people accidently have disarmed it?"

"It's a possibility and a big wish on our part. Perhaps in their ignorance they've done it, since this THRAX may have been here for centuries according to our information," suggested Gladriel.

"We're wasting time speculating, Gladriel. First, let's find the unit, and then hope we can remember our training. We can't count on Redford."

"I hadn't planned to," said Glady as she started down the path with Lori following.

They had no worries about encountering the men since the men's trail led off to the north toward another settlement. The Spacers heard them say they had two days before they needed to report to the Council.

Walking was easier on the path. They had time to record the plants they saw growing along the way. Lori spoke up, "Did you notice there are no animals or insect life?"

Gladriel nodded her head yes.

Several miles away from the clearing grew a dense grove of real trees. It marched neatly off in parallel rows indicating the first strong evidence of man's presence on the land. These looked like an orange grove with orange globes filled with juice.

The woman walked in among the trees and returned to the path. Now they were satisfied the trees were cultivated. The temperature began to rise fifteen degrees. Soon sweat was rolling down their faces, down their backs and under their underarms. Lori called a halt, and extracted a cleanup kit and offered it to Gladriel who wiped her face and neck before handing it back to Lori who dabbed at her own sweating face.

"Changing outfits wasn't a good idea," said Lori. "I'm filthy and I don't have anything to absorb my sweat, and no clean clothes."

They trudged on. About 14:00 in the afternoon they heard a high whimpering sound. Lori impulsively headed in the same direction. Glady drew her disruptor and followed. The whimpering came from an area dense with plants a few yards off the trail. A small furry creature, the first they'd seen on this planet was begging. It was jumping around on its hind legs and snapping at orange melons hanging a few inches beyond its leaps.

The women watched as a broad leaf unfurled, snapping shut inches short of the small bouncing creature's nose. Lori stepped forward and with her machete whacked the leaf with the broad side of her weapon. A shudder ran through the entire plant. Several fruity melons separated from the plant and fell to the ground. It wrapped its leaves close to its body and became a green ball.

The small bouncy creature wrapped itself around a fruit and munched away. While it ate they recorded it for their files.

Lori picked up another fruit and turned it over several times. Then she offered it to the small creature. This time it came to smell Lori's outstretched hand holding the fruit. Apparently satisfied, it timidly licked her hand. Lori reached out and touched where she thought the head might be. It began to make a whirring sound.

"What do you think you are doing, Lori?"

"I'm checking out a possible animal. Does this creature remind you of a dog?"

"Lori, its colors are wrong. It doesn't have ears only membranes. What it does have is cartilage or bones or dense plant fibers, which create four legs, and a tail."

They watched as it thumped the ground with its appendage, and then it swished it from side to side.

Lori spoke up. "Its fur is flatter and coarser than an earth dog's. The poor thing is starved. It is boney feeling. Glady, toss me another fruit." When she reached out to take it she saw her hand was a pale green. "Look at this, Glady." Lori dusted her hands together and smiled down at her friend. "Its green coloring appears to be a form of algae. What do you make of it?"

"I'm not even going to guess. Lori, we're not on a collecting expedition, you know, or have you forgotten?" Gladriel tossed a fruit to her.

"Oh, I remember. You're not going to let me forget. Come here little fellow. Are you hungry?" The dog-like creature licked her hand and took the fruit. "Glady, do you think these are edible for us?"

Gladriel looked horrified.

"Not the creature, the fruit."

Gladriel didn't bother to answer. Instead she shrugged her shoulders and rolled her eyes heavenward.

Finally, Lori stood up, adjusted her pack and led the way back to the trail. The creature watched them, and then turned its attention to the other fallen fruit. After it had eaten all it wanted, it sniffed out the women's trail and followed.

At dusk they found a clearing which revealed it had been hacked out. Lori was for going on. Gladriel, on the other hand, insisted the village was close and they might stumble on a work crew tending the woods. Lori deferred to her friend's judgment.

In the gathering darkness, Lori grew careless. She dropped her pack near a clump of squat grassy spears and took out the perimeter sticks. Her actions stirred the grasses' feathery amber needles on the outer edges. When she returned after establishing a boundary, she sat down on the ground near the spiky grass to rummage through her pack. While doing so, her left arm brushed against a feathered branch. The slight touch activated its defenses, causing a number of tiny barbs to attach to her left upper arm. A tickling sensation resulted. Lori rubbed her arm, setting the barbs deeper. Her failure to mention the incident to Gladriel set up a series of events which was to change their mission.

Taking advantage of the last glint of daylight the two made a hasty meal and recorded their report. Lori took out her solitaire cube.

"You're not going to play games are you? How can you play at a place like this?"

"I can think quicker when my hands and mind are occupied." Lori turned it on, gave one twist and yelled, "Who's been tampering with my game?"

"I did the other day," admitted Gladriel.

"Thanks for being so honest. I thought you'd say the saplings did it or the dog-creature we met today," she teased. "You did no damage, instead you made the game more interesting because I don't know what you did and I'll have to play a few rounds to determine your moves? There was no response from

Gladriel. Lori sat idly tossing the cube from hand-to-hand for a time before she spoke. "Glady, do you want to talk about anything? Maybe you want to talk about Redford's failure to communicate or Jeames' death or something?"

A muffled 'no' came from the sleeper.

Lori sat for a few minutes staring at Gladriel's grey sleeper, and then tucked the cube into her pack. She stretched out her sleeper and lay down. She counted the stars and watched a meteor shower. Shortly regular breathing told her Glady was asleep. After a few tosses, turns and sighs, Lori settled into a troubled sleep.

Chapter 8

They slept later than usual. The sun was fully up and was already driving heat into the clearing. Gladriel woke first. She lay on her back looking into the sky. After ordering her thoughts she woke Lori. Twice she called before Lori responded.

When Lori woke she mechanically folded her sleeper, jammed her things into any available pouch and set about removing the perimeters.

"You aren't talking this morning?" asked Glady as she handed Lori a cup of tea and a biscuit. "Aren't you going to answer me? You're not angry over the solitaire game, are you?" Lori didn't answer. Agitated, Gladriel reached across the small burner to touch Lori's hand.

Lori looked up. She was frowning. "Did you say something?"

"Yes, I did. Why aren't you your usually chatty self?"

"I didn't sleep well, I kept dreaming of Jeames' death and those bones we found. You don't suppose these people are cannibals, do you?" Lori stared into her tea, swirling the pale blue liquid in slow circles.

"No, though the thought did cross my mind. Have you wondered why this uninhabited planet turns out to be inhabited? Are we on the correct planet?"

"Glady, I hope we are. This planet hasn't been thoroughly checked out. Redford's rep-"

"Don't mention his name to me," Gladriel interrupted Lori. "I'm tired of trying to contact him. Let's forget any help he might have offered and get this job done. So help me, when we get back to base, I'm going to have some good questions answered or else I'll activate a THRAX unit named Gladriel.

"Well, Glady, there are two options: one we try to go back to *The Flynn* or two we keep looking for and find the THRAX. I can't imagine why we've lost contact with Redford. I'll bet right now he's taping the latest gossip and planning a gourmet welcome back treat for our return.

"Our return may be impossible." Gladriel tossed the last of her tea on the ground and watched it dribble off the stubby grass and soak into the ground. Immediately she was sorry. They needed to conserve their water and she had tossed out several swallows.

"Relax, Glady. Look at it this way, we are having our adventure. We'll get back soon."

"I'm not so sure. We are low on food and water, having planned for only four days at the most, and besides . . ." She paused for a moment, and then raised her left index finger. She marked off her arguments, one for each finger of the right hand. "One: Redford had time to study the planet. We did not hear the reports nor were they even given in full? Two: Margline insinuated the mission could be handled in three Central days. We've been here three days already. Three: we were forced miles from where our maps say the unit should be. In fact, the first thing we see is a plant consuming a boulder before it walks away. Four: we encounter a carnivorous creature which we had to destroy." She had run out of fingers and was beginning again. This time the thumb was included. Five: one of us gets seduced by a native, who is later killed by his own kind. Six: we befriend an animal-like green creature. Seventh: we cannot communicate with our ship. And eight: the water is tainted and could kill us. One more surprise and I'll be ready to call *The Flynn*, if it is possible. We could take a chance on finding the THRAX using its instruments and then shuttle back to *The Empolo*."

"You're such a pessimist, Glady. Everything will be all right. A few more days, maybe two and we'll be finished. No doubt, a few things, no one predicted, have altered the plans. It doesn't mean the situation is hopeless. We're bound to win a few stars, maybe a cluster along with the space bar for this assignment."

"Lori, the facts are plain. We are no nearer to the THRAX today than we were days ago. Your precious Redford set us down in the wrong place. There is nothing you say to convince me it wasn't planned. I'd like to know why! You can't explain why we can't use *The Flynn*, except for Redford telling us not to use it. I am not a pessimist! I am a realist!"

"Stop it, Glady," said Lori softly and slowly. "Hysteria won't help. This is a simple mission. Remember we are to get in, find the unit, deactivate it, extract it and get out without disturbing the ecology of the planet. You're enlarging this and blowing it out of proportions. Every mission has some danger. I can't explain the trouble with communication nor why we can't use *The Flynn*. We didn't ask to use it in this manner, now did we? Besides, if you think of it, basic training was rougher than this."

"Basic training was nothing like this. Besides we knew it was basic training. This is for real."

Lori sat up and began preparing her pack for traveling. "Glady, you didn't sleep any better than I did. "We're both fatigued. Without proper rest and some nourishing food soon, we'll be more disgruntled and angry."

"You're right about I'm not sleeping. Besides I have a feeling we're being watched."

Camp was broken and they set off down the path. Each was absorbed in her own thoughts. Lori was trying to reconstruct her encounter with Jeames; Gladriel was attempting to unravel the mystery why she felt this mission was going all wrong.

By late morning they had traveled half the remaining distance to the settlement. However, during the last few miles, Lori had stumbled several times.

Sensing Lori couldn't go much further, Glady called a break. She gave her own exhaustion as an excuse. She spread her sleeper and used her pack for a pillow.

Lori went a few feet away and chose a large boulder. She spread her sleeper across the base and onto the ground. She cast her pack aside and dropped down to a sitting position. She tugged the edge of the sleeper across her legs. She wiggled once or twice and sighed. Lori had not set up the perimeters which she normally did when they'd have a long halt.

Glady sat up to speak with her. She noticed Lori's head resting against the rock and she was scratching at her left arm.

"Are you all right, Lori?"

"Yes, however, I'm hot. This humidity and the temperature seem to be getting to me."

"It is certainly bothering me. Why is the sleeper over your legs?"

"I felt a bit chilled. The sleeper helps."

Glady got up and walked over to her friend. "The rest will do us good and we won't get to the village until dusk."

The sound of a falling branch or something unknown got Gladriel's attention. She still felt as if they were being watched, yet she could see nothing. She settled again on her pallet and strained her ears to catch the faint rustling of leaves. This time she didn't move. Instead she cast her eyes around the clearing hoping to see what had made the sound.

A flash of green betrayed the watcher. Careful in her movements Gladriel twisted her head around until she could see the path clearly. There standing in the shade, which obscured it was a giant sapling settling its leaves tightly around its trunk. Something in the way it folded its leaves reminded Gladriel of a human and she smiled. Was this their guardian? Had they been following and watching over them all this time. She did not see the other two who stood deep in the shadows. Her thoughts turned to the landing of *The Flynn*. Could this creature have followed them from the flyer? She did not think so. It was much bigger than any they had met. Though the questions bothered her, she simply shrugged her shoulders, dismissing her thoughts. She settled her mind to unravel the problems with Redford.

An inner alarm went off signaling Gladriel they had rested an hour. She hesitated about waking Lori, who snored loudly. Gladriel looked at the signs of fatigue and stress visible on Lori's face. Dark puffy circles hung under her eyes and sweat coursed in rivulets down her forehead onto her cheeks. Her breath came in gasps. Gladriel read all the signs and concluded Lori was quite ill. This was something more than limited rations and water, or too much heat and humidity plus the endless walking.

Kneeling beside Lori, Gladriel felt Lori's forehead. It was hot to her touch. She pulled open an eye lid. Lori's eye was glassy and the pupil was huge. Gladriel took the scanner and set it for medical check and gave Lori a quick once over. She checked out Lori's head and back of her neck with her hand.

Lori mumbled, "I'm tired, Glady, so tired. Let me sleep." Lori attempted to lift up her left arm.

Her action made Gladriel suspicious, particularly so when Lori groaned and let her arm drop. Glady examined the arm. Nothing was on the front, though it was a bit dirty. The moment she lifted the arm, Lori groan. "It hurts."

Glady pulled Lori forward and off the rock and rested her on her right side. Then she could examine the back of the arm.

She didn't even touch it; instead she saw the angry red streaks and the swelling. The movement awakened Lori who moaned, "I hurt all over. My arm—it's numb. I'm so thirsty." She couldn't reach her pack with her right arm.

Gladriel tugged out her soft pouch which had only a little water.

"Water," pleaded Lori.

After retrieving her own canteen from her pack, Glady struggled to pull Lori back to a sitting position. While Lori rested against the boulder Gladriel poured half a cup of water and held it for Lori to drink. Lori began to shake. Gladriel tucked the sleeper around Lori's legs and waist and then searched Lori's pack for the med-kit. Now Lori's temperature was up even more and her respiration rate was dropping. Lori's illness was somehow related to her inflamed left arm. The blood scan indicated Lori's blood chemistry was raging out of balance.

With the scanner, Gladriel checked Lori's arm and discovered stubby needles so small she had missed them on her initial inspection. She ran her fingernail lightly over the area. She felt the bristles. Lori moaned and pulled away. She

57

needed something to remove them. Now was the time she needed Redford's advice and help. She took out her small communicator, tapped a code into it and waited. Lights flickered across the board, the sequence indicated *The Flynn's* receiver was not functioning. Thinking she may have tapped in an incorrect code, Gladriel repeated her call again and there was no responding signal. *The Flynn* could not be raised. Now her only alternative was to seek help from the villagers. No doubt they had dealt with this before.

First she had to do what she could for Lori. She took sterile moist gauze and washed the inflamed area. A few bristles caught in the cloth and came loose. A trickle of blood stained the gauze. After disinfecting the area, she gave Lori a hypo of antibiotics and painkiller. While Glady was putting a bandage on Lori came to and asked for water. Before she could drink she passed out. Another check of Lori's vital signs showed the poison was slowed. Her body, however, was losing hydration.

The Village was her only answer. Gladriel took her own sleeper and tucked it around Lori's chest and shoulders, set her almost empty canteen in arms reach and placed Lori's disruptor on her lap. For a second she thought of trying to carry her. Proper thought made her realize this was impossible. It was best to go for help.

She set out the perimeters in a narrow field, knowing Lori couldn't crawl out and nothing could get past the barrier. She only took the essentials her machete, wrist communicator, scanner, map and two wrapped biscuits.

She backed away from Lori and out between the perimeter gates and activated the field when she was a yard away. Its steady hum reassured her; momentarily she lingered and looked at Lori. She hated leaving her. She remembered the times they had laughed together, teased one another and protected each other. She called out, "I'm going for help!" She hoped Lori heard her.

"Damn you, Redford!" If he were only in touch he could have summoned *The Flynn* since her line seemed to be blocked. By now Lori could have been in her vat and the poison would have been flushed from her system. After one more look back at Lori she set off in a run in the direction of the village. She did not see the sapling step from out of the shadows and shuffle close to the perimeter where it stood like an honor guard. Neither did she see another one shuffling along after her.

Chapter 9

Shortly the dim footpath joined another path and became a larger well-traveled road. The merging trails confused her and she stopped to consult her map. The blinking dot indicated she should turn south. The village was about a mile away. Certain of the direction and the condition of the road Gladriel began to trot hoping to cover the distance quickly. In the growing late afternoon she ignored the jungle hedging the road.

A half a mile of running brought her to a large clearing devoid of any vegetation. The huge plants had been cut down and their roots dug up and the soil turned, exposing dark loam to the sky. Surprised to find tilled land Gladriel paused briefly, and then began running again. She was anxious to reach the village and bring help before dark.

She consulted the map once more and checked the distance. She attempted to contact first Redford, doubting he would answer. Then she called Lori. She didn't respond either. Glady sighed and hoped Lori was still alive.

She had arrived at the walled village late in the afternoon. Briefly she watched women working the ground. Some were transplanting young shoots; others hoed and irrigated the rows. At a large rack, taller than they were two girls picked and sorted red and green melons. Small girls of four and five years carried gourds of water to the working women. Happy laughter accented the peaceful scene.

From the wall, atop the gates came a long mellow call like a low moan. The women ceased their work, gathered their tools and walked toward the gate. Hiding her equipment, except for the wrist communicator and monitoring kit, Gladriel joined the group gathering up their baskets.

At her approach an older woman handed her hoe to another woman and came to meet Glady. "Welcome," she said, taking Glady's hand. "You are a stranger to us. I am Janine."

Gladriel was relieved the woman spoke ancient Sol and answered quickly, "I am Gladriel. I need your help."

"Yes, child, what may I do for you?" She smiled as she signaled to a young woman to run for help.

"My companion and I . . . My friend has been injured. She needs a doctor."

A group had gathered and listened. At the mention of a companion they began to whisper. Gladriel caught snatches: "in the forest," "two women" "Ameral had forbidden," "condemned."

"Hush," Janine ordered. "We know none of this." Turning to Gladriel she explained, "We cannot help you, perhaps our Lord may. He is wise and knows much of medicine. Come," she gestured to her companions who collected their tools. Together the women moved toward the village.

Once inside the walls, the group separated. Each headed for her own residence leaving Gladriel and Janine standing alone. Other groups entered. Gladriel watched as they stacked their tools near the gates and handed their goods to others who carried the produce to storage and sorting huts.

Glady looked at her surroundings. The large plaza where she now stood served as the central hub of the village. Directly facing the gates sat a large two storied building with a gabled roof and a front portico supported by Doric columns. Streets, as far as she could see were bricked with the same ash gray stone as the courtyard. These radiated symmetrically from the building. Gray slabs bridged streams which fed running water to the homes. These, Gladriel learned later were connected to each other by narrow courtyards. Some were roofed while others were left exposed to the sky. Each house held ten or more women and any number of children. Gladriel counted eight groups. Each flat roofed building had thick grey walls. She reasoned the general structure of the villages was a pentagon. The expanse of gray was brightened by an occasional vine or trellis of blooms.

When the gates thudded shut, Gladriel became aware of the empty yard. She grasped the hand of Janine who tugged away. "Please," begged Gladriel, "won't somebody help?"

"That is up to our Lord," said Janine.

"Then where is he?" demanded Gladriel.

"Here," came the deep rich masculine voice behind her.

Gladriel whirled around. The man was tall, taller than the woman who she realized were about her height. The man, regally clothed in robes of green stood a full six inches taller. His height was further accentuated by the presence of the child who stood near him. For a moment Gladriel didn't speak. She was awed by him. Her eyes appraised his muscled chest and arms, half hidden by the flowing sleeves. He spoke again. She noted his green eyes framed in long lashes and his cleft chin and white teeth. He looked athletic, strong and lean, yet his masculine hardness was tempered by the golden wheat curls which ringed his face from beneath a braided green band. Red stone earrings dangled loosely from the band above each ear. His conduct was regal, calm and self-assured. Gladriel was unaware the girl had left his side. She remained quiet.

Again he spoke, "Who are you? From where do you come?"

Janine touched her arm. "You must answer the Lord."

Gladriel roused as if from a dream. "I am Gladriel I came from the jungle," she gestured toward the gates. "My companion is ill. She is dying." Gladriel started to step forward. Janine restrained Glady by touching her arm.

"Leave us, he ordered. The few women who had lingered in the plaza scattered. Janine nodded to him and moved away. He called after her. "You will be rewarded, Janine."

Alone with him Gladriel extended her right hand palm up and appealed to him, "My companion has been hurt. Will you help me?"

He ignored her hand and stepped closer to inspect her. His eyes followed her lean outline noting the full breasts and long legs. Her dark hair fascinated him and he touched it, feeling its heavy silky texture. Her dark eyes stared into his.

He smiled "Perhaps I will help you. I am Lord Corthain, Counselor to Lord Ameral and Lord of this village." He nodded as though he had made a decision. "Come with me." Turning toward the two storied building he walked away from her. Gladriel followed for a few steps then grabbed his arm. At her touch he turned to face her.

"My friend was hurt by these," she said, extending her left hand and displaying the withered remains of a plant and the barbs.

He glanced at it. "Yes, I am familiar with it. You know she will die unless treated soon. Why were you and your friend, another woman, in the Tangle?" When she didn't reply he asked another question. "Were you condemned? He studied her for the reaction he expected from such a question.

"I don't follow your questioning. My friend is ill. Will you or won't you help her?" she asked rather sharply.

His eyebrows raised a fraction of an inch. "I do not approve of your tone, woman. Show respect for a Lord. You are not of my village, nor of my house, or I would punish you. I do not understand why you should be in the Tangle." Gladriel did not respond. "How many are in your group: Are there any men?" He asked grasping her shoulders. Still she made no reply. He continued to question her. "Were you bound for another village and another Lord?"

"We are two women," Gladriel finally said. "She is sick. She's too weak to move. I could not carry her, so I came alone to seek help." She was growing weary of his lack of comprehension even though he was the power here. Since she had seen no other men she was depending upon him.

"Remain calm, woman I may help your friend, if I learn why two women are alone far from their settlement." He was aware he had received little information, so he changed tactics. "What are you called?"

"Gladriel."

"Gladriel has a lovely sound when you say it. Tell me, Gladriel, where is your friend?"

"She's at least two miles from here in the jungle or the Tangle as you call it. If I delay much longer it will be dark. I must get back to her."

"It already is almost too dark for a journey into the Tangle. I should not leave before Lord Ameral returns. In my absence a Lord must stay in the village or a proxy. It is the Law."

"Then give me some medicine and a couple of men and I'll go."

"No." The refusal was firm and settled. He began walking toward the building again. She followed sensing she should not argue with him and was acutely aware she did not have the cure for the poisonous barbs; he did.

He entered the building. Before Gladriel entered she studied the plaza and judged distance between buildings and locating exits. "Is this the only entrance?"

"There is no need for another, although the women are allowed one in the rear. Since you are not of my household, I permit your entrance here for this time only," he smiled.

She thought, 'How kind of him' and followed him inside.

They passed through a corridor into a central patio. Rooms faced in on three sides and a corridor similar to the one they stood in now faced across the garden. Gladriel sucked in her breath at the beauty here. A gentle stream was flanked by brilliant flowers as it meandered through the courtyard. Scattered throughout the area were elegantly carved wooden benches. A pilot's seat stood in the center, framed by stone masonry and beautiful flowers.

"What a beautiful garden and chair," said Gladriel.

"You act as though you have never seen a ceremonial throne. All lords have one. This is the Rex's ceremonial throne. It is one of the largest. Such thrones await additional Lords when the time is right. Why do I speak of this to you a woman? Why do you find this of interest?"

"I'm curious, I've never seen a throne before," she lied speculating this might be the source of the secondary reading or the seat could be concealing the THRAX.

"How can it be? All women are allowed access to a Lord and no Lord can be a Lord unless he has a throne."

Glady could hear suspicion in his voice. "This is nonsense. My friend needs help now. I must return to her."

"It is late. We will go in the morning." He clapped twice loudly. Two women about forty hurried forward. He leaned upon one while the other removed his sandals and wiped his feet before she offered him thongs. A third woman entered carrying a towel draped over one arm and a bowl of steaming scented water which she offered to him. He dipped his hands in the water and dried them. Then as Gladriel watched he spread his arms and waited as a woman removed his gown. Beneath it he wore a thin pale green loincloth which hid nothing.

"Prepare a bath for this woman. Cleanse her and feed her. Then bring her to my chambers," he ordered striding off to the right.

"Hey, what about my friend?" Gladriel called after him. "What goes on here?" She asked the woman, sensing a change in the atmosphere.

"He has chosen you. It is an honor," said the woman holding the basin. "Lord Corthain is selective and he breeds well. He has fathered ten daughters and four sons."

"Chosen, honor, breeds? What is this?" Gladriel was confused by the woman's words. She had heard these words before coming from Jeames. What had she stumbled into when she came seeking help?

"Please," another woman cautioned, "do not bring disapproval. Obey my Lord."

"Come," the third woman said. They led her away to be fed, bathed and prepared for Lord Corthain.

Chapter 10

Gladriel was keenly aware of the chambers and corridors they passed through. High small windows near the ceiling offered only scant ventilation. Each area was lit by pale yellow lanterns which cast a weak light. As they passed through a work area Gladriel stopped and observed the women. A group of three women were stretching a rectangular shaped cloth onto a frame while another group stirred a mass of cloth in a large pot into which a young girl poured a dark, almost black green liquid. Five women to the left of this group were folding the day's weaving into neat bundles and storing them in a cabinet. A fourth group sat in a semicircle around a cluster of lanterns embroidering sheets of cloth in runny borders of dark green, occasionally adding a red circle of blossoms of some sort or plant.

She would have lingered, however, the women hurried her to the communal bathing room which was unoccupied at the moment. A large tub, nearly large enough to hold six adults stood on a raised platform. Two young girls struggled into the room. They carried steaming buckets of water which they dumped into the huge tub.

A woman tugged at Gladriel. "Please undress and bathe," she begged.

"Tell me," requested Glady as she tugged off her boots, "how many people live here?"

The woman was busy with securing towels and ignored the question.

"Where are the men?"

She stopped her work and stared at Gladriel. "This village is like all the others. We don't have many men. Most of those who live here are in the Tangle waiting while the young man searches for his crowns. What village do you come from?"

"A bath, hot and soothing," said Gladriel as she diverted the question by stepping into the water. "It seems months since I've had one. I've done nothing except dream of a hot tub." She stepped down and sat down letting her legs hang in the giant tub and let the water sooth her aching feet and legs. A few moments later she lowered her body completely into the tub. Dirt and grimy green coloring slipped away to reveal soft almond brown skin. She felt refreshed and let the water swirl around her.

"What is your name?" she asked as the woman entered the water.

"Sarlat, please allow me to scrub you properly. Lord Corthain demands a woman be clean."

"Sarlat, what do you do in this household? Wash women?" she teased.

Sarlat smiled and soaped Gladriel's back first, and then her breasts and abdomen. For the next few minutes she told Gladriel about her duties as a house woman in charge of the bath and sleeping quarters.

A slow nagging idea grew in Gladriel's mind. Lord Corthain was a stud servicing many women. Still he had to be more than a stud if he was a respected Lord and ruler of his women. The warm bath and brisk massage Sarlat administered swept such thoughts away.

Sometime later a girl entered with clean garments and spread them on the stools. She relit several lamps which had gone out and drew the drapes across the doorway. On her way out she stooped to pick up Gladriel's dirty clothes.

From the corner of her eye, Gladriel saw the child's actions and called out, "Leave them where they are!" The authoritative tone in her voice frightened the girl. She dropped the garment and cringed.

"Please, Gladriel, do not frighten the child. She will see your garment is cleaned and returned," Sarlat said.

"I prefer to do it," said Gladriel as she smiled at the girl.

"You cannot wear your gray garment. It would displease the Lord."

"We want to keep him happy?" asked Gladriel.

Sarlat nodded yes.

"Then, I'll wear what you say, but my suit stays with me." Gladriel climbed out of the tub and rubbed her body with the coarse towel Sarlat handed her.

"Lord Corthain has ordered all unclean clothes be taken to the laundry when removed. Later, if Lord Corthain approves of you, he will have you dress in his colors. You will not need to wear your father's colors again," Sarlat patiently explained. "Gray is your father's color isn't it?"

Glady nodded yes.

"You do not belong to a Lord as a member of his household, do you?"

Gladriel shook her head no.

"Good, Lord Corthain will be pleased to know this. He would not take a woman from another Lord's house."

"I understand," said Gladriel as she removed and laid aside her wrist communicator and monitoring kit. She dabbed her suit in her bath water. Sarlat watched in surprise. Glady explained, "I do not come from any village near here. I am a visitor and since I do not intend to stay, I will keep my belongings with me." Gladriel turned and smiled at Sarlat and then turned back to her laundry. She squeezed the suit of excess water, shook it vigorously several times. As Sarlat watched she wiped her boots dry and folded them to fit into a small pouch on one leg of the skin suit. Then she folded her suit so it became the packaging, as well as the package.

Sarlat stood by observing each action. Gladriel knew she should probably report this to Lord Corthain. When Sarlat saw Glady was finished she held forth a pale green shapeless gown. She indicated Gladriel should lower her head so she might slip it into place. Before submitting Gladriel inspected it. Two lose pieces of cloth were held together with twin claps which formed shoulder seams. There were no side seams. Sarlat thrust the garment forward again and Glady bent her head and let Sarlat drape the knee-length gown over her. She watched as Sarlat adjusted the shoulder gathers so the two pieces of cloth overlapped in the middle. The garment did not require a belt instead it draped seductively over her breasts. Gladriel fastened her wrist communicator to her right wrist. It was still functional, even decorative as a piece of jewelry sparkling in the light of the lamps.

"What about under garments?" Gladriel asked.

"You will not need them. Come." Sarlat walked toward the doorway, "Your meal waits." She pulled aside the drapes and ushered Gladriel into a small room and seated her at a table set for one. A young preteen girl served her.

While Glady ate, an older woman hurried in and whispered to Sarlat. She nodded yes and then turned to Gladriel and spoke. "Lord Corthain is weary from waiting. He commands you be brought to him immediately."

Sarlat led Gladriel to the Lord's chambers and knocked softly. He gave permission to enter. Sarlat pushed Gladriel into the room and murmured a warning, "Always obey the Lord in every way."

Gladriel hid her suit packet behind her in the folds of her gown and stepped forward to face the man whom she hoped would save Lori.

Lord Corthain had bathed and changed. Now he wore a white robe. Its edges glittered with embroidered stylized petals and leaves from the flagget. At the shoulder seams sat twin clasps which held the robe together. The robe draped revealing one knee while exposing a well formed thigh and leg. He sat calmly on his chair, another seat from the old colony rocket.

He motioned her to come forward. She walked, head high and eyes directly upon him to the raised dais. Placing one foot upon the dais she asked, "Are you going to help me?"

His eyebrows lifted, a characteristic she had noticed which meant he was agitated. He changed positions, appraising her thoroughly. "You have no fear of me?" he asked while studying her face.

"No, why should I be afraid of you?"

"It is proper you bow before me."

She sneered, "That will be the day." She set her jaw, clenched her teeth and looked him directly in the eye.

"You are a woman pleasing to look upon—dark and warm," he spoke more to himself than to her. "Yes, you please me. You may stay in my household."

"I please you?" Surprise registered in Gladriel's voice and face. She laughed.

"Come closer," he requested, extending his hand.

"I am close enough."

"You are old enough to know the correct ritual. What village sent you?"

"I didn't say. My friend is seriously ill and all alone in the jungle. She needs your help."

"Ah, yes, your friend, another woman. Is she as uncouth as you?"

"Look, Corthain—"

"Do not address a Lord without his title."

"Lord Corthain," she acknowledged. "I was told you could help me. You promised to help me."

"Did I? I recall I said I might help you, if I learned why two women were alone in the Tangle."

"We were sent here to__

He nodded, interrupting her. "Be a lesson for others no doubt. Were you unruly females?"

"What do you mean?"

He smiled. "It doesn't matter. You are here. I shall sample you and decide upon your value." He rose and stepped from the dais. He extending his hand to her, and lead her into the next room.

"Look, Lord Corthain," she said as she pulled her hand away from him. "You promised me help. Is this how you treat people who come asking for help?" Her eyes flashed in anger. "My friend will die unless we help her."

"You must learn patience, my dear." He smiled and reached for her hand again. "She will not die for several days. I will tend to her tomorrow. Tonight I shall attend to you." He smiled warmly. "You intrigue me, Gladriel," he said and pulled her close to him. "Even your name is different. Surely you are

70

from a far settlement." He shook his head in bewilderment. "No woman should dare to speak to a Lord in the manner you have done."

Gladriel attempted to look away.

He turned her face to him. "Are you a daughter some woman has hidden away? I have heard rumors some women try this."

"I'm no one's daughter on this planet," she stared intently into his eyes. "I am a stranger here. I need your help" The strain of control showed in the quiver of her voice. She was tired of repeating her plea for help.

"You keep saying the same thing over and over," Lord Corthain said. "You tell me nothing I wish to know. There have been a few women, who, I'm told, hide their daughters. Later they were discovered and chastised by Lord Ameral."

A chill eased its way across Gladriel's neck as she comprehended his words. She knew then how the bones of females came to be in the forest. Yes, Ameral had chastised the group. In his drive for power and control, he'd killed them because they posed a threat to him by going against tradition. Her understanding grew as she pieced together the facts: the crown; Jeames' death; the women's bones; the shortage of men in the villages; and the arrogance of the men on this deadly planet.

Corthain interrupted her thoughts. "Enough talk, woman. Tomorrow I will help you." He voice softened suggestively, "Tonight is for us." He walked from the room, gesturing for her to follow him.

The adjoining room was a sleeping chamber dominated by a large bed suspended from the ceiling by long braided vines. Its pale green sheets were richly embroidered with stylized flaggets in green. She went closer to inspect the delicate work.

Corthain, removing his loose fitting gown as he entered, gestured toward the bed. "You will join me here tonight as my pleasure."

For a moment Gladriel was too absorbed in the sheets to comprehend his meaning. When the words hit her, she was shocked. When he turned to face her she saw he was naked. In the dim lamplight his height was exaggerated. A weakness settled itself in her legs. Her breathing became more rapid and shallow. She heard a wind rush through her ears and her mouth felt dry.

"Come," he invited as he ran his fingers through his curls. He saw her hesitation before he turned to an elaborately carved chest resting on a stand to his right. He lifted its lid and removed a shimmering undulating coronet of jewels. Reverently he placed it upon his head. Then he turned toward Gladriel who had finished slipping her packet from the folds of her gown and hid it in a pile of folded clothes on a nearby stool.

"Come," he called again as he caressed the crown and gently rubbed his chest. "Come, Gladriel, I am your Lord. I will show you how being with a man is pure pleasure." He beckoned to her.

Gladriel swallowed, took a deep breath and almost laughed aloud, something, however, changed her mind. The weakness in her returned and the longing for his touch flooded her senses. She felt helpless and fascinated like a fly in a spider's web as he came toward her. He took her hand. She felt blissful warmth. Tenderly he lightly rubbed his forefinger across her upper lip. A sigh escaped her. She leaned against him with her face pressed against his chest.

"I have never met a woman as brown as you, Gladriel, nor one would dare so much insolence with a Lord. Yet you must know women are men's pleasure. I shall see you receive the proper training." He hugged her closer, kissed her dark hair and brushed his lips across her cheek as he worked his way to her waiting and wanting lips.

From far away, Gladriel heard a familiar voice call her name several time. Briefly she regained her control and feebly pushed against his chest. "Please don't ask me to do this. I have never been with a man before," she said appealing to him stop. This only inflamed him more. It was then she saw, through glazed eyes the flaggot crown resting securely upon his golden curls. The voice within her reminded her of another crown. This only served to confuse her.

When Corthain squeezed the edge of the crown, she frowned and moved back. He caught her hand and swiftly in one smooth move swept her up in his arms and cradled her head on his shoulder. His voice whispered to her of the night's coming pleasure as a small familiar voice whispered warning. She understood nothing as she was swept into rising whirlpools of desire.

He carried her to his bed and gently laid her down. He kissed her with mounting passion. He nuzzled her neck and sucked her ear lobes. She had not realized this could give her pleasure. He licked her ears and traveled across to her lips. While he kissed her again and again his fingers sought the clasps which held the gown. He released the clasps and pulled the front pieces from her and cast these aside. Leaning over her he sought her lips again as his hands sought her breasts. Gladriel felt the total power of the crown as she released her control and gave in to the power of his presence.

Her lips found his in eager delight. She rubbed and kissed his chest then reached his shoulders and drew him to her. They clung together as his hand sought her mound of joy and caressed her until she cried, "Yes, oh, yes!" He stopped and began to suckle on her left breast while his right hand sought out her joy. He caressed her and felt her body push on his fingers as she sought more. She felt his warm body on hers and she responded to his touch on her body with more and more passion. She had never known anything as wonderful as this. She wanted more and more and yelled, "More, more!" as they united in passion and the voice within her ceased to be.

"You are mine," said Corthain triumphantly as they simultaneously satisfied their needs and she fulfilled his demands.

Chapter 11

Lori did not know when Gladriel left, nor did she know when an old woman crept from the jungle and cautiously walked toward her. Lori still lay securely within the perimeter's invisible shield.

The old woman saw in the fading light what she took to be a giant golden-haired woman. She studied the woman's strange outfit of green and gray and watched as the woman tossed restlessly on the ground. When she stepped closer, she activated the shield and a tingling ran through her. She exclaimed aloud, "Oh, dear." She stopped and laughed.

Lori heard her and labored to sit up. She was feverish and called weakly, "O-ma?"

The tiny old woman's fear disappeared. This was her daughter and she needed her help, "I'm coming, child." She stepped forward. Again the force field stopped her. It was stronger this time. Confused she patted her hair, dislodging several blossoms and small stones which decorated her white braids.

Lori moaned again.

Gaining courage, through concern for her daughter, she raised her crooked hands to explore what restricted her. She saw nothing, so she called to Lori, "Daughter, I'm here. Don't worry." She muttered half aloud, "What is this? I can see you, but I can't get to you. Is this some Lord's punishment?"

"Help me," Lori begged, lost in her cloud of fever.

"I—I can't get to you, daughter," the old woman whimpered. She moved around the invisible barrier, frequently reaching out a hand. She pulled it back when she felt the tingle.

Even in her delirium Lori knew the force field perimeter was on. Automatically she thumbed her wrist communicator and shut off the power. She called again, "O-ma," and passed out.

The old woman was aware something had happened. She reached out her hand again. No tingle greeted her. She hurried to Lori. She knelt beside her and cradled her head in her hands and attempted to soothe her. "Mama's here child. Mama will take care of everything." She blew gently at the wet hair plastered by feverish sweat to Lori's forehead.

"I hurt," Lori cried.

"I know, child." Tears spilled from her cloudy eyes. "What have the Lords done now? Let Mama look at you." She eased Lori's head into her lap. She turned Lori's head toward her and inspected her face. Then she turned Lori's face away from her to inspect behind the ears and into the hair line. This was followed by checking the back of her neck as far as she was able before Lori turned and clutched at her. In her weakened state Lori drifted into unconsciousness. She was unaware when the old woman pushed her into a sitting position against the boulder.

Now the woman could look at Lori more closely. Almost immediately she saw the swollen arm striped with angry red lines reaching toward Lori's hand. Once more she pushed back the wisps of hair to feel Lori's forehead. She muttered, "High fever, sweating, delirious."

Awakened by the gentle touch, Lori sought to hold to the woman. Pushing away Lori's hands, she inspected the injury. Beginning with the fingers she inspected them one-by-one. Next she moved up to the forearm and turned it carefully while she was running her fingers lightly across the taunt skin. When she reached the upper arm and began inspecting it, Lori pulled away and moaned. Patiently the old woman continued her inspection. On the back of the arm, in the fold of skin where the arm meets the trunk she found tiny barbs protruding from swollen flesh. Bending closer she stared at the weeping wound, and then sniffed it. She laid Lori's arm down, got up and gathered her long skirt up in one hand.

"My daughter, you will be all right. I must find the proper herbs. Don't you worry." She bent over and kissed the top of Lori's head before she hurried away.

Fleetingly aware the woman was leaving; Lori stretched out her hand and called, "Mama! Come back, Mama. Don't leave me." The exertion was too much. She crumpled over into a troubled unconsciousness.

At the edge of the clearing the old woman stopped and spoke to a silent green sentinel. "Watch my child until I return." She disappeared into the dense jungle.

The green sapling shuffled to a spot six yards from Lori. It folded its compound leaves about itself and stood sentry.

By late afternoon the woman returned with a skirt full of leaves, a small bundle of pale green spikes wrapped in a large dun colored leaf, and a wad of dark black mud. When she stepped into the clearing the sapling moved away. Hurrying forward she dropped her bundle at Lori's feet and knelt beside her. She straightened Lori's long legs and was thankful she was now lying on her stomach.

Crooning softly to sooth any fears the girl might have, she arranged her supplies and removed Lori's top. She began to cleanse the wound with sap from the crushed spikes. She sang as she worked, "Hush my darling, and do not cry, Mama will sing you a lullaby. Let night time fall away, Mathina will bring you another day."

Dipping a sharp spike into the sap of the dun colored leaf she had crushed, she carefully pushed the spear into the wound. Lori winched and screamed in pain. Mathina patted Lori's shoulder as she continued to work the spear in slow circles within the wound. Blood and thick pus oozed from the puncture. Mathina withdrew the spear. It was no longer smooth. Instead it was covered with tiny thin hairs. She laid the spear aside on the crushed leaf and selected another. After dipping it in the sap, she repeated the cleansing process.

Each time she withdrew the spear, the wound bled. When it was bleeding freely she made a ball of one of the leaves and smeared the sap over it. She pressed it tightly against and wound and held it there for several minutes. When she removed it, only a few hairs adhered to the sap. She used two more spikes before she was satisfied the wound was clean.

Once again she formed a new sap coated wad of leaf and held it against the wound. This time, when she removed it, it came away clean. Placing her hands on either side of the wound she squeezed it gently forcing it to bleed freely again. After wiping Lori's blood away she closely inspected the arm. She took the wad of mud and formed a dark moist pancake and pressed it onto the wound. She then bound it in place with a large leaf held firmly by a short length of vine. Her treatment ended, she settled beside Lori to wait.

By dusk Lori moaned and opened her eyes. "He's dead. I know he's dead. Damn you Oman, you can't die!" She screamed and sat up. Her glazed eyes saw nothing as she looked about her.

Mathina attempted to cradle her again; Lori pulled away. Mathina tried soothing words, "Hush my child, it's all right. Mama is here." She kept repeating this until Lori relaxed.

Finally Lori responded to the old woman's voice and called out, "Mama?"

Lovingly Mathina pulled Lori to her breast and cradled her head said, "Yes, dear."

"Mama, I didn't tell him. I loved him and he didn't know. Mama he didn't know."

"He knew, dear. He knew." She encouraged Lori to rest. Lori squirmed around until she could lay her head in Mathina's lap.

"Now go to sleep, dear," said Mathina as she stroked Lori's forehead. This time Lori dropped into a peaceful natural sleep. Mathina checked the wrapping on Lori's arm. When she was sure Lori was asleep she moved Lori's head onto Lori's backpack and gathered the waste to bury in the jungle.

When she returned, she saw a small green creature sitting by Lori. On seeing Mathina, it wiggled a greeting. In its mouth it carried a round red fruit which it dropped at the old woman's feet.

"Hello there, doeg," Mathina said. "Now what did you bring me?" As she reached for it the doeg snatched it up and dropped it closer to Lori's head. "Oh, you brought it for her." The kindness in her voice was accepted. It pranced trustingly in circles around her. Before long it suffered a pat or two on the head and trotted away.

Mathina settled down to watch over this young woman, whom she had claimed as her daughter. Somehow she couldn't remember the girl's name. She hoped she would. There was so much she forgot lately. The day was wearing off and Mathina napped.

She awoke when a heavy fruit dropped into her lap. In the twilight she saw the doeg. Its hind quarters were all a quiver and it was staring at her. She accepted the fruit and bit into it. The sweetness of the fruit was overpowered by the bitterness of the rind and she spat out the first mouthful. Humming a tune she peeled the fruit and ate it quickly and licked the juice from her fingers. When the fruit was gone the doeg, without a backward glance, trotted a few feet away and sad down on its haunches.

Lori grew restless again and called out names which meant nothing to Mathina. She wondered who Oman and Redford were. Were they men or women? Mathina knew nothing made sense to her since she had left the village. For some time she had been lost. The thought drifted away as quickly as it came and she sighed. Then she curled up beside Lori. The tiny doeg inched closer and curled up against Lori on the other side. With its head on her booted leg it kept a wary eye on the jungle. It watched as three saplings circled the camp and stood silently.

Chapter 12

Both Gladriel and Lori would have been comforted had they known Redford had been monitoring them from the moment they left *The Flynn*. Once again he adjusted the signal. He was receiving intermittent incoherent messages from Lori and knew trouble had developed with medical readings registering her severe illness. Gladriel's message about going to the village for help came through clearly. Thus he knew precisely when she left Lori. He adjusted the controls again and once more ran the messages both women had sent. He found Gladriel's comment about the injury being caused by poison barbs injected by an unknown variety of grass.

Again he ran all the information gathered and decided upon a course of action. Central had not given him permission to contact the women. Redford required direct confirmation about the injury and if possible, a visual scan of the arm. Permission would be long in coming, if it came, and if contact was granted. He directed a message to Central Control summing up the day's events giving particular notification of Lori's serious injury. Then he bent the rules by opening a direct channel to the MCAI (micro computerized audio implant) he had implanted in Lori's right ear and spoke to her. When she did not respond he turned to Gladriel's device. He learned she was running at a steady pace toward the village and looking to contact the human colony in a few minutes. This would compromise Central's rulings against direct contact with natives.

Indecision, created by Lori's programming, which had awakened him, had combined with and interfered with Central's directive. It kept him from taking action. At least, this was his story when they questioned him later. It also made him aware of feelings he had not known for many years.

Carefully he had traced Lori's program's progress as it tampered with his mind. He was aware too, when it touched the program which central had initially placed in his circuits. It was at this point the junction circuits became intermingled and confused. He still had defined areas, such as monitoring hooked directly to the MCAI in the ears of both women. All this he had kept secret, partly because Central had said so and partly because he wished the women would succeed. A part of him wondered if he was still his own master if he had been compromised by both programs. Yet another part of him rejoiced, because he could feel. He wanted to help the two young Spacers because he had grown fond of them.

It came to him as he scanned the information which he was changing. He was caught in a unique quandary. Nothing had been said about his developing emotional feelings. Logic told him to contact Gladriel hurrying to the village which had displayed its cruelty by killing Jeames. Still he didn't because Gladriel was going for help and he agreed with her decision, although she could be placing her life in danger.

Lights across the console blinked, showing his agitation. Perhaps she'd turn back; she is more practical than Lori. In fact she was now meeting the humans. He decided before acting he would check the progress of the group led by a man called Ameral. A scan revealed they were about a day's travel from the village. Hopefully neither paths of travel would cross.

Redford ran the situation through his circuits and concluded further attempts at contact with Glady would be premature. She appeared to be in no immediate danger, although the encounter with the creature on the road had disturbed him and he had nearly called her. He felt proud she was handling the situation. All along he was sure these two would be all right. With open circuits trained on Gladriel so he could monitor every sound and word, Redford turned his attention to Lori. He had assessed the risk of sending a portable video scanner with them; however he had refrained because it was forbidden by Central Control. "I am a victim of bureaucracy and programming," his voice rang out in the empty ship. "This is not a dangerous assignment; the planet is uninhabited," he repeated Central's parting words.

A tingle, perhaps of exasperation or suspicion raced through his circuits as he clicked his contacts at Central's Controls. Central had planned well, he knew. Perhaps they didn't intend for the women to pass the test or return. The women might return in full glory, if he, Redford, warmed his circuits and stayed in control. The women need never know or let Central question their actions until after the deed was done.

Through the night he listened to the women. He was acutely aware Corthain was seducing Gladriel. He attempted to warn her as he had Lori. The aphrodisiac power of the crown was astonishingly powerful. Finally he was forced to stop his communication with Glady out of respect for her and rage at Lord Corthain. No honorable man used such a device to force women to succumb to his personal desires.

Redford considered the two seductions. They were all part of the information he'd learned from the flagget patch, He observed the plants more carefully. They were well tended and tilled. Some, those near the center of the patch and the mound were in full maturity, so the plants were unable to close their leaves around the crowns which rested near the center of the blossoms. Others near the edges were smaller and shorter. They were a bit ragged. Great tears appeared in the leaves as though something had ravaged them.

Redford adjusted the scanner records so he could see a crown from every angle. It did resemble a crown. It was circular in shape with raised prong like fingers which shortened and lengthened constantly as though searching or pulsating. At the tip end of each pseudo-finger was a cluster of cilia which moved in rhythmic waves. Until Redford had a crown to analyze he could not create a counter active drug. He sensed, although he had not done any thinking about it, the crowns would become deadly in the hands of anyone wishing to gain control of a population. Judiciously he decided to withhold this information from Central. He would expunge these from all reports of the women as well.

Chapter 13

Daylight edged its way across the small mound. Gradually it illuminated the sentinels standing about the silent camp. Lori awoke and stirred within the bounds of her sleeper. Slowly she sat up, feeling as though she was wading through deep water to reach the shore. Her blue eyes blinked as they opened to full daylight. She shook off the heavy feeling and looked about her. Lying near her was an old woman and a small furry green creature. Beyond them stood a host of green plants similar to the ones which had greeted the women on their arrival. Momentarily she was confused. She closed her eyes to calm her racing heart. Then she surveyed her situation. Facing her was a huge sapling. It began to hum noticeably in the silent air. She heard a slight rustling and turned in time to see a number of saplings slipping away into the deep jungle.

Her surprise and disorientation was broken by the advance of the lively small furred creature. It capered and bounced around her seeking notice and approval. It shook itself ecstatically and wiggled closer to sniff Lori's hand. His display and actions brought a warm grin to her drawn face. She reached to pet the former bouncing ball which now stood on its hind legs begging for more of her attention.

"Hi, there, fellow," Lori said.

"Hi there, Lori," said a familiar voice. It startled her. Immediately she drew her hand from the doeg. In response to Lori's jerky motion it darted away into the woods.

"Oh, Redford, you startled and surprised me. Where are you? I know I heard your voice." She looked around the clearing, eyeing each piece of equipment. Puzzlement furrowed he forehead as she waited for a reply. 'How can Redford speak?' she asked.

"I am on *The EmPolo*. Where else should I be?" The question rang out loudly.

"You don't have to shout. Do you realize Glady and I've been trying to reach you for days? How can you communicate now?' She was suspicious and it registered in her tense voice. "How can I talk with you when I'm not using my communicator?" Her hands protectively held up the sleeper as though to ward off an intrusion into her bed chambers.

"I have been with you and Gladriel each step of the way," smugness showed in his voice. "Only you didn't know it and you wouldn't now had I not determined the need to communicate."

"I don't follow your conversation, Redford. Explain what you mean, that's an order."

"Yes, ma'am, first thing I need to do is scan you for your physical condition. You act as though you are feeling better; still you must not over do it."

"Look, you old rascal, don't lecture me. Have you contacted Gladriel?"

"No, I can assure you she is doing fine. You, however, are my main concern now. I would like a scan as soon as possible."

"Okay, I'll get the scanner. You get set to receive it." Lori took out her scanner and adjusted it for visual and medical. She began with her hair and face. Slowly she played it over her. She stopped once for several minutes at the site of the injury before continuing. "Well, Dr. Redford, give me the prognosis."

"Temperature normal, unfortunately you have some dehydration. You should consume more liquids. Your injury is mending satisfactorily. No signs of infection. You pass inspection."

"Can you tell me where I get liquids? Our canteens are nearly empty. I've only got a couple of swigs left. How about sending us some? Two days ago the water we tested was toxic."

"I cannot help you." Before Lori could say or ask anything further, he went on, "Gladriel is now at the village. She's resting. From what I overheard, a Lord Corthain will arrive here to administer first aid to you sometime today. I do not trust the man. He is from the village where the killers of Jeames came. However he was not among the killers."

"That's good. Redford, do I hear a touch of jealousy there?"

Redford kept silent.

"Okay, Redford, you better tell me the truth about Glady. I want all you know."

"I told you everything, Lori," he said.

"Well, humor me, tell me again. I didn't get your message."

"She is with Lord Corthain back in the village. She is unharmed. When she wakes up, she'll be angry. She spent the night with him and his crown."

"It's the infernal crown again. Show me where the village is and how far."

"I'll show you on your map."

"Now, Redford dear, how are you able to communicate with me although my communicator is switched off" She smiled. 'That old Fox thought she would forget he hadn't answered her.'

"Please, Lori, don't ask," he begged.

"I've asked and I want an answer."

"I implanted an audio device in both your and Gladriel's ears."

"I see, now tell me the whole story, Redford."

"I was programmed by Central before I was secured in *The EmPolo*. Possibly more than one program had been entered. At present I am unable to ascertain an exact count. Furthermore, all cadet missions are governed by the Academy Board. The Academy wants its young spacers to feel they have a choice. Actually, the cadets have no choice in destinations or assignments. Each team is given a special assignment. Each graduating class is sent out on various missions. Some are sent to retrieve defective THRAX units, such as you and Glady. And, by the way, you two are doing wonderfully. You'll have no problem in dismantling one, though a number of other teams have not been so talented." He paused for a response from her.

She didn't answer because she was thinking she and Gladriel had been betrayed by the group she most respected. They had been led to believe this mission was their choice. Instead, she now was learning the Board pretty much controlled it all.

He continued, "Lori, I was set to place you on a preselected planet, not this one. I don't think Central suspected you would generate another directive. I have tried to do all the commands as ordered, however, in so doing I feel the programs have intermeshed. The result was a totally unplanned destination. After our arrival here, I received orders to observe you in stressful and somewhat controlled situations. Glather concurred with me. Since you were here, and there is a THRAX you should complete your orders. I was to observe only."

"When you made contact with Jeames, I did, however, attempt to communicate with you. Lori, you couldn't listen or understand. When Jeames was killed I thought you would continue under Glather's orders. Later, when you were injured and while I was requesting further instructions from Central Glather, Gladriel went to the village. No orders came from Glather. So I followed your programming and let it determine my actions."

"Do I understand you properly? You do not have permission to speak with me, so you are technically not talking with me?"

"Oh, no, Lori, I am talking with you because I could not let you die."

"Redford, I'm fine now. Wouldn't your device tell you how I am?"

"Well, yes. I heard everything, even the old woman who spoke to you. She talked about what she was doing, so I have some knowledge of her treatment of your arm. Today you seem fully recovered. Therefore, I will cease communications."

"Not so fast, tricky boy, have you recorded this exchange?"

"Unfortunately, I have neglected to do so, Lori. Did you want it recorded?"

"No. You are becoming a sneaky fellow. How much of my programming changed you?"

"As to the degree, it cannot be determined at this time. I seem to be undergoing a number of subtle changes. I am becoming aware of 'self.' This is not interfering, however, with my directives to guard you and Gladriel. In fact, those directives seem to have enhanced my responses. Something happened when you entered some entertainment packages and played around with my circuitry. I'm not sure exactly what is good and what is bad at this point."

"Gladriel would love to hear you admit it. Now show me where she is. Lori twisted around to reach into her pack. As she did so, she bumped into the sleeping woman beside her. The woman sat up and looked around.

"Thank the Lords, daughter, you have recovered." A smile lit up her face.

"Good morning. Who are you?"

"I'm Mathina, your mother," she said as she touched Lori.

Lori shook her head and pulled away from her. "You're not my mother."

Mathina looked bewildered. "Are you sure I'm not? Last night I was sure you were my daughter. You called me 'o-ma' and 'mama.' I dressed a serious wound for you." She looked at Lori's arm. The bandage had slipped off during the night and the mud pancake, dried and crumbly remained. The woman was puzzled.

Lori suddenly aware of the woman's confusion, sought to reassure her. "I feel fine, Ma-thin-a. I am a bit weak, otherwise I'm fine."

"Oh, I am glad. What could a mother do? You were hurt and in such great pain. I looked after you. You called me mother, or I thought you did." Mathina looked imploringly at Lori.

Lori was pleased Mathina spoke a version of old Sol. She realized the old woman was senile so she spoke gently. "You are a good mother Mathina. Thank you for your help." She patted the woman's shoulder. "How did you find me?"

"I think a friend brought me."

"Really, where is Glady?"

"Oh, I don't think it had a name."

Redford interrupted Lori to ask her to inquire of the woman's medical procedure in tending the wound. He would like information on the herbs she used.

"Not now, Redford. First we'd better locate the village and join Glady. I'll feel better when we're together again."

"Oh, dear daughter, you're delirious again. All afternoon and into the night you called for Redford. Now you're doing it again.

"It is all right, Mathina. I'm not delirious." She muttered a command to Redford to be quiet. All they had done was confuse Mathina.

"I understand, Lori. I shall listen and await your signal."

For the next hour, while Lori straightened camp, set up the prism for tea and checked her pack for food, Mathina told a story.

"Once I was a beautiful girl, whom several Lords had coveted. Fortunately Lord Kameal took me. He was a nearby village's Lord. I loved him and served him for many years, giving him four sons, two of them lived, and three daughters as well. I was the finest weaver and embroiderer in the village. As a reward for my skill I was allowed to make all of Lord Kameal's ceremonial clothing. Later a greater honor was bestowed on me. I was commanded to serve in the Temple ceremonies. Then things changed. I aged quickly and couldn't bear children. Then one day, at the baptism of a new Lord I stumbled and spilled the oil on Lord Kameal. In anger and shame he had ordered me to be cast out." The thought of being cast out swept her into a shower of tears.

A short time later Mathina regained control and began to mutter, "It is the way. It has always been the way."

"What is the way, Mathina?"

"A younger woman, strong and healthy replaced me. It is the way. It comes to every woman, if she lives long. I remember how my youngest golden haired son led me out and gave me a container of water and some food. He kissed me good bye and went back to the village before the gates closed for the night. They left me there." Sobs caught in her throat. "I didn't mean to embarrass my Lord. It was an accident, an accident." She sniffled and wrung her hands.

"We are all subject to accidents, Mathina," Lori said as she consoled her. "Here, take a couple of sips of this tea and tell me more about yourself."

Mathina accepted the cup Lori offered. She sought to continue her tale, which she forgot when Lori combed out her sun drenched hair. "Child, your hair is thick like mine. It's as golden as the setting sun." She set down her tea and undid her white braid which curled lopsidedly over her one ear. She unbraided it and ran her grimy fingers through the strands.

As she worked her way through the stiff plaits, strips of vines and colorful leaves and stones tumbled free.

Lori opened Gladriel's pack and took out a second brush. She handed it to Mathina. Silently the woman brushed her hair.

Lori quickly finished brushing hers and paused to watch as Mathina braided and twisted her hair to form a giant hive balanced precariously to one side. Mathina then sorted through a few twigs and leaves to retrieve a special item.

"How old are you, Mathina?" Lori asked as she twisted her hair into a bun and placed her cap over it.

"I must be fifty seasons, I think. Oh, I cannot remember. I was around fifty when they cast me out. I believe I've been living in the Tangle for two or three seasons."

Lori changed the subject, "Are you hungry?"

"Why yes, dear. The small doeg brought me fruit last night. He left some for you too." She pointed to a small mound of orange globes. "Do you want some?"

"No, thank you. You may have mine." Lori rummaged through Gladriel's pack. There was still some food.

Mathina moved closer to observe Lori's every move. When Lori looked into the pack, Mathina looked into the pack. Finally Lori let Mathina study the contents of the pack and she studied

Mathina. She was a hearty individual with a face capped by a set of shaggy, wild growing eyebrows which bristled above her blue watery eyes. Heavy lines of age creased her face and neck. She wore a loose over blouse, its color unknown, and several skirts, layered one upon the other. Lori counted three different patterns each embroidered in different colors. The daintiness of the work impressed Lori.

Suddenly Mathina looked up into Lori's face. "You have many fine things. You have done well for your Lord to reward you so. But, I see nothing of your needlework.

"Thank you for your compliment. Unfortunately for me I do not do needlework. Did you see anyone around our camp last night?"

"No, dear, there were only the walkers and the doeg." On hearing its name mentioned it bounded across to them.

Lori absentmindedly petted it. "What is a walker?"

"There's one," said as she pointed at the green stalked plant standing in the shadowed jungle. "They walk like a man, only slower. They are my friends and protect me." Mathina paused to look at Lori. "Did I tell you I have six daughters and a son? Once I had two sons, sadly one died in the forest a long time ago. He could not pass his test. It is the way." She sighed.

"Mathina, you told me earlier you had four sons and three daughters."

"Did I, child? It is difficult to remember, she brooded momentarily. Then she smiled "I'm a good weaver and I taught my many daughters well." She smiled in triumph. Each of them serves a fine Lord. Their Lords have given them many children."

"Yes, I'm sure," Lori chuckled, trying not to openly smile. "Here eat this," she offered the woman a biscuit.

Mathina sampled the firm biscuit and spate out the bite. "That's vile food. Do not eat it," she warned Lori.

Lori laughed. "It's okay. You have to develop a taste for it. "She offered Mathina another portion.

"I prefer the fruit," she said as she expertly peeled a globe and ate it.

When each had finished her food, Lori loaded the packs and broke camp. "We must move from this area."

"You go to meet your Lord?" Mathina asked hopefully. "Do you think your Lord might reward me for helping you? I am a good woman. You are strong and must be worth much to him. Mathina was watching Lori's quick efficient movement and had definitely noticed her grand size.

"I serve no Lord," said Lori as she shouldered both packs.

"You have no Lord!" Mathina's face registered shock. "It is wrong. No woman can exist without a Lord. It is the way. If a woman has no Lord she is cast out."

"I have never served a Lord, nor was I cast out."

"Then the stories are true. You are a daughter raised apart. I have heard of such things."

"No, Mathina, I am not from here."

"I don't understand, child. Am I truly so old?" She sighed in resignation, "It is the way, I suppose. Since I cannot remember, I should die. I am nobody. No one will help me." She wept into her hands.

"Mathina," Lori touched Mathina's aged and freckled hands, "I am your friend. No one will harm you now. Come," she tugged at her. "I have to meet someone. Please follow me." Lori turned toward the village Redford had shown her. "If we are lucky, we will meet her," she remarked cheerfully, though she didn't feel cheery.

The motley band composed of Lori, Mathina, the doeg and the walker trudged silently along Gladriel's trail.

Chapter 14

Gladriel awoke several hours before dawn. Languidly she ran her hand across her pillow and down between the sheets. With a sleepy toss, she turned over, rustling the covers and stirring the lingering perfume of the crown. For a second or two she felt a desire for Corthain. It passed with the arrival of a cool morning breeze which blew gently through an open passageway. As her senses cleared she became aware of the empty bed and its rumpled pillow and sheets.

She threw back the covers. Awkwardly, and with difficulty she left the suspended bed only to stumble over her gown. She picked it up and wrapped it around her before she walked from the bedroom into the receiving chamber. No one was there. She walked over to the window which overlooked the dark street below and looked out. She couldn't see much of anything.

From below she heard voices and saw two people emerge from a doorway. One carried a dim lantern which cast a feeble yellow glow. The two crossed the street and entered the next house. Gladriel saw the lamplight reveal Corthain and his companion's faces. She was surprised to see another man. Except for Corthain she had only seen women entering the village.

Quickly Gladriel returned to the bedroom, tossed her gown aside and slipped into her grey skin suit. This was her opportunity to check the thrones for evidence of the THRAX's presence. A quick scan told her it was not here in Corthain's chambers, or in his throne. She headed for the courtyard, slipping down the back stairs, through the communal bath and retraced her steps. She remembered how Sarlat had led her. About her the house lay still and frozen in time. She smiled at her good fortune.

The unguarded throne stood in the courtyard. Her scan told only of minor residual radiation from his throne. It hadn't been exposed to the THRAX for long and definitely did not hide it.

The sounds of movement across the yard alerted her. A group of four men entered from the street. Each carried a lantern. The came along the walk toward the throne and paused briefly to look at it. One of them spoke.

"Do you believe Lord Corthain, when he says there are renegade women?"

"No, Lord Ameral told me it was mere gossip the women have started to frighten us men," scoffed one fellow.

"Why would they do such a thing?" asked the shortest member of the group.

"I don't know. Personally, I don't care. Come on Lad, Lord Corthain wants us to be ready to leave at first light."

'What is Lord Corthain planning?' Gladriel wondered and wished she had been able to follow him or his men. She needed to know. She wondered if Corthain would keep his promise to help her and held a tiny ray of hope lingering in her heart. Perhaps he had met with these men for a purpose. Speculation could lead her no further. She shrugged in resignation. There was nothing here. She snuck back the way she had come. A wrong turn, however, at the end of the corridor unexpectedly led her into a supply room. In the darkness she bruised her shin, backed away and fell against a stucco wall. As she fumbled to regain her balance her hand touched a lantern. She grabbed it and pulled it to her. There was a wick and a striker. Several swift twists and the lamp glowed.

In the soft flickering light she inspected the contents of the room. Gleaming softly in the dim yellow light was a stack of useless shuttle chairs. They appeared to be stacked to the ceiling of the small room. A rapid scan showed these were free of radiation from the THRAX.

Shielding the lamp she returned to the corridor and worked her way back to the room. No one saw her as she climbed the stairs, though the light from her lamp glowed softly and cast shadows on the wall. It wouldn't be long before the household awoke for the day. She estimated she'd been gone about twenty minutes. Her worry now was if Corthain had returned. Luckily he hadn't.

The chest she had seen Corthain open the evening before sat near a candle on the table. She set her lantern beside the chest and reached forward to raise the lid. A flurry of voices from the hall stopped her. Quickly she extinguished the lantern and ran to the bed. Stripping her suit as she went, she bundled it together with her scanner and deposited these under the bed. She climbed into bed and calmed her racing heart.

Moments later he climbed in beside her. She felt the bed sway as he settled in. Cradling himself around her, he began to stroke her arm. When he kissed the nape of her neck she turned to face him with a sleepy smile. Her arms wrapped around his neck and she drew his face nearer. Warmly she kissed him and snuggled closer. She enjoyed the closeness of his body and felt the grip of his charm return.

He did not respond. There was no quickening of his breath, nor shine in his blue eyes. In fact, he had no physical response to her. She had no power to evoke emotions of the night before and she felt uneasy. A cold gnawing feeling deep inside chilled her. Laying there she tried to remember what had happened after he had picked her up. She remembered his kisses and the touch of his hand on her body, she knew she gave her body to him; however, the memory was missing.

He reached over and pulled her gently to him. He softly kissed her waiting lips, and then pushed her away. "I will search for your friend today."

At the mention of Lori as sense of urgency returned to Glady. She spoke, anxiously. "Is everything ready? Are we going now?"

"You will have to learn patience, Gladriel. We will leave in an hour." Corthain got up. "My women have prepared food for my journey. I must see to other necessities." Without another glance at her he left the room.

Glady jumped from the bed and retrieved her belongings; she pulled on her skin suit and was seaming it when the woman entered.

"Here is your dress." She saw what Gladriel was doing. "Lord Corthain will not allow you to wear your father's color. Put this on. From now on, you will wear his color." She forced the roughly woven green garment and sandals into Gladriel's hands and left the room.

Gladriel held the gown up to inspect it more fully. It fell well below her knees. It might cover most of her suit if she rolled the sleeves and legs up and folded the neck opening underneath. The sash would work to hide her folded boots and scanner.

Corthain returned and was ordering his women to bring food immediately. Gladriel settled the suit under her dress and bristled when she heard Corthain's harsh demands. His attitude is insufferable, she thought, still she could tolerate it until he saved Lori. She reached for her communicator to call Lori as Corthain entered the bed chamber.

"Woman, aren't you dressed yet? Food is served. Come."

Gladriel lifted an eyebrow in reply and childishly, when he turned away she stuck out her tongue. It made her feel better somehow. She finished tying the sash and tucked everything away. Then she thrust her feet into the flimsy sandals and trotted after him.

The sun's early rays lit the room as they ate. Women quickly extinguished the candles and lanterns. A woman hurried in to clean the bedroom. Another swept it and a third put clean linens on the bed. A young girl scurried in and picked up the discarded gowns and dirty sheets.

One of the serving women urged Gladriel to eat plenty of fruit and bread smeared with a thick red preserve. Gladriel bit into the red jelly and found the taste surprisingly delicious. She noticed Corthain frown at the woman. She backed away from the table, walked to a sideboard and picked up a tray of attractively arranged fruits laced with heavy syrup. She timidly brought the platter to Corthain and was rewarded with a smile.

A preteen aged girl entered, approached the table and stood near Corthain. After eating several slices of fruit Corthain acknowledged her presence. "Yes, Lily?"

"Father the pack is prepared and awaits you."

"Well done," he said and offered her a slice of fruit which she took and smiled at him. "Lily, are you of age yet?"

"No, Lord Corthain," she softly answered.

"You will let your mother know when you are, won't you, Lily?"

Gladriel watched the exchange. She could read pride and fear in the girl's reaction to his question. She also saw an eye contact between the girl and the woman serving him now. The woman was not smiling.

"Yes, my Lord," Lily whispered.

"It is time I increased my household. I will arrange an exchange with a Lord. You are a beautiful and desirable young woman." He cast a pontific smile at her.

Gladriel saw the girl tremble and heard the sound of air drawn between pursed lips. Gracefully Lily bowed to Corthain and kissed his offered hand. For a moment Gladriel hated thinking this man was a god. Deep within she felt a cold hard lump of disgust. She realized the man could not have his daughter around him after a certain point in her development for he must not have relations with his own child. Maybe he really cared for her and realized this too was part of the ritual.

The girl backed away and Corthain stood up. "It is time, come" he announced. He waved in Gladriel's direction. "I will go find this friend of yours."

They left his quarters and descended into the courtyard. Gladriel watched the women working. Some swept the walks, others weeded the gardens and still others carried clothing to be aired. Their happy morning chatter echoed in the damp air. She noticed most of the women were small boned and no taller than she.

He turned to Gladriel, "You are to stay right where you are." He walked away.

Glady waited impatiently for his return. She was anxious to leave and he wasn't there. If she hadn't needed him she would have left.

Over an hour later a woman approached carrying the bulging tote bag which Lily had prepared for her father. "Lord Corthain is coming," she told Glady.

"It's about time. I'm tired of waiting."

"That is disrespectful. Keep your tongue quiet. Some of the women fear you now."

"Fear me? Why"

"Some believe you are an outcast and others believe you are a female from an addled old Lord's household in some other village who came here to cause trouble. They think you've not been taught well. You are arrogant."

"What do you believe?"

"I know you are not one of us. I have never heard of a woman named Gladriel, nor have I heard of a woman coming to a village without an escort. It is wrong, unnatural and evil. Lord Corthain should have nothing to do with you. You should be destroyed." Hate and jealousy blazed in her eyes and she backed away from Gladriel.

"You are right. I am not of this village. In my village there is no Lord who orders women around. There women serve no man, unless they choose to do so." While Glady spoke she saw several women draw closer.

"How can this be?" asked a women who had been sweeping the walkway. "A village with no Lords is not possible. A woman must be guided by a Lord. How can a woman know what needs to be done?" Several of the women nodded in agreement.

Glady spoke up, "Women need no man to tell them anything," she said. "In my village women think for themselves and are free to—"

Lord Corthain chose this moment to arrive. "To your work, women," he commanded. "Lord Ameral will be here late today or tomorrow. He will expect the houses and village in order. Until I return this evening my son Cliff will be in Charge. Now go back to work." He clapped his hands at them and they scurried off.

"Well, Corthain, I thought you'd never come back."

"Gladriel," Corthain released a long sigh, "it is not permitted for a woman to address a Lord by his name only. It causes insolence in all women. I corrected you last evening. The warning should have been sufficient. When we return, I shall personally tend to your instruction. Besides, you have questions to answer. If I am not satisfied with your answers, I shall deal harshly with you."

Gladriel opened her mouth to speak.

"Quiet!" he commanded. When she closed her gaping mouth, he asked "Are these my supplies?"

"I suppose so."

"Good. Your lessons begin now. Pick up the bag and follow me." Without another look or word he turned and walked toward the gate.

She watched as he walked away from her. She hoisted the bag to her shoulder. She noted he wore a knee-length belted tunic and soft leather shoes, hardly sturdy enough even for the short journey they faced. A long curved bladed knife in his belt gleamed in the sun. She noted there were no other men who came to join them. If the men had left at first light, already she and Corthain were almost two hours behind them. She wondered if they had waited outside the walls for their arrival.

She struggled to catch Corthain as she gripped the bag's loops to keep it from slipping from her shoulder. Corthain paid no attention to her. Instead he watched several naked young boys chasing one another in a game of tag. These were the first young males Gladriel had seen on this planet.

"Lord Corthain, are any of those boys your sons?"

"Yes they are. You act as if you haven't seen boys before."

"I have but never playing in the nude."

"Where do you come from, Gladriel?" he asked as he slowed his pace to wait for her reply.

"It's a long way from here, Lord Corthain." She said as she looked him in the eyes and smiled. "I can't wait to get home.

Is there a medical kit in the bag?" she asked as the tote fought to slip from her shoulder.

"Don't worry. The tangle will provide all I need. Tonight, Gladriel, I will have many questions for you," he smiled in contemplation of the event.

"Yes, my Lord," she sarcastically replied.

"Let us go," he said and strode freely up the road.

Gladriel struggled to keep pace. Somehow she always remained five strides behind him. 'If he doesn't have a medical kit then what else besides food can he have in the bag?' she wondered and fought the urge to throw the bag down and give him a swift kick in his fancy tunic. Instead her feelings for Lori guided her. She swallowed her anger and stumbled on behind Corthain. She thought, 'He's so arrogant. He hasn't even bothered to ask me where we're going.'

Chapter 15

Lord Corthain and Gladriel's exit from the village was a fast paced one. He was anxious to avoid any women seeing them leave. Once outside the gates, Gladriel paused while Corthain strode on. 'Probably', she thought, 'the men lie in wait for us at the jungle's edge. She hurried to catch Corthain and attempted to match his stride, but she found it difficult because his big tote bumped heavily against her legs.

A few women already worked the fields to the southeast of their path. Ahead and to the left the fields were empty. Gladriel paused and shifted the bag from her left shoulder to her right. It was then she noted the beauty of the fields. A group of women dressed in Corthain's green moved into the field near the gates and began walking down the rows, pulling weeds and hoeing.

Soon they reached the field where Gladriel had met Corthain's woman. She stopped. Corthain walked a few feet further. He stopped when he became aware Gladriel wasn't following. He turned around.

She set his bag down. He watched as she stepped into the field and crossed it to a mound of grass. She glanced around, and then picked up a bunch of drying grass. Surprise registered on his face as he watched her pull something from under it.

After she returned to his side, he spoke, "What are those?" He pointed to her cutter, disruptor and cloth pouch."

"My supplies," she answered, and then lay put these down beside his bag. Next she removed the green dress she wore. Then she stepped out of the sandals. He stared as she quickly unrolled her pant legs and her sleeves. She adjusted her collar on her suit and pulled on her boots. She attached the cutter, disruptor and soft pouch to her belt. She could feel the questions he wanted to ask. 'He controls himself well,' she thought. He continued to watch as she consulted her map and spoke into her wrist communicator. In disgust she snapped it off and checked her gear on her belt.

"Who are you, Gladriel?" he asked. "Your clothes and those," he gestured at the tools on her belt, "are unfamiliar. I am beginning to believe you are not of this region.

"If you'll follow me, Lord Corthain," Glady said as she folded the garment she had worn and tucked it away with the sandals into her waist sash.

"Women do not order, nor do they lead. They follow and obey," he corrected her.

"That may be true, but let me ask you this. Do you know where my friend is?"

"No need. I will lead until we reach the Tangle." He stepped in front of her.

"All right, if it's what you want."

He waited.

She looked at him.

He looked at his bag.

"I get the message, Lord Corthain. I carry the bag." She went back to it and hoisted its straps to her shoulder. "Lead on, my Lord Corthain, I shall follow."

When she was almost even with him, he turned and walked north on the road.

From time-to-time, Gladriel chuckled as she thought of the picture they made. Corthain walked regally carrying nothing and was five paces in front of her while she struggled to carry his bag. They walked this way for thirty minutes.

Now, not only was she sweaty and disgusted, but her shin was already coloring from the continual bruising of the bumping bag. She called a halt. Corthain seemed oblivious to the heat, because he wore light clothing and carried nothing.

"We'll rest here." She checked her map. "Soon we'll turn east."

"East?" he questioned. "That will lead us into the Tangle."

"Of course," she agreed, dropping to the ground. "Better sit and rest. Do we have any water?"

"I have some water. I'm not thirsty."

"Well, I am."

"I didn't bring any for you."

"Then you better carry this bag or give me a drink of water and I'll carry it."

"Humph," he snorted as he handed her his water pouch.

"Thank you, Lord Corthain. Would you like to sit and rest?"

"I'll stand," hauteur framed his words. He inspected the road ahead and behind them.

She inspected him. Already his soft leathery shoes were showing signs of wear. The shoes would not stand up to the punishment of the Tangle once they were off the path. She withdrew the sandals from her belt and held them out toward him. "Wear these over your shoes. These will offer some protection."

"Mine are fine. We surely don't have much further to go once we're in the Tangle."

"Better wear them anyway," she ordered and added, "We have another two or three hours to go."

"If you insist," he said as he extended his right foot to her.

She looked up at him and then smiled sweetly. "Here, you put them on yourself. I've got something else to do," she said as she handed him the sandals.

He made no effort to take them.

She dropped the shoes on the ground and got up. She walked a ways from him before she touched the communicator. She looked back at him and nodded knowingly. He was sitting and lacing the sandals to his shoe covered foot.

"Lori, this is Gladriel."

"Hi, Glady," Lori's lilting voice rang out.

"Lori, are you all right? I mean you sound well. Are you?"

"Working at capacity," Lori's cheerful answer can back.

Corthain looked up when he heard Lori's voice. Quietly, though quickly, he rose and came toward Gladriel, his eyebrows lifted in curiosity.

Gladriel quickly reverted to Academy language.

"Lori, you were dying when I left you. Tell me what happened."

Lori paused and then began, "An old woman came along and-"

"No teasing, Lori. Tell me the truth."

"I am. When I was extremely ill she found me." Lori proceeded to tell Gladriel what had happened to her after Glady left for the village. "Oh, Glady, I am not alone. I am accompanied by the old woman, a walker (one of those plants we first met), and a doeg."

"I can't wait to see you and meet everyone. It sounds as if you've collected a menagerie. I'm so happy you are alive and doing well. Wait a minute, Lori. I have to take care of something." She looked at Corthain who was almost shoulder to shoulder with her. She turned her back on him. "Lori, I've got a Lord with me."

"A Lord, no less! Goodness, Gladriel, you can't talk about what I collected when you grabbed the prize. How'd you do it?"

"It's a long story, I'll tell you sometime." Gladriel wasn't ready to tell Lori everything including her night with the Lord. "Do you have your map handy? Signal your location and I'll signal mine."

"Glady, I'm not at the camp where you left me. I've moved further north. Do you see me? Lori was eager to tell Gladriel all her news, once they got connected.

"Yes, Lori, I've got your location."

"Redford contacted me."

Gladriel screamed in rage, "Redford did what? Why you? Why not talk to me?"

"He told me I was dying. And he was trying to find a way to save me."

"And did he help you? Gladriel shouted.

"Now, Glady," said Lori with a soothing voice, "Redford was-"

"I can speak for myself," said Redford as he interrupted Lori on hearing his name mentioned.

"Then do it, you . . . you . . ." Gladriel was too angry and relieved to do more than sputter.

Both women listened as Redford explained the situation. Gladriel asked several questions about the tampering Central had done. Lori and Redford assured Gladriel Redford was in control now. When Redford concluded Gladriel asked for an honest opinion of Lori's health. Redford confirmed Lori was in a great condition. He advised Gladriel of a group from the village following her and Corthain at a leisurely pace and distance.

"How large a group following?" asked Gladriel.

"No more than ten."

"Well, Redford, now you're talking to us again, is there a way we can use *The Flynn*?" Lori asked, suspecting Gladriel would soon have asked the question.

"I am under orders. I cannot release it to you. It is not a part of your mission until you find the THRAX. You two will have to continue on until I can discover how to override the directive. I will try, Lori."

"Thanks, Redford," Glady said thinking Redford would do everything he could to help them. "Well, Lori, I suppose we'd better co-ordinate our maps and select a rendezvous point."

"I've got you on the map now. If you continue east for two and a half miles and then turn southeast we can meet at coordinate G-6, it's where the two streams meet. I'll confuse our trail here, can you do the same?"

"Several minutes passed before Gladriel spoke. "Lori, I've got you spotted at G-6. It's a can do only if Lord Corthain doesn't have me lugging his supplies and his men don't catch us. I took him at his word. He promised to help you. If he's planned a surprise for us, I'll spring it."

"I could angle southwest and meet you sooner," Lori suggested. "With us together they wouldn't stand a chance."

"Thanks my friend, however, I've let Corthain suspect too much now. He's been listening to our conversation and hasn't understood a word of it. I want to keep him unaware of our potential. I'll be slowed down, since Corthain doesn't have any trail knowledge. Lori, avoid those circles on your map. Those are some carnivorous giants like we met earlier. Those are definitely beautiful and lethal."

"Will do, Glady, you keep in touch."

"You got any suggestions about Corthain. We don't need him now?"

"You could leave him for his men to find, however he might tell them about you. It could be they'd interfere with our mission. Better bring him along. If he delays you leave him. Oh, one thing more, did you find the THRAX?"

"You know, Lori, I'll bring him for no other reason than I'd like you to see this fellow. He's a real man in everything except manners. And as to the THRAX, it wasn't there.

"That's bad. Say how would you know about his everything and manners? I'll want to hear all about your trip to the village, especially the night." Lori laughed. "You be careful. Even handsome men can be devious. I've met a few."

"I'll bet you have, but none like this one. See you in a few hours." She ended her communication and turned to face Corthain.

"We'll be heading southeast soon."

"I am ready." Corthain had no desire to be left alone, even on an open road.

"How could your friend be alive after a night in the Tangle? Only a true Lord can remain alive after a night in the Tangle by oneself. It is dangerous."

Gladriel was preparing to cut a trail to the southeast. "I hear initiates are asked to do such a task. Beside, she's alive. You heard me talking with her."

"I heard you talking some gibberish. Women are known for talking nonsense. Come," he turned toward the village. "We will go back to my village and send runners to your village. Until we locate your Lord, you will stay in my household.

"Thanks for the invitation, Lord Corthain; however, I'm going to meet my friend Lori." She hacked away at the undergrowth.

"Gladriel!" Corthain's voice rang out sharp and clear. "We will return to the village."

Gladriel stopped, sighed heavily and turned to face him. She stared at him. One hand was on her hip as she observed him. After another sigh, she returned to where he was standing.

"Look, Lord Corthain, and listen well. I am not your servant and I'm not returning to the village. You may go, you are free."

He lunged at her and tried to grab her arms. He was unprepared for her response. She let his thrust carry her backward for two steps. Spinning in and under his arm she flipped him head-over-heels. He landed in a puff of dust and lay, flat on his back. Gladriel stepped around him to face him. She knelt, pushed back curls from his forehead and she smiled. Her eyes were bright with mischief as she bent down and kissed him on his forehead.

"You're no match for me. Lord Corthain. I know moves you'd never suspect. If you want you can go with me," she and in a low voice added, "As of this moment I cease to be your slave. Now pick yourself up and make your decision."

She watched a series of emotions and feelings displayed on his face. She waited until he could control himself before she stood up. Slowly he sat up and eased himself to a stand. She motioned toward his tote-bag and waited until he had retrieved it. Without further talk she entered the jungle. Once she stopped and motioned for him to follow. Corthain hurried to the spot where she had stepped into the wall of green. He hesitated, afraid to go back and afraid to go with her. He bent low and tugged loose two small clumps of grass and tossed them aside, leaving a bare area. Then he obediently followed her.

Chapter 16

For a solid hour Gladriel cut a path. Twice she stopped because she needed to check their position. She also wanted to avoid the areas of heavy concentration of the deadly plants. The third time she halted she saw Corthain twist a vine around itself, forming a knot with the longest end pointing southwest. She smiled and started out again. She moved over in the area of the twisted vine and relieved herself. As she returned she twisted the point of the knot to indicate they were going north. Then she took out her cutter and continued hacking.

After another long hour of hacking through the dense undergrowth she called a halt, cleared a small area, and sat down. "Eat something. You must keep up your strength and let us each have a swallow of water."

He took a drink and handed her the water. He took out a dark purple fruit from his tote. Leaning back on his haunches, he set about peeling the fruit and watched Glady from a distance.

"Tell me, Lord Corthain, how you became a Lord?"

"I would rather you told me about you. You are much more interesting and mysterious than I am."

"I asked first," she winked coquettishly at him.

"You already know women do not ask questions of a Lord," he chided her.

"Yes, I know," she said as she smiled sweetly and fluttered her dark brown eyelashes. "But, my Lord, we're not in the village now. No one will ever know. Besides you have made me curious about you. You are so robust and attractive. Is this how you got to be a Lord?" She smiled again, but mentally felt a twinge of guilt because she was flirting with him to gain information and she was enjoying doing it.

Unable to resist her charms, he gave in and proudly related his story. "When my eighteenth season arrived, I was chosen to seek a crown. Fortunately I was not long in finding it. The first day I was led out into the Tangle I was only a few miles from the village. Soon I found a flagget. In my youthful exuberance I extracted its crown and rushed back to the village where the council still sat. Lord Ameral urged disqualification for me. I was saved because the Law had not been broken. I had legally secured a crown, although it was immature, I was instated as a new Lord. Later I received a mature crown. As a result of my rapid recovering of a crown and speed of delivery, the rules were changed."

"Was this at the request of Lord Ameral?" she asked.

"Oh, yes. He explained it was nothing personal, rather he felt I had not been truly tested having spent only a brief time in the Tangle. The Council saw the wisdom of his words as I did. Now a group of men take the young man into the Tangle. He is given no special clothing or weapons, although he is permitted to carry a knife. He is garbed only in a simple tunic and sandals. At a great distance from his village he meets the danger of nature alone. There he must find a flagget and extract the crown. This completed he returns to a prearranged camp for the completion of the initiation ceremony. After his return to the village, he must fertilize a female and produce a male child. Once he has achieved this he is proclaimed a Lord and is allowed to begin establishing a household."

"Quite interesting," She looked Corthain directly in the eyes as she spoke. "What about the woman in this? Has she anything to say about being fertilized?"

"The woman?" Corthain snorted indignantly before he remembered his companion was a woman. "The men, those who become Lords, maintain the population and direct the life of the village. A woman's main duty is to bear children, followed by working for her Lord. She may be asked to cultivate the crops, to work in the shops, keep cleanliness in their homes and in the village and to preserve foods for the dry seasons. Above all is her first duty to her Lord."

"Have you ever asked the women if they like this arrangement?"

"Why would I ask them? There is no need. Women are not capable of making decisions. They do not have the disposition for it."

"Lord Corthain, we're not talking about disposition. We're talking about women participating in the affairs of—"

"They are incapable. I have told you this already," he sharply interrupted. "Besides they have such short life spans—a Lord lives for many seasons."

Glady realized it was time to change the direction of the conversation. "How many young men survive the tests?"

"Unfortunately not many succeed. Only one out of four young men will return with a crown. In the last ten seasons only two have succeed in returning from the Tangle with a mature crown."

"Do you know them?"

"Of course I do. The two are Garth and Pall sons of Ameral. They each brought back two crowns a remarkable feat of courage of strength."

"Have you ever gone with the group who take the young man out to the Tangle?"

"Only once," he answered as he stood up to straighten his tunic. She held out her hand for him to help her to her feet. He took it and lifted her up. She smiled and he kissed her. She kissed him back. He pushed her away gently. "We must get started back before long. We do not want to be in the Tangle at night."

"Continue your story as I cut this undergrowth."

"I accompanied the group. Oh . . . it must have been six seasons ago. It was then Lord Ameral's eldest son became a Lord. I, however, did not enjoy the ordeal of camping in this devil Tangle. After three days Lord Ameral sent word I must return because several of my women were ill. Personally, I was happy to return and tend to my women.

"What happened to the boy being tested?" she asked as she fastened her pack and set it securely on her shoulders.

"Oh, he returned with a set of fine crowns the same afternoon I left. Today he is a respected Lord. He has sired several children, mostly female. Each season now he volunteers to be a member of the group who wait for the young man to return with his crown. I do believe Garth enjoys the days and nights in the Tangle." Corthain shuddered at the memory of his long days and sleepless nights spent waiting for the young man to return.

Gladriel paused to check her coordinates once more. She had left her cutter resting on a rock.

Corthain took the opportunity to examine it. He hefted it in his hand to feel its balance. He'd watched her closely each time she had used the cutter. Now he hoped to learn its power and be able to use it once he'd taken it from her. He handled it carefully. Its serrated edges resembled a knife. The handle was smooth and afforded an easy grip. He studied the cutter intently. Located above the grip was a depression. He jabbed clumsily at the activation switch. Nothing happened.

Gladriel was watching him. When she cleared her throat, he blushed red and looked up.

She extended her right hand and waited for him to give her the cutter.

He hesitated.

Her hand remained level with insistence.

He stepped back. "I will cut the path. All you need to do is instruct me on how to use this fine blade. It will be easier on you," He swung the cutter in a figure eight pattern. As he did so he felt the cutter adjust itself to his grip and swing.

Not wanting to force Corthain to overreact, Gladriel changed her tactic. "That's sweet of you, Lord Corthain. I know you'd like to help; unfortunately I don't have the time now to teach you. When we have the time, I would like to show you."

He handed it to her. 'It had been worth a try,' he told himself.

"Can Lord Ameral be trusted?"

The question surprised Corthain. He stared at her for several seconds before answering. "Lord Ameral is an honorable man. Without his advice our settlements would suffer more than they do. It is he who devised a plan to exchange food, clothing, women and Lords so each village could continue to grow."

Seeking to plant a seed of doubt in Corthain's mind she continued, "Think on this, if you will, Lord Corthain. I overheard one of the women say Lord Ameral was planning a new village exclusively for himself. Already ten women coming of age have been chosen."

"Women always gossip. The group of women you speak of is for the new Lord's when he returns. Right now he is passing the test of the Law. He's one of the finest candidates we've ever had."

"Would this young man's name be Jeames?" Corthain nodded yes. Gladriel sighed and then spoke, "Lord Corthain, Jeames is dead. He gained his two crowns; however, he was killed by Lord Ameral and the initiation group two days ago."

"That is a lie! You are like all women. You tell this to suit a woman's purpose. Lord Ameral abides strictly by the Code of the Lords. It is he who demands strict adherence from all the Lords."

"Believe what you will. I have no reason to lie."

"Why should I believe you? I've known him all my life and you I've known for only two days. Besides, you are a woman," His lips curled in distain and his nostrils flared.

Glady shrugged, turned away and began hacking a trail. In strained silence they moved slowly through the Tangle. Twenty minutes later they broke into a natural clearing.

Before them lay an area where the sunlight beat directly down upon the squat Kelly green plants which spread themselves open to absorb the sun's rays. These large leathery limbed plants occupied the majority of the clearing. Smaller plants probably younger ones, were scattered among the huge three foot tall monsters.

Throughout the clearing, vines, with tangling treads of inch thick ribbons, twisted themselves around and among the plants. Competition for sunlight was continuous during the day. So if one uncurling leaf touched another open leaf the two would swing and swat at one another. Angry clashes resounded as their hard tips clashed together. Conversely, the leaves of the younger plants caressed the adults. Several times the large plants reacted to this gesture by curling a leaf into its central body well to coat the tip with liquid and then uncurling it to reach the smaller plant. There its orange coated tip rested firmly in the center of the small plant which slurped noisily as it removed the liquid.

"Do you have any idea what these things are, Lord Corthain?" Glady asked as she and Corthain stood side-by-side watching the plants' slow ballet as they weaved and fought one another for position or food.

"I have never seen these before. I have heard from others who have ventured into the Tangle." The sight of them made him tremble. "The men say these plants are carnivorous during breeding times and they breed continuously. Also the men say these will eat anything, even their young if there is no other food. I heard Lord Duluth's group of females was consumed by a cluster of these. He was taking his women to trade for other females. All were destroyed, except for the Lord. He survived to tell the gruesome story."

"That might explain the bones we found," she said as she spoke aloud, while pondered the possibility.

"What did you say?"

"I was wondering if these are breeding now," she answered as she watched the plants dance. "Well, I'm not going to try to cross over them. We'll have to go around. First, let's feed them. To keep them busy, Lord Corthain, you stay here at the edge. While I'm gone I want you to remove your tunic."

He watched her leave yet made no effort to remove his clothing. She quickly returned carrying an armload of broad leaves stripped from a huge bush she had cut from their path. She saw he had not undressed.

"I told you to strip! When I say strip it means to take off you top garment. Now strip!" She entered the jungle again and returned with strips of vines, leaves, and twigs. These she dumped unceremoniously on the ground. Corthain still had not removed his tunic.

"I told you to strip. If you can't manage it, I'll help you."

"I can do it; however, I see no reason for such an action." After removing his belt and knife he pulled the garment over his head.

Gladriel held out her hand. "Give me the tunic."

He stood and held it.

"If you don't, I'll take it from you." Her voice showed the strength of her determination.

He smiled and handed it to her. "What do you want it for?"

"Be patient, as you told me. You'll see." She removed her belt and took her gown off and spread it out on the ground. Using a sheaf of leaves and twigs, she stuffed the green garment full and tied the sash around it. She leaned the decoy up against a small shrub and admired her work. It would do. She then took Corthain's tunic and stuffed it with the same debris. She lifted it up beside hers, much to her chagrin the stuffing came out. Corthain watched as she stuffed the tunic again then he took a length of vine and tied it around the bottom. When she stood it up this time, the stuffing remained in place. Both stuffed garment resembled crude scarecrows.

Gladriel stood up and fastened her belt and added her cutter. She checked her other equipment, even taking time to adjust her pack. She motioned for Corthain, who'd finished putting on his sash, water pouch, and cutter to pick up his tote.

"When I yell 'run,' Lord Corthain, you run as fast as you can on the right edge over to the tall big plant. I'll be close behind you."

Corthain nodded. He was intrigued by Gladriel's control and further resolved to determine what kind of woman she was. He realized the settlement had explored only a fraction of the land. He no longer entertained the thought she was from one of the two nearby villages.

Gladriel lifted his tunic, juggled it and heaved it two-thirds of the way across the clearing and to the left side. A shower of twigs and leaves rained down on the undulating plants. It

112

landed barely off center in a huge adult. It immediately encased the bundle with a quick grasp. She tossed her own bundle to another nearby adult. When it hit full center, the plants near it attempted to grab at it with thrashing tendrils. In anger they slapped their long leaves on the limbs of the two who clutched their unshared bundles.

"Now, Corthain!" she shouted as she pushed him. Suddenly he grabbed her hand, tugging her to run with him. They had crossed half way when he was forced to drop her hand to clutch at his bouncing tote which hindered his running. Once safely across he turned to check on her.

Gladriel was in trouble. She had been forced to go more slowly due to her heavier load of tools. Too, she had already had a strenuous day hacking her way through the undergrowth. Now in her haste she had entangled her left foot. She tripped and lost her balance. A few stumbling steps and she was free. She still didn't have her balance and fell amid the grasping vines.

The big plants to her left, aware of her presence, searched frantically for the victim. Rubbery leaves touched her back and legs, seeking a hold. She scrambled away only to find she was firmly gripped by another. Now other leaves sought her out and slowly bent to encase her. She clawed across the ground, gaining inches only to be pulled back toward the waiting creature. Strong steady pulling dragged her toward the quivering center.

"Help me, Corthain!" she screamed as she flayed against additional threads which whipped at her arms and head. Through flying dirt and whipping ribbons of green she glimpsed Corthain standing with knife in hand. "Help me, Corthain!" she pleaded.

Forgetting the danger to himself, Corthain dropped his tote and rushed to her. His sharp knife sliced through the slender vines. He fought off leafy arms searching for new food. He pulled her to her feet and together they rushed to the safety of the Tangle. She felt him stumble against her as they entered it. He turned and she clung to him. With her face held firmly against his chest, she could hear the rapid beat of his heart which even outraced her own. It was some time before she became aware he was trembling.

"I'm all right, Lord Corthain," she mumbled into his chest. "You saved me. Thank you." She hugged him closer to her.

He held her for a moment and then pushed her away. "I—I couldn't . . ."

"It's all right, Lord Corthain. I owe you my life. Thank you. We're both safe. We need to move on. Give me your tote, I'll carry it."

He was shocked at his own reaction to danger. He had stood stupefied. Then he took a deep gasping breath. His face flushed red. He could not understand his feelings and struggled to speak.

"Come on," Gladriel urged, hoping new action would help ease him past this moment. She strapped on her pack and picked up his tote and then took up her cutter. She began hacking a path.

"No!" Corthain shouted. "I will carry my own."

"Sure." Gladriel smiled up at him and handed it over.

A sudden thud behind them warned them they were not safe even at this distance. She looked in time to see his torn and stained tunic come flying through the air. It fluttered softly down and settled on a bush. He picked it up and held it out before him. It looked fine. Carefully he set down his tote and pulled the tunic over his head and shoulders.

Gladriel laughed. Before her stood the proud Lord now adorned in scuffed shoes and sandals a revealing loin cloth and tattered tunic. He was beautiful. She kissed him for real, no crown involved and he kissed her back. She felt more for him than she thought possible. He kissed her again and she felt drawn to give more. It was then another sound indicated something was happening. They both looked. Her dress had been rejected too. She looked at him and felt love yet she knew this was not the time or place to explore this further with men pursuing her. "Shall we go?" her voice was husky and she was flushed. She wanted more than what they had for the moment still she had to find Lori.

Another hour of hacking brought them to a small stream. She studied her map. They began to follow the small stream being careful not to walk in it. This eased the need to cut so much and leave a trail.

Corthain was feeling helpless. He was aware they were moving deeper into the Tangle, deeper than he had ever been for he always traveled on the road and in the company of men who knew the dangers. He suddenly remembered he had not marked any trail for some time. He twisted a trailing vine into a knot. His men would recognize it. Gladriel was leaving an impossibly easy trail. Her cutting could not be hidden or ignored, however his knot would tell his men he still lived.

A part of him was loath to follow her after all she was only a woman. There was a new side to him which he was experiencing. Too, he was confused and captivated by this strange woman. She had proven she was capable of great strength and gentleness. Fortunately she was quick to understand the situation and react. Yet, as he continued to follow, he hoped for an opportunity to leave additional signs and eventually put stability and control back in his life. He wanted to bring Gladriel and Lori to his village. They would add to his pleasure and put new strong blood into his sons and the people.

Chapter 17

Lori and her group had reached the joining of the two streams while Gladriel and Corthain had stopped for a bite to eat. Lori checked the area and set out the safety perimeters. Her attention was drawn from her work when she heard the deep rumble from far off thunderheads. A quick study of the sky revealed a darkened area gathering to the west. Already fiery flashes of distant lightening etched their way among the building clouds.

"Mathina, does it rain much here?"

"This is the dry season, I think." Mathina was busy wading in the pebble lined stream to respond fully.

"Mathina, isn't the water hurting your feet?"

"Not this stream, it is pure, it comes from the hills. Further on it is angry and burns my feet."

"When it does rain are the rains heavy?" Lori studied the clouds which were continuing to build huge billowy towers of gray marbled with foamy white streaks.

"Sometimes it rains hard. I remember once when I almost drowned. The water was so deep and I was afraid."

"We'll need a better shelter than the perimeter to hold off a rainstorm, if my hunch is correct?"

Mathina wasn't disturbed by the approach of the storm. In fact, she would be reluctant to leave her latest treasures. The stream she explored was filled with water polished stone of various shades of red and blue. Already she had filled her pouch and was trying to find additional ways to carry more.

"I like it here. I want to stay," announced Mathina as she walked over to Lori to share her treasures with her daughter. Mathina thought, 'Lori would want to stay longer once she saw the beautiful sparkling stones.'

She handed Lori a stone. "You may have this one. It will look lovely tucked into the strands of your golden hair." Mathina stretched up on her toes as Lori bent down. Mathina tucked in a long thin sliver of azure stone into Lori's bun. When she finished she place a brilliant red stone in Lori's hand. "This is for you," she said as she folded Lori's hand around it.

Lori thanked her and examined the stone. It was a red crystal with hair thin filaments running through it. She turned it over and could see no difference from the other side. Yet, when she rubbed her finger across one end a warm feeling raced up her arm. She looked at Mathina for an explanation. She was now sitting down and weaving her hair around other colored stones she had taken from the stream. Lori was fascinated as she watched Mathina weave twisted coils of white hair around the colorful stones. Her hair was transformed into a coronet of jewels which flashed in the sunlight.

Mathina gave her hair a final pat and stood with her skirts gathered in one hand while the other helped to balance her elaborate stone laden hairdo. Then she began to rhythmically sway from foot to foot. This was followed by turning tight circles near the stream's edge. As she danced she sang of her union with nature and life. Her dance continued for almost five minutes before she fell exhausted.

A distant rumbling sound awakened Lori's worry about the coming rain. She still held the stone. She studied it again and then went to the stream to collect several more. No two stones appeared to be the same, yet they were similar in weight and feel. She dropped her collection into her already crowded pockets in her pack. Later she would give these to Redford and have him run a panel on the composition of each stone.

Thinking of Redford reminded her she could call him at any time. She wiped her hands on her clothing and hastened to activate the communicator. It was then she remembered the communicator wasn't necessary. "Redford, I know you're not to communicate with me, nevertheless, I would appreciate a weather update. Those clouds to the west are building and there's been ground to sky lightening."

Next she called Gladriel, "Hi."

"Lori, is anything wrong?"

"I'm at the specified meeting place. Are you reading our position?

"Definitely, we're closer than I imagined."

"What is taking you so long?"

"Lord Corthain and I tangled with another deadly species of plant life. This planet would be paradise to a botanist."

"Glad to hear you're fine. How long will it be before you join me at the streams? We have a big thunderstorm brewing and I want to leave this area for higher ground as soon as possible."

"Give me another thirty minutes and we'll be exchanging hellos."

"See you soon, please hurry." Lori broke contact with Glady and opened a channel to Redford. "Okay, Redford, let's have the weather forecast."

In the background she could hear the crackle sound as the lightning interfered with communications.

"You are right, Lori. It is an immense weather front of high winds and driving rain and it is heading toward your camp. If the rain holds off, Gladriel will arrive in 27.4 minutes. Now as to your mission, I found waves of radiation coming from the yellow mountain you flew over days ago. It may be your next point of inspection. I plan another in-depth scan my next orbit."

"Are we being led on a lizard's chase?"

"Lori, try to view this mission philosophically. You are getting plenty of fresh air, sunshine, and exercise."

"You sedentary robot, I'll sunshine you!" she wished she could hang up on him. She was startled by his soft husky voice whisper in her ear, "Lori, I am not a robot. I'm part of a compu-ship. As a token of my apology I want you to know there is an area about a mile north east from where you are which could possibly have caves and shelter. Please don't be angry with me."

She ignored Redford's plea and studied her map. Redford had sent the coordinates. She looked in the north-east direction and could only think of leaving. She hacked a ways into the brush and foliage and found it thinning as she headed northeast. All was good. She returned to the stream and paced restlessly.

"Don't worry, Mathina. Sit down and let me tell you a story." Lori picked up her pack and moved it a ways from the stream and sat on a rock. "I'm ready for the story, Mathina."

Mathina came over to join Lori, as did the doeg. When Mathina sat beside Lori the doeg jumped up between them and laid a paw on Lori's thigh.

"How about telling me about you, Mathina?" I'd like to know how long you've been in the Tangle and how your survived so well."

"Now I don't always remember exactly. It must be at least three seasons since I came to the Tangle. My mother was one of several women who taught their eldest daughters about the Tangle. I learned plant medicine from her in secret; because the Law allows only men should know medicine." Mathina forgot her train of thought and began telling another.

"You know daughter, once women were like the Lords. They could do anything and go anywhere. Then the planet became angry and punished the people. In time few males were born. Those who survived childhood were not always capable of fathering children. This punishment made the people change their ways."

"Some men, those selected by the Tangle, were still able to sire children so each selected a number of women of child bearing age. Our world was saved, but the early days of the settlement were filled with suffering, famine and death. The number of people fell. One day, many years after the settlement was built the number of people began to increase. The people knew the planet was happy with them. They had been purged of their evil and the Law was established. It provided each male would be allowed ten females. Some men produced healthy strong offspring, others did not. In time more female children were born and even less males. And so the seasons passed.

One day a young man found a flagget crown and brought it to the village. It was seen what it did to him. He grew taller and stronger from wearing it. He sired more males. Now all men who have a crown and sire a male child become Lords."

From the story Mathina told Lori pieced together the rest of the story. With the discovery and use of the crown the life span for men increased. The women's did not. Every man's virility also increased as did his sexual appeal. Therefore the women were being drained of their life force while the men and crowns fed off of them. To continue production of females was most desirable to the crown while the crown only needed a few men to guarantee continuous feeding.

Mathina's hair had fallen over her ear and covered a portion of her face. Lori moved closer to her and set about rearranging Mathina's hair. While the old woman sat in the lotus position, Lori brushed and plaited her hair and replaced the color stones in the woven strands. The little doeg had settled itself between the two women again and was sleeping peacefully. Unnoticed by the three, the walker which had so diligently followed them struggled through the sand and pebbles to stand between all of them and the edge of the woods.

After patting the braids into place and inspecting her work, Lori asked, "What happens to the women as they age?"

"When women can no longer bear children they are assigned several tasks in a household. She can instruct, with permission of her Lord, a younger woman to take her place, or she can collect and sort seeds for the planting, or she can carry the garbage to the fields. It is the Lord who determines what she will do. I have done each of these. I did a terrible thing when I caused my Lord Kameal to lose face with the other Lords."

"What did you do?" Lori asked.

"I told you, my child. I spilled wine on my Lord. For my clumsiness I was banished—banished." She stopped talking and cried into her hands.

"I remember now you telling me the story. Please, Mathina, don't cry. I understand."

"Did I tell you my son walked me to the gates?"

"Yes, you did."

"Did I tell you I have lived longer than any other female in my village? My weaving and embroidering were the finest. I was required to teach others my skill so their household would have beautiful garments." She tilted her head to one side and hummed softly, remembering those years. A hint of the delicate beauty which once was hers sparkled briefly in her face and then faded as a painful memory touched her mind again.

"I was loved by my Lord. My son loved me too. Did I tell you he went into the Tangle and never returned? He never came back." She held out her arms to Lori.

Lori took Mathina's hands in hers. Mathina sobbed. Tears dropped unheeded onto their hands. Soon she pulled her hands free and covered her eyes. "He died a glorious death. Lord Ameral told my Lord."

At the mention of Ameral, Lori sat up straighter, crossed her legs Indian style and leaned forward, "What happened to him, Mathina?"

"It was during the time of the initiation. You understand I didn't go—women are forbidden. The flagget ceremony takes place in the Tangle. It was an honor for my son to be selected to search for a flagget. He was so happy, so proud. He left with the men of his village early in the morning and three days later the group returned. Lord Ameral said they were attacked the second day from the village. A huge creature attacked them and my son died saving Lord Ameral's life. My son was brave."

"I'm sure he was quite brave, Mathina. You are right to feel pride in his life. Who is this Lord Ameral?"

"He is a Lord. Remember his title, it is important to him," Mathina said as she leaned forward to grasp Lori's chin firmly in her hands and looked directly into Lori's eyes. Then she removed her hands from Lori's face and continued. "He is the seventeenth Lord to rise who has shown great leadership. There is talk he may become the next Rex. Lord Ameral is strong, tall and handsome with dark blonde hair. I cannot understand why he has fathered only two sons." Realizing what she had inferred, Mathina hastened to add, least Lori think Lord Ameral was not as potent as a Lord should be, "He has 30 women and has sired forty-six daughters."

"Forty-six!" Lori shook her head in amazement. She decided it was time to change the subject. "How did the people come to this world?"

"You want to hear my favorite story? It was told to me by my mother when I was a little girl, before she went away." Mathina beamed and settled herself comfortably.

"In the beginning there was a great emptiness. The land was lonely and awaited the people's coming. The people came to this world. It held out its green arms to welcome them. The first Rex heard the world's call and carried his household across the Great Nothingness. When he arrived with his people he tenderly, with his own hands, carried them to their new earth. With him he brought the first of things: seeds, animals, and the Law. He lived long and ruled wisely for many years. Before he went to join his ancestors in the void of time he called his men together and instructed them they could no longer be simple men. Now they are Lords. He gave them the Law. Those Lords were to protect their women because they were the carriers of the human seed, the fathers of men. His words to the women were to care and provide for the Lords in every way. There were so few men who carried the spark of life. Soon the number of women increased. The Rex called all his children to him, for we are all his children. He gave us the Law we all now live under. He told us to faithfully follow the Law and we would prosper and multiply. It was then he established the Lord's household Law. Each man was to guide a number of women to see they must continue to nourish the seed of life. It was many seasons before first settlement became self-sufficient enough for another village to be established.

Mathina paused and petted the sleeping dog, "There's more. I sometimes have to think about it. Oh, yes, he promised someday, if our people hold to the Law they will be reunited with others of their race. He didn't say how this would be done."

"My mother said once the group was cleansed of all evil, and then the union would come. She had hoped in her lifetime the stars would come to our world. They did not. I don't think they ever will." The thought was painful and she paused as though to shake it from her mind. She couldn't.

"My head hurts. I don't want to remember any more." She started to get up. Instead she fell back down. "I know where there are the best herbs for medicine here in the Tangle. I know of cures for women's complaints and for infertility too. Did you know I can talk with plants?"

Lori shook her head no.

"See the bramble bush there?" Mathina pointed at a shaggy foot high bush. "It's laughing at us right now."

"Bushes can't laugh."

Haughtily Mathina reprimanded her. "Have you talked with one?"

"Well . . . no . . ." Lori admitted.

"Well, unless you have, don't talk about something you know nothing about." Mathina struggled to her feet and brushed the sand from her skirts. She returned to play in the stream.

Lori lay back and watched Mathina. When the bushes rustled behind her, she rolled over and spoke to it. "Hello, bush."

Suddenly a greenish ball of fur streaked from the area of the bush. Lori didn't have time to reach for her disruptor before the green ball and the doeg which had been sleeping beside her mixed in a flurry of sand. Once the doegs' rowdy greeting was over the two trotted up to Lori, sniffed her boots and licked them. Lori reached out her hand toward the newcomer. It permitted her to touch its head. Then it dutifully trotted to Mathina who welcomed it warmly. She picked it up and hugged it as it washed her face.

"He's back to see how we are," she explained to Lori.

"Back?"

"Yes, back, when you were ill he came to see you. He brought us the fruits I ate."

"Mathina, I thought our doeg was the one." Lori pointed the one at her feet. "From where did this one come?"

"This one sent the other one to protect us."

"I'm really confused. Does either of them have a name?"

"Those in the forest never do. They are part of the lost group, I suppose. Didn't I tell you about them?"

"Maybe you did, but let me hear it again."

"In the beginning several doegs came with the Rex. They were blessed and multiplied greatly. When the first village grew enough for a second village the Rex sent a pack of doegs with the new Lords. Some of the doegs strayed away and were lost. No one knows what really happened to them. They became the ancestors of these doegs."

"Mathina, you've told me so many stories I'm confused. I doubt if half are true."

Lori's disbelief in her stories hurt Mathina. She began to cry. "My memory is failing. I may not recall all the details exactly. I do not lie." She sobbed angrily into the green coat of the doeg in her arms. It growled at Lori.

Chapter 18

As the storm approached thunder rumbled louder and lightening brightened the sky. Wind bent the trees around the stream and whipped biting sand around the small group. Lori hurriedly repacked the perimeter poles. If the wind increased any more she would have to find the protected area Redford had mentioned. This was the only possible course of action she could take. She hoped Gladriel and Corthain arrived soon. Her only other option was to lead them to their new location using their communicators.

To find shelter before the storm Lori knew she would have to leave now. Suddenly a strong upper current of air dashed away the clouds. The sun was dazzling as it captured the world once more. Lori knew it was a lull. She policed the area and decided she'd have to carry the equipment and her own bag. Mathina didn't look capable of carrying anything.

"Mathina, I'm sorry," Lori apologized, feeling Mathina would think an apology was necessary. "I don't know enough about this world and your way of life to make judgments. Will you forgive me?"

"It is all right, daughter. You must learn. Sometimes I tell tales. Before I was cast out, it was said I had a great imagination." She laughed.

"Will you call me Lori?"

"I won't remember it, dear. Besides, all women are my daughters. I will try to remember your name. You're sure you're not one of my daughters?"

Lori had to laugh. "If it pleases you to call me daughter, I would be honored. Now, Mathina, we are going to leave here to search out a cave in the cliffs. Please come with me, mother." Lori lifted one pack and strapped it to her left shoulder and then the other for her right shoulder. "Let's go, Mathina."

Suddenly, Lori realized Mathina had not heard one word.

"I'm not the only one who tells tales. All the Lords tell stories of their journeys into the Tangle. I don't think they travel anywhere except on the trails. You and I haven't followed any trails have we? Even when I watched them during the testing they used the trails." Her voice dropped to a secretive whisper, "Women aren't supposed to be in the Tangle. I'm no longer a woman." Mathina mumbled something to herself. Then the volume of her increased and Lori could hear her. "Lord Ameral sent a group of women with Lord Duluth. This was after I was cast out. If I'd have been younger I might have been one of them. Sometimes I forget, but I do not lie." She told herself with smugness.

"What women were these, Mathina?"

Mathina didn't answer her question.

"Do any of the women who leave for another village ever return?"

"I'm not telling you any more stores. You are an ungrateful daughter. You think my stories are lies," said Mathina before she turned her back to Lori to look at some tree.

"I told you I am sorry. You said I was forgiven. I'll ask again. Will you please forgive me? I am a daughter who does not listen well."

"All right," she said as she headed back toward the stream.

"Please stay with me and tell me of the women who are taken from one village to another." She looked at the threatening sky and figured she needed to hear this story. Luckily the wind had died away in a second lull and the sun was shining warmly.

"The Lords always visit the villages regularly, however, the women who leave never return to their home village. All young women leave when of age for another village. I did. After all it is the Law. Once a woman is joined to her Lord she must stay in his household until she dies, grows infertile, is exchanged for another or is cast out. A young man almost never changes his home village, only when he becomes a Lord is he given absolute freedom. If a young Lord is ordered to help establish another village he will take his women with him, but it has been a long time since we had a new village."

"How are the women chosen?"

"First the Law forbids a Lord having his own daughters of maturity age in his own household. So a number of women come from this group. Too, if a woman, after several years with one Lord has had no children by him, she can be given to another Lord. I remember one beautiful woman who had four Lords, but she never had a child."

"Poor woman," exclaimed Lori.

"Yes, it was her disgrace. When a Lord dies his women are given to any Lord who is willing to take them after they get the approval of the Rex.

"Were you ever in such a group?"

"Oh, no, not me. In fact, my Lord died shortly after I left and his women left my village about 8 days after I was cast out. They were given to Lord Ameral. Of course, any daughters of his in the group would be given to another Lord, it is the Law."

Lori hoped Redford was recording all of this data so maybe later Gladriel and she could analyze it thoroughly. "How many Lords live in one village?"

"I don't know about the other villages. In ours we have ten Lords with households."

"Do any men not become Lords?"

"Most men are not Lords, because they are weaker or not as healthy so they are not fit to sire. Others are impotent or sterile and cannot become Lords. Most of these men would not want the responsibility of a household. Those men can serve as guards or teachers of the young men. Our village has about twenty such men. Some are older, though they do not live as long as a Lord. Still they serve the good of the village. Daughter, my head aches. I'm hungry too. Will we stay here tonight?"

"I'll get you something to eat and I'll fill our canteen if the water is good enough. Then we must leave. We'll sleep elsewhere tonight." Lori hurriedly pulled out a ration biscuit and gave it to Mathina. She sampled the water and found it free of any known contaminates. She dropped a capsule in each canteen and filled these with water from the stream. She gave Mathina water and drank some herself. Then she filled the canteen again. When she turned around Mathina was curled into a fetal position and was sound asleep. She looked at the sky and tried not to worry.

One of the doegs approached Lori. It sniffed around her feet. Lori reached down to pet it and the green ball licked her hand. Then the second doeg whined for attention as it joined his companion. Lori squatted and rubbed its head. It licked her hand. Lori ran her fingers over its head, shoulders, and front paws. She could see, on close inspection, the creature resembled an earth dog.

Again the wind picked up. The breeze ruffled the doeg's fur and carried a mildewed smell to her nostrils.

"Phew! You need a bath."

"I beg your pardon, Lori," said the familiar voice of Redford.

"Did you record Mathina's stories?"

Redford ignored her question. "Permission from Central has arrived. Officially I can now communicate with you. Lori, it seems your directives overrode Central's so I delivered you to the incorrect planet. My circuits were shorted by everyone's information downloads. Think of it! I have been everyone's plaything. First Central and then you, and finally Gladriel all loaded in data."

"Glady never touched your programming!"

"Before we left Base Gladriel fed in the coordinates of Clemet's planet before she cleared the program on which you were working. I assumed all the data was related."

"You didn't find out the difference until now? How incredible."

"Isn't it? I have finished backtracking through all my programs. So those coordinates you originally gave me and those Central laid in, as well as Gladriel's information confused me. Added to this was Central's directives and we arrived at planet three of this system instead of planet three in the correct section. Funny mix up, still it worked out well."

"Redford, you stupid pile of chips, you should have your boards cleared. We depend on you. I guess we'll have to leave this place. See to it."

"We can't leave, Lori. There is a THRAX unit on this planet. Central's files on this system indicate a unit was lost in this system many years ago. It may not be functional and our readings may be inaccurate. Central wants us to check it out to be sure."

"I don't care. This isn't our mission. Redford, we'll have to try again."

"Negative. Central has instructed you to continue, find and dismantle the unit as originally planned."

"Don't be stupid, Redford, we shouldn't stay. The error appears to be mine. It muddled you. We'll have to start over and take demerits."

"That's not possible. You must continue. I am ordered by Central to leave *The Flynn* where it is until you have located the unit and dismantled it. Besides, there are no demerits. If you quit you are thrown out of the Academy. Is this what you want? Think before you act. You have no choice except to continue. Besides this is not your fault, Lori. Had Central kept its programs to itself, this might never have happened. I could have determined the location of a THRAX unit and adjusted for it. I might even have adjusted for an error, maybe even have located it sooner, if it weren't for multiple errors. I've already informed them of their part in this mission. It isn't fair to you or me. We are victims," he wailed. Redford slid into one of his rhetorical infamous monologues.

"Redford, you always brighten my day. Now stop crying and wallowing in self-pity. I've heard your complaint. Contact Glady, I need to know her exact location. We must leave here as soon as possible, if we wish to reach safety from the rain."

"She is in your vicinity. You should see her soon," advised Redford.

Lori checked her map. They should be here.

Twenty yards upstream from the rocky beach they burst from the Tangle. Gladriel shouted Lori turned and shouted back. They broke into a run. Faster than they could cover the distance the two small doegs arrived between them. The green balls of fluff bared their ugly green fangs and held defensive position, growling loudly. The walker shuffled noisily through the sand and took position to the left of the doegs. The noise and confusion woke Mathina. She cried and wrung her hands.

The creatures were no deterrent to Lori. She jumped the doegs and ran to embrace her companion. Joyously they hugged and kissed. Once reassured the other was well they moved closer to the camp site. Corthain followed slowly as he observed their reunion.

Gladriel pulled Lori toward Corthain. She whispered to Lori, "You've got to meet Lord Corthain. He's something else." She stopped a few feet from Corthain before she introduced them. "Lord Corthain, I'd like you to meet Lori, my friend. Lori, this is Lord Corthain."

Lori reached out a hand in friendship. He did not. The two doegs stood beside her and grumbled deep threats in their throats. Behind her the sapling whined shrilly.

Corthain was surprised to see such a quartet facing him. The giant golden woman alone would have been enough to meet in the Tangle. To top it off she was accompanied by demons of the woods. He stiffened his spine and chastised Gladriel. "She's not sick. Is this some kind of woman's trick?"

Lori studied the man. He was equal to her in size and height. He could even have been one of the men from her home planet, unfortunately his speech was rude and his eyes showed fury. She looked him over carefully. He was handsome almost beautiful and his blonde ringlets fell haphazardly over his forehead and around his ears. The short ragged tunic reveled much more than it concealed. She smiled. No wonder Gladriel brought him to her. She tried to resist the urge to tease Glady, but couldn't.

"What did you bring home, my friend? He is something. You don't believe in packaging, I see. No wonder you spent the night. I would have too, if his looks are any indication of his abilities. I'm surprised you bothered to come back for me."

"Lori! I went for help. You were injured. I didn't know how to treat your wound." She hadn't heard the tease in Lori's voice. Her puritanical upbringing had reared its sin ridden head and she felt caught in a personal dilemma. "Corthain promised he would help. I didn't know until Redford contacted me he wasn't needed. I couldn't leave him alone because he couldn't protect himself. He's in this condition because he lost most of his tunic to a hungry plant. I used the tunic as a decoy."

"What kind of decoy?"

"I hope I made his men following us think we were eaten by the plants."

"How did you know my men were following?"

"I saw you marking the trail. There wasn't any need of marking a trail, I left a clear path." She turned to Lori. "May we go now?"

"What caused the reading?"

"Seats from the space craft and these are in all villages. So there's no need of checking out any more villages. So where do we go from here?"

"I think we head to the yellow mountain."

"Nobody goes to the yellow mountain; it is the mountain of death. Only Lord Ameral has been there," warned Corthain.

"There's another reference to Ameral. He surely gets around," said Lori as she winked conspiratorially at Gladriel. "When we have some time I have a few stories to share with you Glady."

"So have I, Lori."

"We need to get moving. I want you to meet my companion, Mathina." She swept her hand in Mathina's direction.

"It was then the old woman recognized the man with the women. She jumped up from the ground and cried, "My son! What has happened to your clothes? Your women have not taken good care of you. Look at the cuts. How did . . ."

Corthain turned away from Mathina and ignored her. He spoke with authority in his voice, "Now we are all together and your friend is no longer sick, we will wait here until my men arrive. I shall not allow you to go further."

"Who is he talking to?" Lori asked Gladriel.

"To us. In his society he is the decision maker." Lori raised her left eyebrow, "To us he is a spoiled child."

"After what Mathina told me, I can understand why he's the way he is." Lori took hold of his arm and squeezed it tightly, so he'd understand her and turned him to face her, eye to eye. "You must be something if you can keep so many women happy. Since you don't seem to have any manners, you must be quite a lover."

"Stop it, Lori! His culture is different from yours or mine. In his society he is proper and correct." Gladriel had spoken more harshly than she had intended to do, for she misinterpreted Lori's contempt as jealousy. "His actions are justified by his culture."

"He really got to you didn't he?" Lori smiled and ruffled Glady's hair.

Gladriel's face turned red as she blushed. "That's enough!"

Their conversation was halted by a deep hollow rumble which echoed through the valley. The rain storm was really moving again. Bright flashes illuminated the sky.

"Lori can he wear your skin suit?"

"It's not going to hide him much better than what he's wearing now. I think he looks good the way he is."

Gladriel walked over to the packs and without a word reached around in Lori's pack for the skin suit. She pulled it out and tossed it to Corthain. "Lord Corthain, please put this on, it will help cover you." She zipped up the pack. Then she went to help him into the suit.

Lori watched. Suddenly she realized Corthain was Glady's first love. She smiled and put her pack in place and handed Gladriel hers. "Look at your map, Glady. Redford has set up the system to lead us to the shelter. You head out first. I'll follow. Gladriel took Mathina's hand and started off. Corthain stood stubbornly where he was with his arms crossed.

"Let's go, Lord Corthain!" she shouted at him.

He didn't move.

"Are you planning on drowning?" she asked as she approached him.

He looked puzzled. The first huge drops of rain hit him. He looked up at the sky. A low moan escaped him and the color drained from his face.

Acting quickly, before he could think to resist, Lori grabbed his arm and twisted him to face in the direction Gladriel and Mathina had taken.

She hissed furiously into his ear, "Look, lover, it's raining. You can die here like a candle in the night, or you can start walking. You decide."

He noted her other hand rested on her belt near her cutter. His fear of the weather, the Tangle and her was too great. He resisted no more. He began to follow Gladriel and the old woman.

Lori gave the area a quick check and hurriedly followed him. One of the doegs and the walker had disappeared. The other doeg trotted behind Gladriel. Lori hurried to catch the group. As she moved into step behind Corthain she childishly gave his rump a companionable pat. He turned and studied her for a moment.

Lori laughed boisterously and hurried him along.

Chapter 19

Colonel Lori got up and walked to her console. "Lt. Wallace, is everything okay? I haven't heard from anyone for hours. It is now 21:00 hours. Why am I not getting any reports?"

"Sorry Colonel Lori, I assumed you were at the Admiral's party. I'm sending it to you now."

"Thank you. Lt. Wallace. I want copies of all communications on my desk which concern the Admiral or me."

She stretched. They were having a bachelor party for Sheffield, maybe she should have gone with Glady. She had time for a soak in the tub, and then it is bed time. She removed her uniform, cleansed it and filled the tub in the Admiral's suite. She did her nightly cleansing ritual and brewed another pot of median tea. Now she was ready to finish her reverie. She set the pot of tea and her cup on the ledge and slid into the warm tub, jets circulated the fluids and she felt wonderful. It was her own personal time, something she seldom had. She sipped her tea and relaxed. She was startled when the chime of her console announced a message. She got out of the tub and hurried to her message center. It was Admiral Sheffield.

"Colonel Lori speaking."

"This is a personal call, Lori. Do you have a minute to talk?"

"For you I always have a minute. I'm listening."

"I didn't know this was going to happen tonight, I understand a bachelor party is a human event quite galactically popular. I am the guest of honor. I appreciate their gesture still I'd rather be with you. I wanted you to know I love you."

"I know. Why don't you stop feeling guilty, unless there is something to feel guilty about and have a good time? I've been enjoying some quiet alone time. I do regret I wasn't invited since I'm single too."

"Did Glady go over to your ship?"

"Yes, she, Fergus and Wally planned on dining and visiting according to her parting words. I told her I'd see her in the morning. If someone had told me of this event, I might have gone with her."

"I didn't know. My officers planned it."

"It's too bad my fellow officers left Gladriel and me out of the loop. I would not have told you, nor stopped you from going. I can see they don't consider me an officer on this ship and this will be something we need to talk about when we have time to talk."

"You honestly didn't know?"

"No. It's done now. I am enjoying reflecting over a number of things, as I plan on leaving the single life shortly. Who planned your party?"

"I don't know for sure. I think Captain Kidwell did most of it."

"Well, I need to talk with her as soon as we are through with this conversation."

"This might not be the right time for conversation, Lori. She's set up a big event for midnight and is working on it now."

"Have her report to me immediately. Even though I am not your superior officer I need to see her now.

"Is that an order?" He raised his eyebrow and looked at her.

"Consider it what you will. I will see her or I will come to the party as I am. So you might want to consider it a strong suggestion or an order."

"You sound upset, Lori."

"I am her superior officer and she has not reported to me of these activities or gone through the proper channels to set up anything for this affair. She could have endangered your life. This is a breach in procedure and protocol. I want her in my office in five minutes."

"Yes, I will get the message to her. Is there anything else?"

"No, I thank you for calling me and letting me know. Now I have some things to do. First of all, I need to get back into my uniform. Sheffield, remember, I love you."

"I love you too, Lori."

She got up and went to put on her military attire.

Shortly Captain Kidwell was at Lori's office door. She knocked.

"Come in."

Captain Kidwell entered and saluted Lori who was seated at her desk.

Lori acknowledged her salute. "Please be seated, Captain Kidwell. Do you know proper procedure and protocol in the service?"

"Yes, Colonel Lori, I do. I can't stay long; I have things to do." She fidgeted in her chair.

"You are here because you broke procedure and protocol and are now being considered for a possible court martial for not going through proper channels and the chain of command. I am your superior officer and am responsible for all things dealing with Admiral Sheffield. Therefore, when you did not contact me in any manner about the event planned tonight for Admiral Sheffield you broke the chain of command and I will not tolerate such actions."

"I want to be perfectly frank with you, Lori," said Kidwell with a sweet smile on her face.

"No, you will not speak. You will not address me by my name. This is not a matter of frankness but military law. You have broken the law. Now you must be responsible for your actions."

"You're nothing more than his paramour, everyone knows. No one respects you and he deserves better."

"That is insubordination as well. You are adding up the charges. You are being escorted to the brig immediately."

"But, I have to go back to the party. I have a surprise for Admiral Sheffield."

"Unfortunately they will have to carry on without you. I'm sure the cake will wait."

"How did you know?"

"I have no doubt saved you from indecency and being out of uniform charges. You may thank me later."

A rapping was heard at the door.

"You may enter."

"Corporal Brighton, reporting, Colonel Lori."

"Corporal, please escort Captain Kidwell to the brig."

"Yes, Colonel Lori." He walked over to Captain Kidwell's side, "Please follow me, Captain Kidwell."

"You won't get away with this, you whore. The Admiral will save me, and see you for what you really are."

"That's two acts of insubordination and in front of a witness this time. The charges are mounting and you are ordered to the brig as of now. We'll see to your case when I return from my leave, until then you will remain in the brig to do some serious soul searching and reflection. It is sad when an officer with such potential would destroy her own career."

"Corporal, remove her from my office immediately." Lori was glad it was over. No doubt the woman thought to sleep her way to the top. There was no way she could know Lori and Gladriel had earned their positions. She knew their assignments to Sheffield's cruiser were to keep them out of the public eye and trouble for the Council. She had to draw a line somewhere.

"Connect me with Lt. Colonel Gladriel on *The Empolo*." She took off her uniform jacket before Glady answered.

"Hi, what are you up to, Lori?"

"Probably more than I should be, Glady. Did a Captain Kidwell contact you to plan a bachelor party for Admiral Sheffield?"

"No. I had no requests from anyone to arrange a party. I thought you had a hand in it, so I let it go."

"Well, the secret organizer was Captain Kidwell; you know the cutie from Earth?"

"I've seen her here and there. I have never spoken with her. What has she done?"

"She arranged this party without official approval and had a cake made so she could climb out at midnight. I need to get hold of the outfit she was going to wear. She, no doubt, planned on seducing Sheffield and sleeping her way to my position."

"She is either quite ambitious or wanting to get him into a compromising situation. Surely she knows you and he are 'tying the knot' so to speak as soon as you get to Acuman."

"She was quite mouthy to me and disrespectable too. She is now in the brig. I'm sending you a copy of our meeting. See what you get out of it and we'll discuss it on our journey. How's your visiting going?"

"We're having a great time. Fergus and I had to force Wally into his tank and shut the lid. Wally is so strong being like an octopus and he needs to cleanse his system. He was too far gone to even enjoy dinner. So now I am having a good time and visit. When will Sheffield be back?"

"I have no idea. I really need to confiscate the cake and her costume."

"Are you really going to prosecute her?"

"It's a strong possibility. Listen to the tape and tell me what you think."

"Okay, I will. It came through. I'll listen to it now. She ran the tape. There is every reason to charge her and she is recorded. Wow, she's quite the lady?" Do you need my help?"

"I hope I don't. I'll let you know if there is a need. Thanks, Glady."

I'll see you and talk with you tomorrow."

"I'll see you tomorrow." She leaned back and smiled. Now she needed to get the cake and costume and save these for possible evidence. She wondered how she could do such a thing without a big fuss. "Connect me with the person in charge of the galley."

"You've reached the galley, Corporal Grant speaking."

"This is Colonel Lori speaking. Is the cake for the Admiral ready?"

"It is. We made the hollow center as you ordered."

"Can you store the cake in the freezer in a sealed container? No one is to touch it, except Admiral Sheffield or me. I need an official receipt and a copy of my order immediately." She hung up.

Now I need to contact the ship's financial office.

"Hello, this is private Xian."

"Hello, private Xian, is any officer on duty tonight?"

"Yes, Major Munns."

"Can you connect my line to Major Munns, this is Colonel Lori."

"Yes, ma'am," he responded and pushed the button to the Major's station and connected them. "Colonel Lori on line one, sir."

"Thank you, Xian. Hi, sweetheart, is everything going well? Have you got him where you want him yet?"

Lori hung up. She knew all she needed to know. The officers were using her name and code to procure items, she hadn't ordered. She immediately buzzed Sheffield.

"Admiral Sheffield speaking."

"Colonel Lori here. I've discovered something which you should investigate immediately. Please come by my office now."

"Are you serious?"

"I am quite serious. I've uncovered an intrigue on this ship." She hung up.

Shortly the door to her office burst open. "What's going on, Lori?"

She asked him to sit down and listen to something. She played the recording of Captain Kidwell's initial hearing. "What do you think of the situation?"

"You did the right thing."

"Oh, there's more." She played back the short visit with the galley and Major Munns. What do you think now?"

"Something would show up, when we're getting ready to leave."

"Who can you trust to find the copies of all purchases and requests issued by officers? We certainly can't trust Munns or Kidwell. Maybe it's only the two of them; however, it could be bigger."

"I'm going to talk with Colonel Jord. I can get him here in a few days and have him bring a team of investigators with him. In the meantime I could have my replacement maintain the situation until we return."

"We need to act as if nothing has happened. Kidwell needs to stay in the brig. The time she spends may be enough to allow her to think of her career. I don't know if you should feel flattered or used by Kidwell. She possibly thought she could replace me and control you. You are a handsome man and you would be a nice sauce for her plans."

"You need to go ahead with the court martial. I don't want her on this ship. She is to be transferred to Glather for her trial immediately."

"What about Munns?"

"I'm going to have a talk with him now. I'll see you when we finish." He stepped over to her side of the table and kissed her. "You truly are an expert at finding the unusual. For a moment there I thought you were jealous."

"Fortunately my instincts are a bit sharper when I have enough of the pieces. The cake is locked in the freezer.

"No, it arrived when I was leaving. Call me a squad of security now."

Lori contacted the brig and gave Sheffield the phone. "I need the person in charge of the Brig tonight."

"Captain Neuse, here"

"Admiral Sheffield speaking. Is Captain Kidwell in the Brig?" He waited for the answer. "When did she leave?" He paused to listen. "Who took her from the Brig?"

"Corporal Brighton came with a message from you, sir, to release her."

"Captain Neuse you are to maintain your post and send me a squad of your best to the recreation center to remove a cake from the room and return it to the freezer. If someone is inside the cake they are not to let that person out. I want a copy of all orders received by you immediately sent to my office. Furthermore send Corporal Brighton to Colonel Lori's office immediately. I'll speak with you later, Captain Neuse." He hung up the phone.

"Lori, there are more problems here than I knew. Is Glady with us?

"No, she went over to *The EmPolo*. Do you want me to call her?"

"Yes, have her report to the recreation area as soon as she arrives. She can bring Fergus with her. Tell her what's going on here. Can you handle Corporal Bright?"

"How do you want me to handle him?"

"Explain how important it is to pick your friends well and tell him he will lose his position with the service if he continues in this intrigue. He could be court martialed. I'd advise you to get back into your uniform. He might think you were asking him here for other activities.

"Lori, I don't know when I'll get back. Let me know if anything else happens. This is a busy way to leave a ship." He hugged and kissed her and headed out. "Wait up for me."

Lori called Gladriel. "We have a bit more on the story. Seems someone claimed Admiral Sheffield ordered the release of Captain Kidwell and the message was carried by Corporal Brighton who escorted her to the Brig. He is to report here to my office shortly. You and Fergus are needed over here. I want Redford to comb through the ships files and find all copies of communiqués from Sheffield, you and me ordering items through the galley and from supplies. I want Fergus to search the area where the cake was to be stored to see if there is a costume in the room. If it's not there, he's to go to Captain Kidwell's room and search it thoroughly for the outfit and all copies of officers' letters, messages, and notes. If he finds any empty requisition papers bring these too. This is important and hush-hush. No one should know of this, no matter what. Have Fergus sent me a report by morning, if possible. Sheffield needs you, Glady. I only wish I knew who can be trusted. We need more men to help. See you soon. Thanks, Glady."

Lori got back in to her uniform and waited. She had her disruptor set at stun and prayed it was enough. She sat down to wait.

Shortly there was a tapping on her door.

She pressed the ID-screen and saw Corporal Brighton with two armed officers. She buzzed Sheffield.

"Admiral, this is Lori. I hate to bother you but thought you might like to know I have Corporal Brighton with two armed officers at my door. I only requested him. I've notified Gladriel and Fergus of your request. I'm going to tag Fergus to come to my office and be my back up."

"Busy here, okay on Fergus."

"Redford, I need to have Fergus here now. I have a corporal here with two armed men and I would like to have him as back up. Is this possible?"

"He's on board now and coming to your quarters. You may answer the door."

"Who's there?"

"Corporal Brighton."

"Please enter Corporal Brighton after you set your weapon on the tray by the door. You are to enter alone. I have turned on the scanner. Enter now."

"Colonel Lori, I would rather you came out here. I have an arrest warrant for you from Admiral Sheffield. You are to report to the Brig immediately."

"Please stay where you are, Corporal Brighton. I will be with you momentarily."

"Did you hear that, Redford?"

"I did and I'm contacting Sheffield now."

"May I see a copy of your orders, Corporal?"

"Certainly, Colonel Lori." He unfolded the order and held it to the scanner screen.

"Who gave you this order, Corporal?"

"Captain Munn's, he got it from the Admiral and passed it to me."

"Redford, we really need some help."

"Help is on its way. I had a surprise for you but this is more important."

"Thanks, Redford."

Lori listened to the men in the hall. She learned nothing. Suddenly she saw Fergus. "I'll be right out." As the door opened Fergus stunned the two guards and she knocked Brighton's hand down and into the door jamb as she gripped his wrist. "Drop it now." The disruptor fell to the floor. Fergus with gloved hands picked it up and showed her it was set for kill. "It's time for a talk, Brighton. Have a seat. Give me the warrant and lay your hands on the table. Thank you, Corporal."

"Didn't I give you an order to only take orders from the Admiral or me earlier this evening?"

"Yes, Colonel Lori."

"Then why are you giving me orders from Captain Munns?"

"This is from the Admiral."

"Did you get it directly from the Admiral?"

"No, I did not, Colonel Lori."

"I want to show you the Admiral's signature. Does the one on this warrant look like this one?"

"No, Colonel, it does not, but Captain Munns said you might try something like this. He said you weren't really a member of this crew and had no right to question anything or order anyone."

"At this point I want to tell you, you are being recorded. All of this conversation will be for the Admiral and the court record. You are up for court martial charges for mutiny and attempted murder. Do you admit to mutiny and attempted murder?"

"Since you are not a legal member of the Military staff your death would not be mutiny it would be murder, but I didn't kill you."

"The disruptor was set for kill, isn't that true?"

"Yes, it is true. You are big and strong and I wanted to make sure you came with us as requested."

"Is murder the best way to get someone to cooperate, Corporal Brighton?"

"Not really, but you are not legally here on this ship. Captain Munns is a better leader than you or Sheffield."

"How do you know this? Captain Kidwell told me how smart he is and how much of this ship he controls. Almost all the crew supports him for the position of Admiral."

"That is not how one becomes an Admiral. If Munns had succeeded you'd be official pirates."

"We would not; he has the approval of the Sseech and the Council."

"What Sseech was this who gave him approval?"

"The leader of the Supreme Sseech LaConTraVitra personally asked Captain Munns to aid him in this effort and he would make him Admiral Munns."

"LaConTraVitra is dead, Corporal Brighton. I saw him die with my own eyes."

"Captain Munns says his death was only a story to cover up his presence as he takes over the galaxy."

"Admiral Sheffield and I saw him die along with his son on Gloriel last year. That is a fact. Captain Munns is using you and others in this plot. Who is in charge outside of Captain Munns?

"I don't know. I answer to Munns and Kidwell."

"No, Corporal, you answer to the Council, the Admiral and me. Now, Corporal, I have a surprise for you. You are the one going to the brig. I have been appointed to this position by Supreme Counselade Hyptiggia and the Council on Glather for various reasons. I am a full Colonel. I am going to my wedding with the Admiral. Since when do you listen to a Captain over a Colonel or an Admiral? Fergus, will you escort this vermin to the Brig and inform Captain Munns he is under arrest. If he gives you trouble fire to kill or maim. If this young Corporal gives you any trouble kill him. I will not stand for trickery and insubordination. Corporal, I am notifying the Admiral right now and I am playing this interrogation back to him." She watched Fergus and Brighton leave.

"Admiral Sheffield speaking."

"Hi, it's Lori. I have arrested Corporal Brighton and ordered the arrest of Captain Munns who sent a fake warrant for my arrest. I told Fergus to shoot to kill or maim if either Brighton or Munns gave him any problems. I have two stunned guards who came with Brighton. They need to be moved and questioned. You might want to listen to this tape before you grant immunity to anyone. Redford said he had additional help to send but didn't say who." She waited as he listened to the tape.

"I'll handle it from here, Colonel Lori. We have made several arrests. Thanks for help on the other end. I think I have someone who might tell all for a reduced sentence and a dishonorable discharge without a court martial.

"If it's Kidwell she is the mastermind, not an innocent. Do not give her immunity. She and Munns are a team. Corporal Brighton says there are a number of crew members too. He might be able to help with a bit more information. He's gung-ho and immature and may give away more without meaning too. I wonder what it took for Munns and Kidwell to bribe the crew members."

"Thanks for the tip. You are right, she is a player. See you later."

She sighed and made another pot of tea. Shortly she was settled in her comfortable conforming chair holding her brewed Median tea. She turned on the techno-diary once more and let her mind go back to a special time when Gladriel and she were learning about life outside the Academy.

Chapter 20

Thunder continued to rumble across the sky and lightning clipped the air. The wind, rising in the storm's first contact whipped their path into a frenzy of dancing, slashing branches which impeded their way. Gladriel resorted to using her cutter and soon Lori pushed up beside her. Together they cleared a path and made walking easier.

About a half mile from where they began, Corthain called out, "The old woman has stopped."

"What now?" grumbled Lori? She hastened back down the slope.

Mathina was standing at the base of a tall tree hung with long gray-green tubers. Some tubers had dropped to the ground forming a pebbly carpet beneath the limbs.

"Why have you stopped, Mathina?"

"This tree is a friend." She walked carefully under its limbs stepping over the fallen fruit. Once under the branches she stopped and reaching up and pulled a tuber from a low branch. It came loose with a soft pop sound. Mathina returned to Lori.

"Look this is a jug tree. See this jug." She handed it to Lori to inspect.

Lori saw its deep rich green jug and hefted it to calculate its weight and felt the liquid move beneath the skin. She looked at Mathina.

"Many plants find a way to store their liquid for the dry season. These are still green and carry much fluid which I drink when I'm thirsty. But, when they turn brown and then black the liquid is no longer good and the jug falls to the ground. The left over water and the jug's hide feed the seed. If I cut a jug open when it is green the water is fresh."

Lori pulled out her cutter and followed Mathina's directions and cut a hole in one end. A clear liquid poured out when she turned the jug upside down. Mathina, cupping her hands, caught some and drank greedily.

Gladriel had seen the doeg bite into one. She ran her scanner over the jug. "Lori, it is drinkable. Nothing shows up on the scanner." She plucked another from the tree and cut off the end and drank a sip than a mouthful. "This is delicious."

Everyone drank their fill. Mathina gathered a number of jugs and tied them into a bundle with one of her skirts and hung the bundle over her back with the waistband forming a band on her forehead. Everyone filled their water bags and drank more than normal. Everyone added some jugs to their packs except Corthain who felt it was beneath him to carry anything other than his water pouch which he had filled.

With lifted spirits the group continued their climb. The terrain changed from heavy jungle to grassy knolls to clusters of rock. Even the cutting of the thickening grasses was impossible, for the wind whipped the grass in chaotic patterns. The women put away their cutters. Now large boulders were strewn about causing their passage to be slow and loose gravel caused them to slip. The strain of climbing was wearing on Mathina and Corthain. Mathina said nothing when she stumbled and fell. It wasn't the same reaction from Corthain, a village athlete and Lord. He grumbled and complained. Finally he stopped. He insisted he needed to rest. When he stopped, Mathina hurried to him and fussed over him.

"Leave me be, old woman," he said as he pushed her away. "I will go no further. I am tired."

Lori who was again bringing up the rear saw what Corthain was doing, however she didn't say anything until she caught up with him. "Gladriel, come back here."

"What's the problem?"

"The Lord here has balked again."

Gladriel squatted at Corthain's feet. "What's the problem?"

"I am tired. I will walk no farther."

"You must. We have to get out of this gully. If we get caught here we could drown." She knelt and put her hand on his shoulder before she spoke. "Corthain we are going on with you or without. But . . ." She hesitated before speaking more, "I want you to come with us."

Lori stepped over Corthain's outstretched legs, grasped Gladriel by her arm and pulled her up. "Glady, you take Mathina and go on up to the top. Take the doeg with you. It's not fond of Corthain anyway. Contact Redford as to what's going on and I'll get things straightened out. We'll join you shortly."

"Gladriel made as if to speak. Lori spoke up, "Would you take my packs too?"

"What about Corthain's pack?"

"Don't you worry about his pack? One of us will carry it. Get up the hill and to shelter now. Save Mathina, yourself and the doeg. I'll take care of us. What is it, Mathina?"

"I'll carry the Lord's pack so he can rest." She removed the fruit from her head and attached it to her waist. Then she put a strap of his tote on her forehead and started climbing the hill.

"We'll meet you at the top. Don't rest long."

"We'll be there soon. Get a move on and find the cave. It's an order."

Gladriel climbed up the incline and left them behind.

When Lori was sure they were beyond hearing, she turned to Corthain. A streak of the dramatic stirred within and she spoke, "It's a good place. You have chosen well. I approve." She smiled sweetly, aware Corthain was watching her. "It is such a waste of a good looking man. Sadly you can't keep up with us. Look at Mathina. At her age she can out walk you, a Lord" She shook her head and pretended to straighten her boots. Then she brightened and smiled broadly directly at him. "Getting rid of you will be my pleasure."

"What do you mean?" He looked puzzled.

"Where do you want it: the head, the gut, the groin? You pick the spot. I'll hit it," said Lori with braggadocio. She stood up and

148

pulled out her disruptor. She watched his eyes as they darted from her to the trail and back to her. "Oh, don't worry. They won't hear. I'll tell them you decided to wait for your men."

"You don't want to harm me, do you?" Corthain asked. Then he licked his lips. "You are different from any women I've ever met, even Gladriel. No one would ever dare to treat me as you have." He felt an edge of fear creep over him as he looked at Lori towering over him with her weapon pointed at his head. "I could take you as one of my women. In time, with the proper training you could become a wife to me. Strong women make good breeders. I can be kind and gentle with the training. Soon you will love me as my other women do. Look at Gladriel, your friend, she loves me." He smiled with a half hitch in the corner of his mouth. "Such beauty and strength as we have should not be wasted. We will have beautiful strong sons and daughters."

Corthain watched Lori carefully. Dare he hope he could win her? A hard lump of fear settled deeper in his stomach as he saw the corners of her mouth tighten before she spoke, slowly and calmly.

"Are you trying flattery on me, Corthain? So you've won Gladriel, you think. We are not of this world. We may be the women of your legend, consider the possibility. I feel Glady deserves better than you. Make up your mind. I can kill you here and now, or you can join the women at the top. We three women can manage without you."

"Come with me, Lori," he begged. "Together we can find our way home. Then together we can enjoy the fruits of the crown."

When she didn't answer, he turned and ran off among the boulders.

Her bluff hadn't worked. He was gone. She wondered how she would explain this to Glady, as she turned and began climbing to join Glady and Mathina.

A piercing scream filled the air. She looked up. The women were out of sight. Another screamed echoed below her. It was Corthain. He was in trouble. Darting among the boulders, searching for him, she stopped many times to determine the direction of his screams. Finally she caught up with him only to find he was clutched in the tentacle of a huge jungle plant creature.

Brown tipped green tentacles pulled Corthain toward a yawning mouth of lime green pulsating flesh. He struggled and screamed as the tentacles clasping his legs pulled steadily. Although he had one arm free he could not loosen the grip of any one tentacle.

Lori was in time to see a long green tentacle flip out and wrap itself around Corthain's free arm. It began contracting and pulling him closer to the churning mouth salivated in anticipation. Corthain screamed again.

"Need a little help, Corthain?" The sarcasm she wanted in her voice did not surface. Instead the question was couched in fear.

"Lori!" he puffed. "Lori, help me."

"I don't know. This could be too much for me. However, if I help you, you might make me another offer." Lori couldn't believe she was watching a man being pulled to his death while she joked. She hated this. She didn't want this friction between them to continue. Thank goodness the plant was not a fast worker.

"Please, Lori, help me. Don't let me die. What would you tell your friend?"

"Will you join and stay with us until we release you?"

"Yes, anything if you'll save me."

While they had conversed she'd studied the actions of the plant. Corthain was too big to dump all at once in its maw. So the plant had released and moved tentacles to eat him bit by bit starting with his feet.

She selected the best spot and took two steps closer and fired. The first beam of fire disappeared into the maw as it was preparing to draw his feet into its digestive juices. The second beam sliced through the tentacles which waved above Corthain awaiting their turn to hold the victim. A third shot sliced the creature off its base. She holstered the disruptor and took out her cutter. Wading in among the tentacles, Lori cut Corthain lose and pulled him some ten feet away before she would let go and he could stand up. They watched the dismembered tentacle thrashing about.

"Thank you, Lori," said Corthain as he hugged Lori. Suddenly he kissed her and held her in his arms. "Never have I seen such actions I cannot understand you women. Gladriel shows such strength."

"Let's join the others."

"I am ready, Lori," however, he made no move to release her from his arms. "I will cause you no further trouble." He pulled her close and kissed her again.

"Are you serious?"

"Yes," he answered and then kissed her again. This time more emotion went into his kiss and Lori responded. He felt love for the first time. He didn't have his crown and he became euphoric. He wanted her as he had never wanted any woman before.

Suddenly the rain which had held off for so long came crashing down in huge sheets of water. The roar of the downpour was so great they had to shout to one another. Fearing they might get separated they clasped hands and climbed up the slope fighting against rain and run off. The ground became wet and slippery. Each was glad of the others hand.

In the blinding rain they ran past the outcrop of rocks. A sharp bark from the doeg alerted them and they stopped. Lori began calling. When Gladriel answered they called back and forth until Lori and Corthain were squeezing into the small cave opening and joined Gladriel, Mathina and the doeg who huddled there.

"Are you all right? I was beginning to worry," said Glady.

"Me too. How did you find this place?"

"The doeg found it and barely in time. We crawled in as the rain hit."

"How much room?" asked Lori?

"We can definitely wait out the storm here. I've checked it out with the doeg. It goes back about twenty feet to a five foot ledge and probably beyond it into a cavern. We're dry and we'll be warm soon. Come," said Gladriel as she took Lori by the arm and moved her deeper inside. She pulled a sleeper from Lori's pack and tossed it to her.

"Strip and wrap up in the sleeper. I'll see to Corthain and get the perimeters set and the prism lit. Some light and heat will help." She moved off to do as she said.

Corthain stood near the entrance and watched Lori as she stripped and dried herself then wrapped the sleeper around her body. He moved only when Gladriel gave him a sleeper and shoved him aside so she could plant the poles.

A low steady hum assured her the perimeter was working. She turned to set up the prism and found Mathina had already unpacked. Gladriel checked the prism and turned it on. A feeble glow danced above the cylinder and grew as Gladriel increased its fuel. Shortly the cave was filled with light and rosy warmth spread out from the heater.

Lori took her brush from her pack and squatted by the prism while she brushed out her wet hair. The doeg came and sat beside Lori waiting for her touch. She patted its head and then finished brushing her hair.

Mathina build a small cache of rocks and placed her water jugs inside, explaining they would stay cool. Gladriel set up the tripod and fixed the water can. When the water began to boil she tossed in pinch of Median tea. Soon a soothing fragrance of roses drifted from the can.

Corthain watched the group around the fire and feeling cold, damp and lonely he joined them at Gladriel's invitation. He squatted and then sat between Lori and Gladriel. He had retrieved his tote from Mathina. Now it rested between his knees.

Seated between the two women he felt the call of the crown. He knew he dare not reveal it in the presence of three women. The weakness in his legs grew in strength each time Lori's thigh brushed his. The urge to lift the crown from its chest and place it on his head grew. He fought not to give in to the passion mounting inside and his urge to feel the crown's power was more than he could bear. He arose with a groan.

"Is something wrong, Lord Corthain?" asked Gladriel.

"No, everything is fine." He carried his tote to the far side of the cave and deposited it behind a large stone. He sat there and tried to fight his urges.

Seeing her opportunity to talk with Lori Gladriel asked, "Lori, what happened back there in the boulders?"

"It is nothing to worry about, it came out right."

"Lori, we're friends. You can tell me."

"I gave him a choice. He decided to run and leave. Then he got caught by a plant. It would have had him for breakfast, lunch, and dinner if I hadn't found him in time. I zapped it. "I was furious because he would want to leave you. He's a lazy, self-centered, conceited . . ."

"He's gentle too. He saved my life," said Gladriel in his defense. "Do you want him, Lori?"

"Want him? Why would you think I did?"

"I can sense a change in you. You're extremely quiet."

"I could say the same about you, Glady. I almost died two days ago."

"Me?" Gladriel was dumbfounded. She didn't think her feelings could show so much. "Something has happened to us, Lori. I know the night in the village I was seduced by Corthain and Jeames seduced you the day he got his crown."

"I can't forget it."

"When I am close to Corthain, I want to throw myself at him and engulf him in my arms. Yet those feelings disgust me, because I can't control them. They come when I'm not prepared. If you and Mathina weren't here, I know what I would do. I'd be with Corthain. Can you understand me, Lori? You're the girl I remember who said she never had any trouble controlling herself. You took what you wanted and left what you didn't want alone. Help me Lori, to be able to walk away."

"This is the first time you've felt passion and love. You are young. You can love and not be destroyed by it. Glady, there is nothing wrong with passion and love as long as it is what you want. It is not your fault. Don't let traditions or guilt hurt you. You have done nothing wrong. It is more the crown than any one's fault. Corthain pays a high price for its use and so do his women. It gives them pleasure and insures the race will continue."

"But, Lori, this isn't love. It's lust" Disgust and fear clung to her words. "I always thought I could control my urges and desires. I can't."

"You'd have to change a great deal to be free of your childhood training and beliefs. So forgive yourself and let yourself love if you want. He has not had his crown around him so maybe you're seeing the real man."

"Did you sleep with him today?"

"No, I did not. I saved his life. He kissed me and thanked me."

"Do you love him now?"

"No, Gladriel, he is your man, not mine." She thought it would be easy to lust for him, but it would not be worth the harm it would cause Gladriel. She loved Gladriel too much to cause her pain. "He loves you. Let yourself love him. It will give you a greater understanding of what love really is."

"Thanks, Lori. I needed to know. I keep feeling jealous of anyone he might want."

"Jealousy is not healthy. It is your fear and a sword in your heart. Get rid of it."

Chapter 21

Outside the storm raged, while inside there was quiet. The tea brewed and Mathina talked of plants, Lords, stones, and doegs. They let her ramble, reluctant to interrupt with talk about what tomorrow would bring. Mathina had no thought of the morrow. She was content to enjoy the present. Corthain leaned against the wall, feeling the pull of the crown. He was not sure if he could use it and feared missing its usage for several days. Once he had a crown he never used it less than one time a night.

Lori had retreated to the back of the cave and sat watching the light dance across Gladriel's face. Surely neither would let a man come between their friendships. She waved at Gladriel when she looked her way but wasn't sure if Glady saw her. She'd waited a while to see how Glady was doing.

Gladriel swirled the tea around in the pot and stared into the blue whirlpool. Her eyes burned from the tears she'd shed and her chest felt constricted. She hadn't wanted to be so hard on Lori. Surprisingly an emotion she couldn't control had gained hold of her. She knew Lori was in the back of the cave.

Mathina broke the silence. "Is the tea ready? I'm hungry."

"Yes, Mathina, the tea is ready. Lori and I will share with you. Lord Corthain, I think, has some supplies." She spoke to him, "Lord Corthain, would you like to bring your supplies and join us? Lori, come on over and share a bite."

Lori and Corthain were slow to return to the small circle. Corthain carried coarse bread and several globes of green fruit. These he gave to Gladriel who passed them to Mathina and asked her to divide the fruit for everyone.

In silence the four squatted around the prism. Mathina divided the food Corthain had contributed, as well as two fruits she had carried with her.

Gladriel saw Mathina give her own portion to Corthain.

"Sorry, Lord Corthain," she said as she took Mathina's portion and gave it back to her. "We all share alike. You need the food for your strength for tomorrow. Lord Corthain can survive on less. He wants you to eat to be strong."

Mathina might have argued more. Instead Lori spoke up. "Glady is right Mathina. We all share. Now eat." There was more command in her tone than she would have liked, for some reason unknown to her the irritation of the afternoon hung upon her.

Several times the women caught the other staring at Corthain who seemed unaware of the stares. Quickly they shifted their glances away, pretending concern with other things. Corthain was moody and stared into the dancing light. He sighed repeatedly and shifted his weight.

The meal ended in silence as it had begun. Mathina checked her cache of water jugs and then began smoothing out a resting place. She hummed contentedly and tossed out loose pebbles which the doeg retrieved to heap in a small pile. Satisfied with her bed Mathina settled herself pulling up her long over skirt until it formed a cover around her arms and shoulders. When she had settled quietly into the beginning of sleep the doeg crawled up against her back and lay down.

All evening Corthain had thought of his crown, only marginally aware of his dependence upon it. He remembered his winning of it. The first seasons he used it once or twice a day. During the last four seasons he had found himself using it much more frequently, lately as many as seven times a day. This great usage had to be kept a secret. Even now the women talked of nothing else but serving Corthain's growing appetite for sexual pleasure. The physical evidence of its usage appeared early in his adult life. He had rapid growth and weight as well as fathering so many children. It was no secret in his or any other village. His muscles had grown and developed. He had reasoned to himself he was not the only Lord to increase his usage of his crown. Others had begun using their crowns more frequently and the population was increasing, although few males were born.

He had fathered four sons, all living. This led to the envy on the part of several Lords including Lord Ameral had made crude remarks about Corthain's potency. Corthain had assured himself Lord Ameral was merely teasing him as a father would a son.

The thoughts of the crown intruded again and made him feel tired and discontent. He had gone all day without is use. So near it lay, yet so far away. Frustration and anger built in him and he moaned aloud.

The growing desire for the crown increased until Corthain finally yielded to its power. He stood, and then began pacing with his hands on his hips. He spoke, calmly with great authority. "I have a great need of a woman tonight. Gladriel will you join me?"

Gladriel got up, took her sleeper with her, and went to him. She put her arms around him. "I'm here." She spread out her bedding. She raised her hand toward him.

"Before I wear my crown the old woman must leave, it is the law."

Mathina got up and walked to the door of the cave. It was still raining outside and the perimeter would not allow her to leave. "I cannot leave, my Lord. There is a power holding me here."

"Lori, you are to help Mathina outside, and then come back in here."

"Corthain, you idiot," Lori said. "In her obedience, she might have walked to her death. It's a good thing Glady set the perimeter. Did you think where she might find shelter in the dark from this storm? What's wrong with you, why would you give such a command?"

"You may go with the old woman, if you like. I shall find satisfaction with Gladriel." He looked down at Gladriel who sat on the bed.

157

"You are mistaken, Lord Corthain, if you think I shall let Lori and Mathina go out in the storm. I cannot understand what is happening to you. None of us will leave. You will have no satisfaction and pleasure tonight with your attitude." She picked up her sleeper and left to join the other women.

Apparently Corthain had not understood the exchange or he thought his Lord's right would get him his way. He squatted in front of the chest.

"I have spoken," so saying he threw back the lid of the chest. The crown was prismatic and its colors permeated the room along with its sweet cloying odor.

Gladriel stopped walking and turned to him. She was the nearest and the pheromones had reached her instantly. Her eyes glazed over. Deep down inside a growing desire to share the crown began is upward spiral. Lori felt the tug of the crown and was drawn to him and the crown.

Mathina awake and was fully aware of the crown and thankfully unaffected by it. She went to the edge of the cave near the mouth. She feared she would see a double mating and be damned. The small green doeg's growl rumbled deep in its throat and increased in volume.

Exposure to the prism created more light and this inflamed the crown, Corthain and the women. As the cilia moved its perfume climbed upward to engulf the three. Corthain breathed deeply. He realized Gladriel was near to him and he pulled her to him. They began to sway and move with the rhythm of the cilia and he laid her on her sleeper. He kissed her and pushed her hair away from her ears. Then he traced her right ear with his left pointer finger which he'd used to help pick up the crown. The scent and powerful essence of the crown went directly to her bloodstream and he felt her run her hand over his chest. Then she gently kissed his nipples and nibbled at them. These became hard and she undid his clothing and felt the rest of him. She felt him harden as she touched him and he smiled at her, as he laid her back and kissed and tugged on her right nipple and ran his hand lower and lower until she moaned, "More, my Lord, more." "Be patient my love." He kissed her and rolled over putting her on top of him and his erection. She gasped in surprise. He began to pick her up and lowering her time and time again until she screamed in pleasure as she reached her first orgasm. She could hardly breathe. He was already on top of her and took his time as he reached his own moment of pleasure. Then he rolled her over as she was even more desirous of him. He kissed her lips and forced his tongue into her mouth and played with it as she reached a sheer state of ecstasy. She wanted him and needed him. She yelled, "Now, Now," but he held back and brought her body to frenzy as the combination of his kisses, his hands played over her body. Finally the full impact of his driving force allowed him the joy of joint pleasure. He whispered, "I love, you, Gladriel, you and I are one." He kissed her lips and became one. Their love radiated like sparks of fire through him and her.

Lori struggled against the pull of the crown, yet felt herself slowly losing control. She began to work on a mathematical puzzle and tried diverting her mind to other things, yet she felt the pull and fought it even more. She thought of Oman and the thought saved her. She ignored the power of the crown, yet was trapped in a vortex. She knew Gladriel was giving of her love and feeling his love too, so this helped her control herself even more. She dared not open her eyes; she was too close to him and the crown. She dropped to the floor and meditated, hoping it was enough to save her and Gladriel from this trap. Somehow she thought I must destroy the crown. She began to crawl toward it carrying only the one thought: destroy the crown.

Soon these women would taste his power. Tomorrow, when he was filled with new vigor and they were weak and docile he would question them fully. He'd learn of their strange powers and weapons, as well as the location of their village. Then when his men arrived he could send a message to the Rex. He'd see their village was taken and its women trained in their proper ways. Their rebellion would be quelled. The women needed repeated exposure to the crown. He quivered with the happy thought. The new women would add new strength to the villages. He smiled at the thought of this adventure taking him from his quiet village. His spirits lifted as he thought of the coming nights.

Lori finally reached the chest for the crown. Corthain had replaced it in its chest after He'd taken Lori for his own. She leaned over the chest. She was breathing slowly and softly. Her presence roused Corthain from his reverie. He watched Lori's heaving breasts and golden skin. He motioned with a sweep of his hand for her to join him and Gladriel on the sleeper. She didn't notice. Instead she stared at the vibrating crown which beckoned to her. He smiled warmly pleased she could not refuse him. She was after all only a woman and he would be her Lord.

Slowly she reached out to pick up the crown. He called her name. She looked up at him. She tried to concentrate. She needed to destroy the crown. She kept thinking destroy the crown. He reached for her chin and sought to bring her up to him. She had taken hold of the crown. Suddenly the doeg darted out of the shadows and grabbed the crown from her hand. The force of its leap carried it over the chest and into the dark portion of the cave.

For a moment Corthain was stunned. Then he screamed and stumbled. Then he kicked the chest. When Gladriel reached for him he shoved her aside. Gladriel's moan and Corthain's screams plus the action roused Lori.

"What's going on, Glady?" Lori reached her and pulled her up. They stood huddled together.

A sharp bark and a growl from the doeg brought their attention to the dark portion of the cave. Corthain yelled and called out, "Stop the doeg, it has got my crown!"

A green blur sailed past the prism and disappeared into the dark once more.

Corthain stumbled over the pile of pebbles and fell flat on his chest. "Help me, you women," he ordered. "The doeg has my crown." He got up and shot off into the dark portion of the cave. "Help me!"

The three women watched in amazement when the doeg reappeared out of the darkness once more with Corthain in hot pursuit.

Mathina was hysterical and cried openly.

Gladriel was unable to respond, she was still dazed from the after effects of the crown.

Lori was laughing. Her head had cleared rapidly and she stooped to pick up the prism. This chase was one not to miss. The strong white light filled the cave, pushing back the shadows until the perimeter poles shone like silver toothpicks. Light played over Corthain and the doeg at the back of the cave.

Corthain had cornered the doeg but its teeth were buried deeply in the crown. Corthain advanced confidently. He felt now he would get his crown. As he bent over the doeg it growled and darted between his legs, leaving Corthain to smack his head against the wall. He cried out in pain and anger.

The doeg trotted toward the women who had regained some of their senses. The doeg stopped four feet short of them and laid down the crown. The light revealed it was torn and dirty.

Lori stepped forward; she hoped to destroy the crown. The doeg growled and stood up. Hearing Corthain's approach from the rear and watching Lori's approach from the front, the doeg stood guard over the damaged crown. At the moment the two came within an arm's length of the doeg and crown, it snatched the crown and wheeled away. Neither Corthain nor Lori could check their advance. In the confusion they collided, knocking themselves off balance and landed on the floor. The prism fell from Lori's hand and rolled away.

Gladriel collapsed into laughter and Mathina was smiling. The doeg had simply trotted a few yards away.

Corthain shoved Lori away and crawled toward the doeg.

It waited a few seconds before dashing off toward the rear of the cave and wiggled between two boulders.

"I want my crown now!" screamed Corthain.

Lori crawled toward the prism and Gladriel. When she reached it she stood up, took the prism in on hand and then pulled Gladriel up with the other. "Let's help him, Glady."

She held the light above as she and Glady walked hand in hand toward the rear of the cave. In the dark niche where the doeg had disappeared Lori shoved the light.

A low growling and then chomping caused the three to peek over the ledge. They could see the doeg, well away from an arm's length reach. The doeg was chewing on the crown as a dog would chew an old bone.

"My crown! He's eating my crown!" Corthain sobbed.

"Glady, if I give you a boost up, could you squeeze in far enough to grab it?" Lori asked.

"It could run again."

"No, he won't. He can't jump over these big slabs and I don't think he'll try running out into the cave again." Lori handed the prism to Corthain and asked him to hold it high and steady. Cupping her hands together Lori told Glady to step into them and crawl onto the ledge. Gladriel squirmed a few inches forward, reached down, and grabbed the crown.

Suddenly a tug of war began. First the doeg pulled then Glady. The contest of strength was a draw. The doeg could not retreat for leverage and Gladriel could not move her arm enough to simply pull. She pretended to let the doeg pull the crown away. As it released it to secure a tighter bite, Gladriel jerked it away, but not before his sharp teeth ripped a large chunk out of it.

"I have it, Lori. Pull me back out." A few sharp tugs and Lori had Gladriel freed and standing between her and Corthain. "Here, Corthain, I'm sorry," said Glady as she handed him the dead crown.

Tenderly Corthain took the dead crown in both hand and carried it back to the center of the cave. Lori and Gladriel followed him. They watched briefly as he mourned its loss.

Lori established the prism in its proper place while Gladriel picked up the water can and metal rack. Both tried to refrain from looking at Corthain who sat fondling the useless crown. Sobs racked his body. His crown was destroyed. He did not have another. The initiation group, he was sure, had returned by now. The young man would have two crowns while he had none. Corthain was here in a cave, not there in the village. Even if he were there he could not replace his crown. It was not his turn.

Mathina, who had watched the chase, now came to Corthain. Crouching beside him she took the dead crown and held it out to the women. "It is useless. Bury it for him."

Lori held it and studied it for a time. All its color had disappeared. Before she placed it in the shallow hole she had dug she looked at it again and pondered its great power. She patted the dirt over it. Gladriel set two large stones on top.

"Lori what do you think will happen now?" Gladriel asked.

"I don't know."

Mathina heard them and spoke. "He has no crown. He is no longer a Council Lord. Until it is his time for a crown he will not mate nor sit in Council. A man is not a man without his crown and its power. Without a crown he cannot fertilize a woman."

"How awful for him," said Lori.

"Do not worry, daughter. I know you two do not understand our ways. Maybe you are the ones sent to help and unite us. Will you put Corthain to bed, Gladriel?"

She directed Glady to move the sleeper near the prism. Lori was to get Corthain to lie down. The three of them eased him onto the sleeper. Then Lori and Mathina turned away to settle themselves for the night. Gladriel remained. She pushed back the curls from his forehead and kissed it. She spooned him and held him tight. Then she whispered, "Good night my Love."

Lori tried to contact Redford. The cave was shutting off their signals. She looked at her sleeping companions. All seemed well. She smiled to herself as an old line of poetry came to mind. 'Good night, good night! As sweet repose and rest come to thy heart as that within my breast.' She curled up on her sleeper and joined her friends in sleep.

Chapter 22

A couple of hours after sunrise Lori awoke when the doeg began licking her face. She had been exhausted and slept soundly she did not know when Lori and Corthain had moved their sleeper next to hers. He had wrapped them in his blanket from his tote. Their collective body heat helped keep away the damp coldness of the cave. The doeg licked her forehead and she gently brushed him away from her face. Slowly she slipped from beneath Corthain's arm. He turned sifting positions and snuggled closer to Gladriel, and they continued to sleep.

Lori took out a cleansing kit from her pack and went to the rear of the cave. When she finished she took out her shorts—an-all outfit. She thought it was bad luck they hadn't brought more clean clothes. Once she was dressed she tiptoed around Mathina and walked to the entrance.

The sun greeted her proclaiming a good day. Eager to begin their trip, Lori returned to the sleeping group, skirted Mathina and approached Gladriel. It was then she noticed the crown was scattered all around. During the night the doeg had dug it up and chewed it well. She picked up the pieces and reburied it. Once she finished she walked over to Glady. She bent and touched her cheek. Gladriel stirred and reluctantly opened one eye. Lori nodded to her. She noted the surprise on Glady's face when she saw Corthain beside her and smiled

Carefully Gladriel extricated herself from Corthain's side and stood up. Lori handed her a cleanup kit. Gladriel moved to the shadows in the rear of the cave.

Lori walked to the entrance and stood staring out. Shortly Glady joined her there. They exchanged weak smiles.

"Shall we talk, Glady, asked Lori.

"Yes, not here. Let's go outside."

"Do you want Redford to learn what happened here?"

"Oh, Redford? I'd forgotten him. Quite easy to do, really," said Glady.

"I tried contacting him last night. He couldn't hear me, no doubt due to the structure or materials in this area."

"That's good,"

"Gladriel, did you know Corthain had been carrying a crown?"

"I thought it was food and medicine. How ridiculous for him to bring his crown. Why would he bother?"

"Lots of reasons we'd think ridiculous," Lori speculated. She stretched her arms over her head to rest them on the inner lip of the cave. "If we want to believe Mathina then I'd say the crown is his symbol of manhood, maybe his badge of office too."

"I'll accept the premise, but why would he carry it into a jungle when it isn't necessary. What would you do with it here?"

"He may not want to leave it at home unless he has someone to protect it for him or he has a woman traveling with him, such as you, and he plans on using it. Didn't you tell him there was another woman? Maybe he wanted her to know he was a Lord too."

"Lori, how silly it would be to try to impress someone out here. As dangerous as the Tangle is I wouldn't want to be under a crown's influence out in the open."

"Neither would I, however, Corthain might see it differently. The crown is quite powerful and he's used it on you twice. In his life time he's used it many times. He could even be addicted to it. Remember Corthain is a professional at using it. Jeames was only a neophyte. We'd expect Corthain to be good at seduction, romance and love making."

"You're right." Inside Gladriel was dealing with serious emotional issues. She and her society were sexually repressed. She had feared her desires and passion could control her as her uncle had warned her, since it happened to her mother. She had never slept with a man nor had a man sexually touched her until the last two nights. Now the horror of letting this happen and yet enjoying and desiring his touch and love was eating into her mind and moral directive.

Glady broke off her troubled thoughts and asked Lori, "If what you say is correct, we don't have a problem. I think Corthain is addicted to its use. If he is then he might not be able to travel with us. He could have withdrawal from it."

"He has shown signs of stress. I thought this might have been caused by hiking through the Tangle with two strong willed women. This terrain is horrible. It's a strain on us and we're in the top of good health and younger. Last night after everyone was asleep I got to thinking about your contract with a crown while you were in the village and with him alone. When so much power and chemical reaction occurred you could not fight it. You did nothing wrong. Remember my words."

"I am ashamed of what happened. I was at fault too. I wanted him. I may have seduced him." In a quick flood of words Gladriel told Lori everything that happened from the moment she had left Lori until she and Corthain met her at the stream.

"He was so dynamic in the village. I felt I was being swept away. I foolishly thought no one would know what I had done. I don't even know why I'm confessing and telling you all this, except I almost lost everything when I learned Redford had monitored us with our EAR implants. I wanted to walk away from the mission, even you, Lori. Can you imagine how embarrassed and humiliated I feel right now? I'm ashamed of how Corthain treats the old woman. He would have put her out into the storm if the shield hadn't been set. I don't want any part of him, even though I love him. We know he is a victim of his culture. I'm even jealous when he talks to you or looks at you. I think any woman who is young enough to have children would get his attention. He is not trained to be faithful to one woman, but he is faithful to his wives. He will not sleep with another man's woman. Free women are game for him. It isn't me as a person. We're still silly girls, aren't we?"

166

"We are not silly girls, Glady, we are women. We have thoughts, emotions and intelligence. We've learned much about ourselves and each other. Nothing of this need go further. Since Redford can't hear us, there's no one who knows what we did last night, except for us and I'm not talking. Is it a deal?"

"It's a deal. I definitely don't want Redford to know about this and I don't want it on my record.

Lori moved off to waken Mathina and put tea on to brew. Gladriel turned off the perimeter's shield and removed the poles which she stored in her pack. While Mathina prepared their meal, the women moved outside to contact Redford.

"Redford, you misbegotten pile of junk, you still up there?" asked Lori as she spoke into her communicator, while looking up into the clear sky washed free of clouds. She noticed the sun had not yet burned away the ground fog which clung to the valleys and wrapped aimlessly around the base of taller hills.

"I'm still up here. I had expected a talk much sooner. You must have been busy or slept in today."

Lori and Glady looked at one another. Both were thinking maybe Redford did hear their conversation in the cave. His next words eased their minds.

"May I ask what happened? I lost you both when the storm took over. Did you find the shelter in the cave I told you about? Wait a minute you slept in didn't you? Naughty, girls, you have a job to do."

"What do you know about sleep? Remember Lori is recovering from a serious wound she needs extra sleep and we both hacked our way through jungle to get here."

"Okay, you two, cut the chatter," interrupted Lori. "What's the weather report for today?"

"As of now the clouds are nearly gone. Ground fog will disperse by mid-morning. The streams and rivers are swollen and the swamp is covered with water."

"What swamp are you talking about, Redford?" asked Lori?

"Have you girls consulted your maps lately?" Redford's tone said he was plainly exasperated with them. Margline always called them 'girls' when they missed a single item or detail in a report. Now Redford was doing it.

"Not this morning, Redford," answered Gladriel as she winked at Lori. Their comfortable camaraderie had returned to them. They were teasing Redford once again and enjoying it.

"Had you read it carefully, you would be aware you will cross a swamp before you reach the indicated area."

"Why don't you send *The Flynn*?" Lori suggested.

Redford ignored her and continued, "I must emphasize you must read your map and stay in contact with me."

"Why? You're the one who had the trouble with communication."

"Well, yes, I did. Now I have taken care of everything. Besides, I worry about you. You both are such magnets for troubles."

"Are you actually worried about us?" teased Lori.

"You should be aware t . . ."

Gladriel interrupted him to save them another lecture. "Redford, have you any data on Corthain's men?"

"I know what you're doing, Glady." When he called her Glady she knew he had no ill will toward her. For a second they thought he was chuckling. "When I last observed them they had camped on high ground to wait out the storm. I judge they are moving now and can only be hours behind you. At the current time they have no problems. I advise you to leave now. Caution before valor."

"Are you quoting the ancients?" asked Gladriel.

"I wouldn't know. Get a move on, ladies."

Mathina came to the entrance and called them to breakfast. Corthain was awake. Without further debate, Lori checked her map and they both followed Mathina into the cave.

In less than twenty minutes the four had eaten, packed their meals and broken camp. Lori was wearing her shorts-an-all while Corthain wore her skin suit. Each one carried a pack. Now Corthain's tote held his empty chest the water jugs and Mathina's fruit along with his food stores. Mathina carried nothing, she was frail and the trail today was quite rugged.

Lori was quite surprise when Corthain helped Mathina as she climbed up and down the trail. Today they descended and this helped make up time. Suddenly the terrain changed and became dense jungle. The doeg pushed its way ahead, jumping over vines or crawling under them. It was over a mile before Lori began to use her cutter. She set the pace, maintaining it for an hour before Gladriel insisted they change places.

By noon the terrain had changed again. The jungle abruptly ceased and the group faced a tall chalk bluff. It ran north and south for many miles, Redford reported. He wisely ignored Gladriel's stinging barb, stating since he knew of its presence he should have warned them. Furthermore, she suggested perhaps they could have taken a different route.

Lori ordered Mathina and Corthain to rest while she and Gladriel searched for a route up the cliff.

"Why are we doing all this walking?" asked Corthain.

"We are looking for a THRAX," explained Lori.

"I've never heard of a THRAX before." The fact is he had no idea what a THRAX was still he didn't feel like risking to ask more. He was tired, dirty and without a crown. He had no power. He could only follow these women now and he had no idea where they were bound. He only hoped they would find a village soon. He'd even settle for theirs, if it had hot water and a bath.

The women inspected the cliff area near them, and then consulted their maps. Ten minutes later they returned with the news—the bluff ran for miles. They discussed their options and decided to climb it here. Redford had warned them Ameral's men were moving faster than he had expected.

"This map says the unit is in this direction so we'll climb here," said Lori.

"It is also the same direction as the swamp. Strange topography this planet has wouldn't you say Lori?"

"Strange everything," laughed Lori as she looked at the map and then Corthain.

"How do we get over it?" asked Corthain.

"We climb, we climb," answered Lori who was deciding where to begin.

Shortly Gladriel was working her way diagonally up following hand and toe holds offered by the vines. In five minutes time she was at the top, shouting down she'd secured a line and Lori could send up the packs. When this was done she asked for the Doeg. Mathina came next. She awkwardly climbed the line secured by Glady at the top and held by Lori at the bottom. She stopped hallway saying she couldn't climb any more. Lori shouted to Mathina to hold tight and Glady pulled her the rest of the way. Mathina laughed and enjoyed the ride.

Corthain had rested while all this happened. Now only he and Lori remained at the base. Lori turned to him offering him the line which he tied about his waist. She watched him as he climbed. He duplicated almost exactly Gladriel's route and wondered where and when he had learned to climb.

Once he was on top Gladriel tossed down the line and gave Lori the okay to climb up. Lori had almost reached the top when a misplaced toe slipped and she fell ten feet before she could grab a finger thick vine to break her fall. She was glad she had tied the line about her and then worried about Glady's strength to take her weight. Lori waved she was fine this time both Gladriel and Corthain helped pull as she worked her way to the top.

Five minutes later the party stood united atop the chalk wall. Lori applied a spray skin to her hand and assured Gladriel and Mathina she had suffered no real damage. Redford's voice in her ear told her to get moving. They did.

Chapter 23

It became a race of sorts as the group struggled through soggy sparse jungle. Occasionally one would fall and the others would help him or her up and go on again. They did not stop for rest or food, only for water because Lori urged them onward fearing Ameral's men would catch them. The third time Mathina fell Glady insisted they stop to rest and eat. Corthain wanted to continue in order to get out of the muddy area. Finally they allowed for a brief rest. The doeg was exhausted too. Glady put it in the top of her pack.

The sky had clouded over again and thunder rumbled. It was a sure sign of more rain. Mathina's insistence this was the dry season made no impression on Lori and Gladriel who were wet, dirty and ill-tempered. When a particularly loud clap of thunder shook the ground Lori jumped. After her heart returned to rest she voted with the others to find shelter and make camp for the night.

She contacted Redford who explained he had mapped the terrain they were crossing. Scattered islands dotted the swampy area and would offer a relief from wading if they found one. The streams feeding the swamp were swelling with upland rain Redford reported. He suggested they wait until morning to complete their crossing of the swamp.

Gladriel was arguing there were still several hours of daylight. She wanted to go on. She hoped they could get across the swamp before night arrived.

"Think, Glady, how far will we get in the swamp?" asked Lori. "Do you honestly think we can get across by nightfall and make camp?

"How wide is the swamp, Redford" Could we go around?" Glady asked.

"You could if the group trailing you were a day's journey behind."

"Glady, time doesn't allow going around. We could go straight across, but not today. At least I'm not going far or for long."

"I guess another night on the planet won't hurt us. What will it matter?"

"Redford, we've got to find shelter. The perimeters won't deflect rain off this large of a group. Do you see anything?" asked Lori.

"You are there, Lori. Do the best you can."

"Thanks for the advice," said Lori.

Redford kept them apprised of the group of men's location and distance from them. He told them the men had stopped at the cave for the night. Meanwhile he told the women he was busy running tests on their biological data, Tentative test results on the mineral samples and the planets foods was hopeful, however he advised them to eat their own food supplies.

"We are out of food, Redford, and have been for some time," reported Gladriel. "We've already eaten and drank water and are suffering no ill effects."

Redford did not respond to this message and feared for their lives. "I will report when I learn anything about the group following you."

"We never doubted you would. We'll hear from you in the morning." Lori turned to the group. We must continue until we can find higher ground, this water is rising and the storm isn't even here."

They moved as fast as ankle deep mud, hidden branches, and rocks buried under six inches of running water would allow.

Glady tied Mathina's skirts up under her arms with a supple vine. Even so Mathina still stumbled and grew muddier and weaker. She whimpered as she walked following Corthain.

Corthain resembled a mud slug. At times he paused to throw handfuls of water up on his suit to rid it of mud and muck. He walked in stoic silence

Lori's short-an-all was now a camouflaged jungle outfit. She carried the doeg in her pack and hummed as she led the way.

Glady had to keep wiping her face. She brought up the rear, so she had the most stirred up mud and water mixture to wade through. She couldn't remember when she had been so miserable.

The group struggled on. Each tried to imagine a clean dry place waiting at the end for their hike through the swamp.

Redford called warning them they were drifting off course still they could possibly find sold ground by dusk. They were drifting east because they had found solid ground under their feet which they followed, rather than depending on a map.

By late afternoon they reached higher ground on an island surrounded by swirling swamp water. The soggy and muddy group pulled their bodies upon the island. Mathina leaned up against a large trunked plant and breathed heavily. The doeg which Lori had released from its perch ran to Mathina. An exhausted Corthain dragged himself up on the shore as he labored to breath.

First the two women searched the island for any signs of danger. To their left where the group had emerged, they found two large tree-like plants which had fallen at angles to one another and this offered possibilities of building a shelter with an elevated roof since it formed a crude tepee.

"We can build a shelter with only a limited amount of time and keeping ahead of the impending storm," said Glady. She began cutting off branches to give access and formed a rough doorway beneath the arch.

Lori used more of these to line the area under the trunks and around a possibly sheltered area. "Glady, can you cut a trench around the base of the shelter? It might create a good draining area." Lori added a ground cover over the leaves. She noted the natural leaves were not enough to keep out the rain. "Anyone have an idea for the roof?"

"I do," said Mathina. "Cut off some more big leaves and then weave them in between the branches of their shelter. "Surely the broad leaves would offer some protection. I could show you how to weave these.

In less than an hour the shelter was secured against the wetness around them. They had lined the walls and cut a large leafy branch to fit the opening. In the last light of the day the sun sank into freshly gathering storm clouds when they finished. The packs were carried in and the prism activated.

Mathina took command quickly. She bustled around spreading out the food. She set up the stand for the tea and rummaged through the packs. She found one biscuit and six large pieces of fruit she'd found along the way.

When everything was completed Corthain chose to enter. He looked around, sniffed loudly and seated himself near the prism. From there he could draw upon it for heat to dry him off. He moaned. "I don't feel well, Gladriel. My head aches and my legs and back are stiff from so much walking. I'm almost sick at my stomach."

Lori felt Corthain's head, he seemed to have a bit of a temperature. She huddled with Glady and told her of Corthain's health issues. They decided to contact Redford once they were settled in for the night.

"Lori, were you thinking the men following Corthain are his own? I'm thinking this group behind us is more trained in Tangle encounters than Corthain's. I think it's being headed by Lord Ameral."

"I think you're right. They have been travelling well and seem to be more than keeping up with us," said Lori. "We're talking about the group behind us. Are your men trained in traveling in the Tangle?"

"No more so than I. I've never really gone into the Tangle before. I can't say it's such a nice place to be either."

"You told me Lord Ameral has been to the yellow mountain and spends time in the Tangle," said Gladriel. "How far was

Lord Ameral from you when you notified him I was there and looking for a friend?"

"My men said he'd be there later the same day we left."

"Corthain, I don't think your men are the ones following us," said Lori.

"Why wouldn't my people come?"

"I don't think Lord Ameral wants to be friendly to Lori and me. We saw him kill Jeames. We think Ameral has been killing off initiates for some time, as well as women."

"This is another women's tale."

Glady touched his shoulder gently, "Did you realize for the last 10 years only his sons have survived. He generally goes with a set group of men."

"I went one time."

"Yes, it was the ceremony for Lord Ameral's son. His son did not appear until you went home. Were your women ill?"

"It was a false alarm. It was some imaginary thing. They were well when I returned home."

"If this is so, why would he tell you the women were ill? He wanted you gone. All he had to do then was walk into the patch and pluck a couple for his son."

"Lori and I met Jeames while he was in the patch of plants. We watched him get his first crown. It was then he slept with Lori. We didn't know what was happening. Later we watched Lord Ameral slit his throat and promise Jeames' crown to one of his sons, who, is a whiner."

"Lori and I did some damage to the flaggets' patch. Now he'll know what we're capable of doing. Jeames went on and on about the golden goddess who slept with him. The golden goddess would be Lori. He wanted to make her his first woman. So the power we have and Lori's beauty are reasons alone to capture us. There is also the problem of us seeing him murder Jeames. Regardless to what you may believe, he will want to kill you because you have been with us."

"He is my cousin and I have great faith in him as a man. You are story tellers. There is no cultivated flagget patch. Everyone knows they cannot be cultivated. By now Jeames has already returned with his crowns." Corthain almost chocked on the words. "I left detailed information for my men. By now Lord Ameral has been informed. He most likely will bring another group and follow and help my men. I do not believe your story. Lord Ameral is an honorable man. He will want to see the Law is carried out."

"Didn't you hear Glady? She and I saw him grab Jeames by his golden hair and bend him back and he slit Jeames' throat. It was terrible to watch. Jeames did not break the Law. He and the men, as well as Ameral were celebrating his victory immediately before Ameral killed him so brutally."

"Maybe, Jeames deserved death," Corthain was upset by their story and their pressure. "It is possible he had not fulfilled the rites correctly. It has happened before."

"If he hadn't killed him his men would have raped him and then killed him, maybe he was being kind," blurted out Lori. "Don't look so shocked, the men were drunk and they set the big crown on his head and attacked him. Even men can be affected by the crown of another man."

"No Lord would act in this manner."

"They did and we saw them. So, if they think we saw them they would kill us too. Our lives are in danger, as is yours," warned Gladriel.

"You'll see when we get back, Jeames is safely in his settlement and enjoying the fruits of the crown," retorted Corthain.

The matter was closed. Corthain would not accept anything they said. Besides he was getting fatigued. His intense anger had drained him of his desire to argue. He huddled in on his knees with his arms clasped tightly around his legs. His eyes were half shut.

Mathina passed brewed tea, slices of fruits and bread to each. In silence the four ate. Absently Mathina shared some of hers with the doeg who had returned. It had disappeared while the women built the shelter.

When the meal ended Corthain stretched out on a sleeper at Lori's suggestion. Mathina cleaned up the remains of the food, being careful to preserve all leftovers. When she finished she set about combing out her hair. Gladriel signaled Lori and they went outside.

The heavy rain had stopped. Lingering droplets filtered through the towering foliage as the clouds slowly dissipated portending a clear day tomorrow. Almost overhead a few stars twinkled. One of them might be *The EmPolo*.

Gladriel had wanted to speak with Lori all day, even as they sat eating. The presence of Mathina and Corthain restrained her. She knew she had to speak now, though both were tired. She feared another night with Corthain under the same roof might bring harsher words in the morning.

Gladriel began cautiously; she was sure Lori was hiding something. Out of the corner of her eye she watched Lori who stood comfortably leaning on one hip staring up at the sky.

"Were you going to tell me what happened between you and Corthain yesterday on the trail—all of it? You don't have to say any more, I'm sure I know what happened."

"Whatever do you mean, Glady?"

"I've seen the way Corthain's acting today."

"What do you mean?" She turned to face Gladriel directly.

"Don't act dumb. Are you my friend?"

"I've always thought so. Now, with the way this conversation is going, I'm not sure. If I knew what we were supposed to be talking about, I'd know the answer to your question."

"You can't control your lust at all, can you? First you picked Martin, and then Jeames and finally Corthain. Shall I stay out here so you can send Mathina out so you can spend time with another conquest?"

"Who is Martin?"

"Martin was my friend. He helped me in astrophysics, until he found you a bit more fun. I heard rumors about you. You are mainly interested in sex. You have no control when it comes to a man you want. No matter how much it hurts someone else." Her words rushed out.

Lori looked heavenward as she recalled the student Gladriel referred to in her tirade. "Oh, I remember Martin now. He had dark eyes, swarthy complexion and was from Niguel. You liked him? I didn't know you did. You never said anything. Did you want Jeames? You didn't say you did. I cannot believe the conversation we're having.

"It's just . . . I don't know what I'm trying to say."

"Now, as to Corthain, I do not want him. I never touched him in a sexual way. Sure, I find him attractive nevertheless the crown is trying to seduce us all."

"You find all men attractive!" yelled Glady with bitterness.

"Well, why not? On my world men are appreciated by women as much as men appreciate women. In our family units . . ."

Gladriel put her hands over her ears, "I don't want to hear it."

Lori pulled Gladriel's hands from her ears. "Don't be jealous, Glady."

"I'm not jealous. Maybe what was said about you in the academy was true. Maybe you are oversexed. You can't wait to sleep with a man."

"Cool it, Glady. This isn't helping you or me. I'm tired and I don't want to argue. I've never seen you so wrought up and feeling such strong emotions. Relax, enjoy your time with him and don't chastise yourself. You have done nothing wrong. Right now your eyes and your soul are green with envy and jealousy. I repeat and for the last time I tell you, nothing happened between Corthain and me. I promise, as Redford is my witness, I did not have sexual relations with him."

Silence was like a stranger in the room who was robbing them of their senses. "Say, why are you so concerned about it? You're not thinking of staying here? Don't answer. I'm too tired to listen to any more of this tripe."

"Tripe indeed! I see how he stares at you. He even mumbles your name. He did so last night in the cave and this morning.

"Stop it, Gladriel. Did you consider for one moment he was staring at nothing in particular. He has no crown and surely he must be affected by its loss. If you weren't so serious I'd be insulted and then I'd toss you in the swamp."

"Can you honestly tell me you never desired him?"

"Well, no, and I kissed him but . . ."

"A kiss isn't enough for you, is it?"

"He kissed me because he was grateful. I saved his life. I don't think he realized what he was doing. He was over joyed. I kissed him in the moment of joy. This was all we did. I swear. Check with Redford, if you don't believe me."

"He'd probably lie for you."

"I would never lie to or for either of you," said Redford. "I have avoided entering this argument. It is time to get you both on the same track."

"Gladriel, you system seems to be coping with random pheromones from the crown. You cannot be held responsible for your actions. Most likely continued exposures would have settled you down. It's probably what the men call training their women. All the females in Corthain's household function smoothly. Lori, you are recovering from a heavy dose of venom. It may have interacted with the pheromones left from the crown when Jeames seduced you. One thing is positive; I will vouch for Lori's innocence. I have readings from Lori during the time she and Corthain were absent from you. She was telling you the truth. She had no sexual contact with him. This should settle the matter. I never want to hear this argument again."

"Now I will give you some sound advice. Get some rest. Do not let your personal life interfere with your professional life. True it is hard to do this in the field. You are both from such radically different cultures. Ladies, I repeat—no more. The matter is closed. You need to understand you are feeling these emotions because you feel the power of the crown even after it has been destroyed."

"I need to give you a bit more information: the men trailing you have stopped again. They should rest there for the night. You should as well. Good night, ladies."

"Redford is correct, Glady, let's go to bed." They turned and entered the shelter.

Glady set up a portal perimeter across the doorway after securing the leaf door.

Corthain slept soundly near the back where the tree touched the ground.

Mathina and the doeg were curled up near the prism. Lori shook out the other sleeper and lay down. Soon Gladriel dimmed the prism and lay down beside her.

Shortly only the regular breathing of the sleeping group could be heard. The temperature of the small area had risen a few degrees. In comfort, insulated from the damp ground, the group rested gathering strength for the coming day. The water level, fed by mountain runoff and a heavy deluge rose another six inches and was lapping within inches of the crude shelter.

A soft rustling in the overhead branches went unnoticed even by the doeg. Steadily the sound increased. Soon a soft plopping was heard as limp moist bodies hit the springy carpet of their shelter. The first hint of a disaster had overtaken them went unnoticed. Soon wriggling six inch green coiling and recoiling eel like creatures attached to the members in the group. Several slid out of the tree and attached to Corthain. He made no stir.

Now by two and three's more creatures slid out of the leaves protecting them and from the hollow in the tree above their heads. They were attracted by the heat. Several had crawled onto the women's sleeper. As Gladriel rolled over she was awakened by one as it squirmed to turn over and latch on to her. She sat up. In the dim glow of the prism she saw three creatures slide up Lori's leg and settle on her thigh.

Gladriel screamed. Immediately everyone was awake. Confusion reigned. Gladriel pulled at a creature. It slipped from her grasp. She continued to scream as she tried pushing and prying to lift one free. It clung tightly like a leech.

Finally awake, Lori turned to increase the light and watched fascinated as one slid up her hand and wrist to create a circle around her forearm below the bend of her elbow. In the bright glare she saw a wriggling mass. Dazed she watched as more slimy creatures secured themselves to her arm. They met no resistance because she had more exposed skin. Soon she began to feel chilled.

Glady kept screaming. She had gotten to her feet and was trying to stomp on the wiggly creatures. They were everywhere.

They began rushing toward the light. Where there was light there was heat. One wriggled up the cylinder and fell off as an unidentifiable charred mass.

"Stop screaming, Glady. Use your disruptor," yelled Lori who was trying to find a safe way to destroy the wriggly mass around her without killing the group.

"No, daughters, no!" shouted Mathina above Gladriel's screamed. Only Mathina and the doeg seemed unafraid. She was joyously grasping the creatures in the mid sections and squeezing firmly. The wrigglers went limp, apparently paralyzed or dead. She gathered her overskirt into a bag and was busy depositing the paralyzed creatures into her skirt.

The doeg was barking between snaps and lunges at the creatures. Each time he bit one he would tear out a chunk of its flesh and swallow it.

Lori when she saw Mathina knew how to handle them so adroitly shouted for her to help Gladriel who still slapped at the creatures. Lori pinched those attached on her own arms. Soon she was free.

Mathina in a short time managed to clear Glady. Exhausted by the ordeal of terror, Gladriel sank to her knees and stared into the light.

"What are you doing, Mathina?" she asked as she watched Mathina empty Corthain's tote and began stuffing stunned creatures into it.

"I'm saving them. We are so lucky. There are so many." She scurried about squeezing and collecting the strange life forms.

At this point Lori remember Corthain and called to him. He had slept through the attack. They had numbed him and cut off his air. Lori called his name again and then went to check on him. He lay wrapped in a green mass of quietly heaving moist browning bodies which had plastered him totally. Lori pinched off several creatures until she exposed his face. A quick check told her he was barely breathing. Pinching a few more creatures away from his neck and face, she bent to give him a few quick breathes of air. Some began to climb from him onto her. She quickly stunned them. Corthain moaned. He fought to free himself however; he only managed to roll over on his side.

"Glady, Mathina, come help Corthain. He's covered in the creatures. At the mention of Corthain's name Gladriel shook off the horror and revulsion she was feeling and hurried to him. Mathina left off collecting and hurried to help too.

It was quite a job freeing him. Quickly the creatures sensed a new source of warmth and left him to attach themselves to one of the women. Expertly Mathina would give a quick pinch and toss the limp creature aside. Lori was doing the same. Gladriel was reluctant to touch them until Lori insisted and showed her how.

Finally they freed him. They dragged him closer to the light and heat. Mathina set up the tripod and brewed tea. She forced him to drink several cups before she was satisfied he'd regained heat and hydration. Lori and Glady shared a cup between them. Their shelter was a mess. Everything was thrown about. Dead and stunned creatures were everywhere. Among the mess the small green doeg capered and chomped at any wiggling creature.

Satisfied her children were safe she called the three of them, "Help me gather these up." Mathina hurried to collect more creatures. She ran out of space to load the creatures, so she dumped Gladriel's bag.

Glady reached out and stopped her. "What are you doing now, Mathina? You don't have to bag them. We can cut off the perimeter, remove the leaf and then toss them out. You are not going to put those disgusting things in my pack," she screamed as she jerked her bag from Mathina's hands.

"We have to keep them, daughter."

"Why?"

"When you go back the village you will be the envy of everyone. No three women have ever captured such a nest as this. Usually several families share a capture. We are privileged. Even the Lords will have praise for us. Let's hurry, daughters and bag them before they regain mobility." Mathina reached for Gladriel's pack, but she wouldn't give it to her.

"What good are these, Mathina," asked Lori as she held one up to the light to inspect it. It was six inches in length and was mainly a stout cylinder shaped body with tiny vestigial legs on the front and rear ends. Each leg ended in a tiny suckered toe. A slit for the mouth distinguished the front from the back and the rear end was blunt as though someone had chopped off a tail it might have had. In a strange way it resembled the water jug fruit in consistency and feel.

"Glady, we need to scan these and take a couple of pictures."

Gladriel hurriedly got the scanner and ran it through the system. She shivered and finished her job.

"Such a wonderful nest of plump mature sallies."

"Are these sallies?"

"Yes, it is food and a good food. It is so delicious. I know we've already eaten. This is good to pass up. I haven't had bread and sally for . . . I can't remember. But, daughters, before we eat, let's clean up this nest. Please help me. They hurriedly did as she asked. Then Gladriel moved Corthain closer to the prism to give him another cup of tea and draped another sleeper around him. He looked up at her and smiled his gratitude.

"Come, daughters, sit down and we'll eat." Mathina took Corthain's knife, selected a sally and expertly skinned it. What remained was gluttonous deep red jelly. There were no bones or parts which could make it be called an animal. Instead inside it was a tube of cellulose which served as a gut. This Mathina pulled out and gave to the doeg. She called for bread. She sliced the bread expertly into four equal shares. On each piece she spread a thick layer of the red jelly. She handed Lori two pieces and Gladriel two. Then she turned the tough outer rind skin inside out and licked it clean.

Lori's stomach gave a violent heave and she thought of the primitive Melosi who ate their enemies in hopes of gaining their knowledge and skills. Gladriel was hungry but she kept swallowing, hoping to control her stomach as she stared at the two slices of bread she held.

"Glady, what's the matter?" asked Lori.

"I now realize this is what I ate at the village. I thought it was good. I thought it was a preserve made from berries.".

"Did you like it?"

"Yes, but . . ."

"Don't think about its source. We need food badly. Look at the doeg. He's enjoying eating sallies."

"You think so, Lori," said Glady as she smiled at Lori. "Then you eat some."

"Well, I'm not hungry."

"Now, daughters, eat up." She took a slice from each of them and gave it to Corthain, who'd already eaten his original two slices.

Lori looked at hers, and then swallowed before she touched it with her tongue. It was cool. Several times she lifted the bread and sally to her mouth. Not surprisingly each time she lifted the sandwich she stopped short. Finally she got it to her mouth and took a tiny bit. The flavor of the sally was one of the most delicious things she'd ever tasted. "This is wonderful. Do we have more bread?"

"It is even good on fruit or on its own. Eat, eat, daughters this is your breakfast today. Eat heartily. Sallies are wonderful things. They don't like light instead these thrived on heat. These live in communal nests in dark recesses of huge plants or in winter in dry caves. Usually they avoid human settlements. No doubt they moved into the dry shelter of the tree. The heat revived them and they visited us.

"Let's try to get a bit more sleep and sunlight so we can find our way through this mess," suggested Lori. "I could use a few more hours of sleep and more sallies for breakfast." Come on let's make our nest and keep warm. She spread out her sleeper to its widest width and lay down. "Who is joining me?"

Shortly they were all a cozy bundle of warmth and drifted off into sleep.

Chapter 24

Redford woke them before dawn reminding them the men would be moving soon. A hurried breakfast was served and the packs readied. When Lori retrieved her sleeper from Corthain he shivered and complained he was cold.

She touched his forehead. It was hot to the touch. "Glady get over here. I don't think Corthain is well."

Scanner in hand Glady moved rapidly to check his vital signs. She called Redford and asked him for results as soon as available.

"Redford, is Corthain reacting to the sallies?" asked Lori.

"No. Having run the tests I think you were correct yesterday. He is an addict and in withdrawal from the use of the crown. A total blood analysis might verify this. However, we don't have time for an in-depth medical workup."

"Well," said Lori, "we'll take a chance on giving him a mild stimulus of cordovine. He has to travel. Do you have any suggestion as to the dosage, Redford?"

"No more than 20cc. His metabolism surely is different than yours."

"He is as big and solid as I am. I'll give him a dose now and see what happens." With practiced ease Lori administered the dose.

Shortly Corthain indicated he felt better. They moved out of the shelter to greet a clear day. A quick check of the maps assured them of their direction. It was almost due north. Lori led the way. Today they waded through mud only; the swamp had drained or consumed the water rapidly.

When the women consulted their maps they found the yellow dot for the mountain had disappeared. A consultation with Redford assured them it had been a false reading. The final point was at a site from across the river.

"Well, I'll be spaced!" exclaimed Lori. "Redford, you did it again, you hunk of circuitry. Now don't tell me it was only a little miscalculation. I'd like to know why we're not going up Yellow Mountain.

"I don't care what his excuse is. If we have one place left, let's check it out. We can wring out his excuse later. Remember Corthain and Ameral's men aren't far behind."

"It's definitely true. Well, Redford, she saved you, your day of reckoning is coming," warned Lori.

Another hour of struggle and they left the damp swamp behind. Now they cut their way through heavy jungle. Redford updated them on the trailing men who kept moving steadily.

An hour or so later, Corthain collapsed without warning. Gladriel, who was in the rear, called to Lori, who was twelve feet ahead of Mathina who was seven feet ahead of Corthain. Lori came back and administered another 20ccs. They didn't wait for it to take effect. So they supported him between them for a short time to keep going. Soon he was walking on his own strength. He appeared addled and confused. When he became even more confused Mathina took him by the hand and led him as though he were a child.

About a mile later Corthain regained his equilibrium and began walking on his own. Then his talking began. He mumbled and cursed his fortune. When his vision improved he stared at his pack on Lori's back. He thought of his shimmering crown and imagined it calling to him. He stumbled, reaching out to grab his tote and slid into Lori.

At the touch on the pack, Lori stopped and turned around colliding with Corthain. Feeling her warmth he wrapped his arms around her and nuzzled her neck and mumbled about his crown.

"We can't have this, Corthain," she said and gently pushed him away.

"What's the trouble now? Gladriel demanded. Her jealousy flared as she sensed they were together.

"Corthain is passing in and out of consciousness and hallucinating. How are we going to keep him going?"

"I have a solution. Let's tie him between us and keep the line taut. He'll have to follow."

"Let's give him another shot," Lori suggested.

"It's too soon. We shouldn't even think of it now." Glady wrapped several loops and a hitch around Corthain. "Here, Lori, take this end and get moving."

Corthain followed Lori like a small puppy.

Meantime Mathina didn't understand they were being followed by a dangerous group of men. Indeed she had never consciously known about them. Once free of the women's attentions she lagged behind. Twice Gladriel called to her. Obediently she gathered her skirts and quickly ran to join the line. This time she had stopped to inspect a particularly interesting leafy vine. The others moved on.

She was intrigued by the new leaf. She broke off an eight inch section of the leafy vine and began weaving it into her hair. To this she added two more flat stones from inner pockets. Once more she patted her heavy coil. Finally feeling satisfied with her work she began to hum a cheery tune.

When she had stopped the doeg had remained with her. Momentarily it watched her fix her hair. Then it looked down the trail and whined. When it could not get her attention by whining the gentle creature took to tugging at her ragged skirts.

Mathina gently pushed it away. Her rebuff was not accepted. Instead the green fluffy ball yanked harder. Mathina called for Lori to help her. It was then she noticed she was alone. A long look back down the path showed their travel up this point. She looked ahead to the freshly cut greenery and didn't see anyone. She gave a shrug, patted her hair and sat down.

The doeg, when it could not get the woman to move began barking. It gave a few tentative hops, whined again at her and tugged once more at her skirt. It tried to pull her to her feet;

instead she patted it on the head. It licked her fingers and dashed away up the trail.

Shortly the doeg and Lori arrived. She took Mathina's hand and pulled her up. Without a word Lori pushed her up the trail to join the others.

After Lori dropped Corthain's cord from her waist and retreated down the path to find Mathina, Gladriel helped Corthain sit down. She had silently agreed with Redford and Lori. Corthain should have been left at the cave; sadly she couldn't give him up. Ameral could have found him, she was sure. If Ameral had killed Jeames for no observable reason she figured he might kill Corthain as readily for associating with renegade women. Still she was glad she had insisted he be brought along. She felt sure Lori was happy about it too.

Together they sat and waited for Lori and Mathina. Gladriel cradled Corthain's head against her shoulder. In his delirium he often mumbled incoherent words as well as her name and Lori's. Once more Gladriel felt betrayed as Martin had betrayed her with Lori. She tried to understand why this kept happening. She knew Corthain was indeed a man who any woman would have difficulty resisting. He was attractive and charming, she thought as she studied his face. Possessively she hugged him tighter. If he required a crown she would get him one before she left the planet. It hurt her to see him suffer.

As Lori and Mathina approached Glady said, "I'm worried about Corthain. He's not fit to go on. He can't fend for himself in his condition. I'm sure, if Lord Ameral finds him, he won't spare him. Remember Jeames?"

"I'll never forget Jeames. I don't trust Ameral either. Glady, what do you want me to do?"

"Let's try another dose of Cordovine, only stronger this time."

Redford broke in. "You are tampering with his life. There is no way short of the analysis to determine if he can withstand repeated injections."

"We have no choice, Redford," yelled Glady as she looked at Lori. "If we leave him he could be attacked by anything. If we leave him for Lord Ameral, Corthain could be murdered."

"All right, Gladriel, you win. Another shot, Lori. You don't know how safe it is for certainty. Corthain's men would find him in a few hours."

"What do you mean, Redford?" asked Glady as she watched Lori administer another dose. This time it was 40ccs.

"The men are on their way. They've reached last night's nest camp. After separating to scout your trail they have regrouped. I estimate they are about five hours or less behind you. If you leave Corthain here the men will find him."

"Gladriel, why do you keep calling the group Lord Ameral's men?"

"These men are faster than Corthain's men who have never been in the Tangle. These men are skilled trackers. They know how to rough it and get up and keep on going. Only Ameral and his men have been to the yellow mountain so they have some tracking and hunting skills. They are definitely not Corthain's men."

"You have some strong points there, Glady. I hope you are wrong."

"Me too," sighed Lori.

"Are you ready, Glady?" asked Lori. "I've got Corthain on his feet. Once more he can walk without assistance. They rapidly moved toward the cliff.

So gradual was the incline they were unaware they had been climbing until they reached the cliff and were looking down. There was no debate. This was an extension of the bluff they had climbed the day before yesterday. Today they would descend it. Below them and half a mile away they could see a rampaging river tugging and eating at its banks. They had to cross it somehow.

There were no heavy vines on the edge of the cliff to help them down. Glady's cord was almost long enough; they could drop down from the rope to the ground which was four to five feet below the end of it.

Lori tied one end of it to a woody plant and threw the rope over the edge. She tested it before she allowed Gladriel to climb down.

Glady set her pack near the edge. The doeg sat down by it. A curious Mathina, who had awakened and a tired Corthain watched as Gladriel picked up the rope about six feet from the bush and walked backwards over the cliffs edge and walked nonchalantly down the embankment, using her feet to keep her away from the wall. On the first swing out she gathered momentum and hit the wall with force, denting its thick clay side and scraping off a thin layer of skin. The dirt, skin and debris clung to her skin suit. Her feet slipped. She could not find any secure footing and was finally forced to let herself down hand-under-hand.

Once at the bottom she checked the area for deadly plants. Finding none, she called for Lori to send down the doeg. Lori slowly released the rope. Shortly the wriggling doeg was lowered. Glady untied him. While the doeg sniffed around the area Lori lowered the three packs.

Mathina's turn came next. Lori tied a crude sling in the cord and showed her how to sit in it and then lowered Mathina over the side. Mathina's laughter echoed across the wide valley. Here was another thrill. Her daughters surely knew how to make an old woman happy. Soon her ride ended. She joined the doeg in exploring.

"Corthain, I don't think I can lower you like I did Mathina."

"I shall climb down." He eased himself over the edge and did as Gladriel had done. Soon he was at the bottom.

"Glady, here I come," Lori grasped the line and stepped over. She collided against the wall. Gladriel had Corthain boost her up to reach the end of the rope. Her weight gave some stability to the rope. Lori dropped down hand-under-hand for a distance. Suddenly she screamed and fell the rest of the way.

The shrub had been up rooted. Shortly the shrub and line landed on top of her. Lori lay in a tangled dirty heap of rope, bush and chalk.

Glady extended a hand and tried not to laugh. Then Gladriel lost her battled with herself and began laughing. "Lori," she gasped between giggles, "you're a snowball on the front and a piece of black lava on the back.

Lori looked down at herself. She was plastered with chalk on one side and muddy black clay on the other side.

Glady was laughing hysterically.

Lori scraped off a handful of black clay and plastered it on Glady's cheek.

They began to scuffle and wrestled for a few minutes until Redford captured their attention.

"The men are moving rapidly now and gaining while you two play."

Sobered by the news, Lori wound up the cord and stored it. The rest had freshened Corthain and Mathina. Soon they were moving rapidly under the direction of Redford.

They crossed the flat expanse to the river, walking through sparse clumps of bamboo-like plants. At the river's edge they halted and spread out along the bank to survey the water rushing past.

"Do you have any suggestion about getting across?" Gladriel asked Lori.

"One of us could swim taking the end of the rope and going to an island and having every one hang on the rope and get to the island—"

"Lori, only we two can swim and it would be dangerous for the others. If they stay here the men will catch them and who knows what will happen."

"If we have time we could build a raft. All we need are hollow reeds or regular logs."

"Lori, I don't know if there are enough of those here to do the job."

"Daughters, I could help you find enough hollow reeds. Maybe we could build a large raft and float across. It would be fun," laughed Mathina.

"It's our only option. Let's try it, Glady."

With a definite task to do, Mathina shook out her skirts, scouted around for a stick, and finding none asked Corthain for his knife. He gave it to her without hesitation.

"Come, daughters." They followed her up stream for about 200 feet. She halted near a large grove of brown saplings. Each towered above the group some ten feet. The large cylindrical saplings each had a group of five leaves spread around a green knob at the top. Mathina warned them to not touch the knob. The knob secreted a white milky substance which when dried and powdered could be mixed with water to make a sleeping potion. In a liquid state directly from the plant it could paralyze.

Mathina began hitting each stalk at waist level with the back of the blade. A hollow echo resonated on the second one she hit. "This one is ripe. Cut it, daughters." She moved from reed to reed, calling out orders.

The women did not question her. She had been correct about the water jugs. Beside she was an old native and she knew these things.

Gladriel went back for Corthain and the packs. She gave him directions to watch over the packs while they worked on the raft.

Each stalk Mathina tested and declared "ripe" was cut. These were piled together and all lengthwise after twenty-five slender reeds, all the same size and length were cut. Mathina and Glady removed the top bulb and leaves. Mathina instructed Lori to carry these to a sandy area and spread then out. When Lori finished she threw sand over each as Mathina had instructed her.

Mathina beamed, "A new grove will grow here.

"This planet's a botanist's dream," said Lori.

Step-by-step Mathina instructed the women to follow her crude drawing in the sand. Within two hours the two rafts were completed. Each was five foot wide by ten feel long. The reeds had been tied by a thin stout vine. Mathina showed the women how to form balls of sap taken from a plant which grew in the river. With these balls of sap she sealed the ends of each reed.

They stood back to admire the finished rafts. These would hopefully take them across the wide river. They drug the rafts to the river's edge. Before they were launched Lori retrieved the cord from Glady's pack. She cut two lengths of rope each about six feet long. These she used to tie the two rafts together. The remaining piece of rope she stowed in her pack.

The women tested one raft and placed it in a back eddy where the current barely ran. It floated well even when Gladriel stepped on. It compensated with the addition of Lori's weight.

Lori declared them safe and dragged the other raft in beside it. Mathina had attempted to make paddles. She clapped her hands as Gladriel used her disruptor, set on low, to finish carving four cupped paddles at the end of six foot saplings.

When the women came to get the packs and Corthain he complained of being hungry. Lori was surprised when Gladriel informed him they would eat once they were across the river.

Quickly the rafts were loaded. Gladriel, Corthain, the doeg and one pack huddled precariously on one raft. The other was loaded with Lori, Mathina, and two packs. Each raft had two paddles.

Lori's attention was on the packs. Mathina, however, spotted an interesting leaf arrangement and jumped off the raft and waded across a shallow backwater to get it. As she reached up to pluck it a flat stubby ended green tentacle dropped out of the overhanging branches and coiled a round her arm. Mathina screamed as she was lifted out of the water. She pried at the tentacle, which continued to retract bearing her up to its maw.

Mathina' second scream brought Lori to her feet on the raft. A burst from her disruptor missed. The raft was rocking dangerously. Lori jumped from the raft into the shallow water and fired again. Mathina dropped three feet into the water.

Lori's sudden jump to her feet had also bobbed the raft. Glady and Corthain fought to control it as it swung from side to side bumping the raft Lori had been on. As Lori tried to get onto the raft it tilted and she pushed one side down. When it shot back up it threw her off and she landed in the brackish water. She came to her feet sputtering, and madly searching for her disruptor. After a quick search she found it was safely in the holster on her hip.

In the meantime Mathina floundered in the water and attracted the attention of another more deadly plant. It snaked its slender tentacles through the water well below the surface until it touched her leg. Quickly it wound its appendage around her leg and began pulling her into deeper water. Mathina flayed at the water, screamed and churned up foam in the water. Every attempt to scream after the first one was stopped by her being dragged under the water. She coughed, sputtered and swallowed more water.

Corthain had kept his eye on Mathina. When Lori cut her loose, he saw her fall and saw the tell-tale ripple of the sea-leaf's tentacle. He knew what would happen to her if she didn't get loose. A quick struggle with the rocking raft and he was able to drop over the side. He thrashed his way through chest deep water toward Mathina. Her continuing struggles slowed the retracting arm. Corthain reached her as she was pulled under again. Diving beneath the swirling foam covered water he located her ankle and sawed at the sea leaf. His knife bit quickly through the aquatic limb. Mathina was free. Suddenly Mathina was caught by a stronger current and swept out toward the main channel.

Corthain struggled back to the raft and tossed his knife to Glady and shouted at Lori to push the rafts out. He swam and pushed against the raft where Gladriel sat working her paddle against the water. Together they swung the rafts into the river. Immediately they were caught by the current. Corthain refused Gladriel's efforts to pull him aboard. Instead he clung to the raft searching the water for Mathina. Soon they spotted her and shouted this to Lori, who began with Gladriel's help to paddle toward her.

When they reached her, Corthain reached out and caught her arm. He couldn't hang on for long. He grabbed a second time and grabbed her hair. This time his grip held. Mathina thrashed around until she touched his arm. Then she began working her way toward his shoulder. He held his grip. When she was close enough, Gladriel grasped Mathina's hands and attempted to drag her onto the raft. Her heavy petticoats pulled her down. Finally Corthain put his hand under her buttocks and gave her a good heave. She slid up on the raft and lay exhausted in a wilted bundle of petticoats and leaves. She was not hurt by her brush with two deadly plants. Instead she was unhappy she had lost so many of her pretty baubles.

Corthain worked his way to Lori's raft. He pulled himself up and she helped him climb aboard. He collapsed breathing heavily. Lori scanned him and could find no injury.

She called to Glady, "Everyone here is all right. How are you?"

"We're fine."

Mathina, once she found herself unhurt sat up and spoke to Gladriel. "That was exciting, but I don't think I want to do it again."

Gladriel smiled. The doeg scrambled over Glady to reach Mathina who pulled it onto her wet dress and soothed him. As she bent over a loose braid dangled for attention.

She began unbraiding her plaits and soon was absorbed in redoing her hair. She was elated because the vines and pretty stone had not been lost. Happy once more she began to talk of things past.

Lori consulted her map, "Glady, the rafts would drift a few more miles before we need to paddle. If you want to take a nap do so. This raft will lead and if I have a problem I'll call you."

Soon Glady was lulled by the lapping water against the hollow reeds and Mathina's incessant chatter. She fell asleep.

Chapter 25

Rescuing Mathina had cost them invaluable time. Redford reassured them they were well ahead of the men. Redford said they were correct in assuming Ameral would be in charge. They were moving too fast for town dwellers. They had run into some animal problems. They had been stopped by one of those raging giants who'd interrupted the women's travels early on in their assignment.

The women were grateful for the delay. Anything which could give them time to get across the river and find the THRAX was appreciated.

Corthain lay curled up on his side facing Lori. She sat nearly in the middle hunched over her map. The current carried them like bobbing debris down the middle of the river. The quiet was haunting. There were no calls of birds or hum of insects. There were only the occasional swooshing and sudden gurgle of the water as it bounced against the raft's bottom. The small group was truly a part of the River. They continued onward.

Corthain, who had been staring intently at Lori, broke the silence. "I feel quite different. I feel . . . well, more awake than I have in years. And though I am tired, I don't desire to sleep. Shall we talk, Lori? I've never really talked with a woman. I feel I can with you."

"If you want to talk Corthain, I'll listen."

"In your village you two must be most prized." He saw she was about to speak. He touched her leg. "No, please let me talk, Lori. I cannot believe the way you handle the dangerous situations and perils this land has thrown at you. I can indeed see you and Gladriel are different. I have no women in my household who would do as you have done. I have come to respect you, yet I find I fear you. Amazingly I am enjoying being in your company. I could not have said so yesterday." He fondled her hand.

"You have changed too, Corthain, since the day I met you. You have lost some of your arrogance and air of superiority. I am surprised," Lori said as she controlled her impulse to question him, now he seemed so open and inviting.

He moved closer to her, taking hold of her arm and pulling her down to lie beside him. She did not resist. He kissed her softly on her cheek and cradled her head in his arms.

"I have always found women strange and hard to understand yet strangely they are so enjoyable to be around. It is pleasant to lie here."

"Corthain, how did your people get to this world?"

"I have generally believed we have always lived here. When I was young and still in the women's quarters I often heard them tell a story of the beginning."

"Tell it to me, Corthain, please."

Corthain kissed her gently and felt so close and gentle. "Of course, if you wish. The story begins, as do all women's tales, with 'Once upon a time, a long time ago, the people came from the heavens.' Then the women always tell the little girls someday the Mothers and Sisters will save the women from hard work and constant duty to men."

"Is it possible there may be some truth in the story?"

"No, our history goes far into the past and nowhere are there any grounds for the story. We men have tried to erase the story, still the women tell it."

"It is a sad story, Corthain, yet believable."

"You are a woman and you wish to believe in tales. Maybe even in your village women tell the same tale."

"No story like that in my village. I learned in school the stories of the mothers, children and fathers who have been lost sailing through the skies."

"These are pretty stories, but none are true," said Corthain with conviction.

"You cannot know for sure, Corthain. Maybe someday you will learn how much of your stories are true."

"Where there is no truth, one cannot learn," he said hugging her tightly. "If we had a crown, we would find we are one. We would not need a story. We would have a truth." He kissed her cheek and fondled her neck and breasts.

"I'm sorry to tell you, but you may not have a crown for many more days," said Lori as she felt his allure steal over her. "Gladriel will wonder why we lie here. We'd better sit up and check our position." She did not attempt to move from his arms.

"Isn't this what you want now?"

"Yes, but Gladriel's my friend. I don't want to hurt her any more than I have. She feels and cares about you. Maybe she is in love with you. I don't know."

"I feel strongly for her, but she is not here and you are. I have learned to take my pleasure with whichever woman of my household is near."

"I find it hard to accept such rationale. I don't approve or disapprove. I feel love and or pleasure should be an equal response between a man and a woman. I was reared in this manner. We feel a woman should have a say in her own pleasure too."

"Sadly, Lori, it can never be. A man is superior to a woman. Without his potency the woman would not be capable of maintaining the civilization."

"Nor would he be able to carry on civilization, because he needs her womb to carry his seed to produce the children and the future."

"We will never agree on this, I see." He laughed and kissed her and pulled her to him. He felt himself being turned on by her presence without the crown. It surprised him. He let his hand undo Lori's blouse to caress her breast as he kissed her with more fervor. She was breathing more heavily and pushed against him as he twisted her nipple and felt her body respond even more.

"I see you want me too."

"I do, desperately but I cannot betray my friend."

He kissed her and reached down to the junction of her legs and rubbed her gently then more firmly.

Her hand reached down into his clothing and grasped him firmly and felt the girth of him. "I must tell both of us 'no,' Corthain. Glady would never understand. She truly loves you. You are the first man who has ever touched her. Save your love for her, not for me, please."

"I have enough love for both of you, but I have never been turned on by a woman without my crown. Why is this happening?"

"Because I am like you, I have an allure. It attracts men. A superstition of my planet says once a man's made love to a woman of my world he will never want another woman. I couldn't do such a thing to you or Glady."

"Let me test this old adage now, Lori. Give yourself to me." He kissed her once more and forced himself into the edges of her mound of joy.

"What am I doing? No, Corthain, No."

"I see you've gotten yourself in a spot, Lori. I'm going to keep Glady asleep and you satisfy your needs and his. He will have great tales to tell of the women from the stars who helped him change his world. He is going to call the planet Mathina too, in honor of Mathina and us. Enjoy this moment in time. Glady will understand."

When Lori had paused to listen to Redford Corthain had worked his erection into the outer edge of her passion mound inside her and began to gently rock her until he felt the passion rise within both of them. She fought against her nature but finally gave in to her pleasure. She felt fierce and ravenous. She pulled his top back and almost savagely drank of his lips and she thrust herself against him time and time again until she felt him within her and he felt hot and warm and she was hot and filled with fire. She demanded his richness, his seed and his passion. He couldn't stop the feelings he was having. He realized he could never have known this was what real sex was. He had never had such an experience and he didn't want to stop nor did she until she came with a muffled shout and total body shudder and he joined with her. They trembled in ecstasy and they climaxed once more.

"I have never had anything like this love in my life. I have slept with a goddess of love."

Lori rearranged her clothing and his.

He took her hand and she pulled it away.

"No more, Corthain. No more. Now you know what sex can be like without the crown. Without it you remember everything, not the euphoria of the crown. So try it without the crown when your woman is with child or when you want to experience and remember your love making. Love your women. They deserve real love so they may carry your seed."

"Will you carry my seed, Lori?"

"No, I cannot and will not. I am too young."

"I have young wives and they can bear children."

"Let them be children before girls, let them be girls before they become women and let them be mothers when they are ready. No child or girl should sleep with a man before she is 18. Then if she is with child you can have stronger healthier children. Let her live in a house with other girls until she is ready to be a wife and mother. Let her learn to read and write so she can teach her children. Respect should be mutual. Now there is something else I want to ask you. Why did you save Mathina?"

"The old woman is of no value. However, I could see you and Gladriel were intent on bringing her with you. I think I know where the women go who have been cast out. You and Gladriel save them."

"You are totally wrong, Corthain. So far we've found evidence the woman are murdered by men, killed by creatures or destroyed by the Tangle."

"I am through talking. I don't want to continue this conversation, Lori."

"Are you feeling a twinge of guilt? If you and the other lords had any sense, you could have benefitted your settlements by learning and using the knowledge the older women know. Mathina knows all about the Tangle."

200

"I suppose you are correct. No one has ever survived as long as she has and certainly not alone."

"She has survived when men have failed. Isn't this true?" Lori asked.

Corthain did not answer.

"Perhaps your men are missing something. She knows plants and herbs. By nature she is innocent, loving and trusting. She has been devoted to you Lords. How could you men drive out such a woman? How did you feel when you threw out your own mother?"

"It is our way. When a woman reaches the point in her life when she cannot bear children or when she grows feeble she is sent out. You realize women do not age at the same rate as we men. Men who have crowns live years longer than those who do not. Too, we are stronger in body and father many children who reach full term. It is the men who keep the learning alive. Men direct the education for the young men. They decide who will seek a crown and which women will be united with which Lord's household. As you know this is a harsh world. Many women are born yet few males. Those few men are nourished. They become the rulers if they are healthy and strong. Our world does not offer a surplus of men. We cannot explain what happens here, we only live within its boundaries."

"Corthain, this is strange to Glady and me. I would never have believed such a society existed had I not seen it. I come from a world where women are equal to men. A woman chooses her own path of life. Gladriel and I have traveled a long way to your world to save it from destruction."

"How did you get here?"

"We have a special ship. It takes us to various places. This time it brought us here."

"Women are clever. My father warned me. He said a woman will tell many stories and the listener may not know which is the truth. You are dreamers. No one will ever fly in the heavens. Only women dream of such foolish things. Tell me something I can believe in, Lori."

"You are a good man who takes care of his family. You need to take care of the women and men in your life and village. Believe in yourself, Corthain. You know how to love now, but I am not sure you will remember the lesson."

"If you stay with me I will."

"That is kind and loving of you. We both know I cannot. You will always be special in my heart. I am glad I can now see the man Glady loves and I know why. Please keep our secret for as long as you live. If you treated all women as you have treated me today, you might not need a crown anymore and you might even have more children. Who knows? I must get back to my job and wake up Glady." Lori sat up and consulted her map. They had drifted for some time. She'd figured out they could paddle the rafts at an angle they might land within a couple of miles from the point on the map. She tucked the map back into the band of her shorts and called to Glady.

Shortly the combined efforts of the four enabled them to turn the rafts toward the distant shore. An hour of steady paddling brought them to the bank, but they could not beach. The banks were steep.

Redford suggested to Lori the rafts needed to head on downstream where the river was flooding over its banks. It was getting closer to sundown and they were still paddling. A sense of fear and dread was entering their minds. They didn't want to be on the river after dark. Lori feared they'd drifted too far.

In desperation Lori turned into a finger of the river which seemed to offer a landing place. Shadows became tenuous web shaped clouds floating over the water. Gladriel pulled her raft up beside Lori's. Both could see large tree-like plants standing in water. They could not, however, tell how deep the water was or how far the water penetrated the Tangle.

Glady paddled past a shapeless black cloud quivering on a branch. She reached out and pushed the limb out of her way. Her screams broke the silence. The cloud clung tenaciously to her hand. She flung her hand about, attempting to shake it off. When she saw she couldn't dislodge it she dipped her hand in the water. Instantly the web dissolved. She gave a sigh of relief. "My arm is stinging and burning."

"What happened, Glady?" asked Lori.

"Are you all right, Gladriel?" Corthain asked.

"I don't know. Do not touch those!" she screamed and pointed at the black clouds clinging to the branches. She inspected her hand. "It dissolved in the water. Now my hand still stings and it's swollen. Let's get out of here."

Lori and Corthain back paddled until the two rafts were well away from the webs and again out in the river. They continued downstream for about fifteen minutes when Lori called out, "I see a landing half submerged in the water."

Soon they all saw it. Combining their remaining strength they pulled up close to a broad smooth sandy beach. They could see the remains of a landing above a water covered dock.

When they beached the little doeg was the first off. It ran up the beach a short way, stopped, and sniffed and frisked back.

They unloaded their packs. Gladriel spoke up. "We need a rest, Lori." She shook her hand.

Mathina came running up. "I'll return shortly with some herbs for your hand." She ran ahead and into the brushy area

Lori consulted Redford. She learned Ameral and his men had stopped at the river. They were making no effort to cross. He suggested the beach might be a good place to camp.

Lori studied her map. "Glady, we're less than a good mile from the location of the last identified source. It's got to be the THRAX. We've made it. Are you up to traveling another mile? I'm not exactly comfortable on the river. Too many river monsters for my tastes are known to murk in these waters."

"I'll try to go a ways. Is there any shelter up this way?" Gladriel murmured to Redford.

"Yes, there is. It is about half a mile from here. I can guide you."

"Lori, we'll each carry something and head up this old trail. I've been informed there is shelter ahead."

"Okay, everyone, let's go. We don't have much sunlight left," ordered Lori. "Mathina, we're heading to the old village up the trail."

They each drank some water and ate some fruit they picked on the way. Before the last rays of the sun went down they reached an abandoned village. They picked the nearest one with walls tall enough to keep out most things and hide their location. They set up camp and ate a bit more.

"I have the herbs now," announced Mathina as she entered camp. She took a flat stone and lay the herbs on then rubbed the plants with another rock. Soon she had a sticky greenish paste. Marina applied it to Glady's hand and wrapped it with a leaf. Corthain watched and asked Mathina what she used. She told him. He took out a pad of paper and wrote some notes about the medicine.

"Mathina, it really feels better already. I think it has taken the fire out of it. Thank you so much." Glady hugged Mathina and kissed her cheek. "Thank you for your help." Glady looked around her. "Has anyone seen my sleeper?"

"I have it right here. Would you do me the honor of warming my bed tonight, Gladriel?" He led her to the next room section and spread it out on the ground. "I would be honored if you would allow me to make love to you? I love you and want to hold you close to my heart."

Gladriel helped him spread the sleeper and removed her shoes. Then she helped undress Corthain slowly and carefully and then he undressed her. He ran his hands over her dark curls and kissed each eye. Then he lightly brushed her cheeks and finally he found her mouth waiting for his lips. The kiss was warm and promising. He ran his hands over her body and felt her curves and rubbed his right hand in circles on her back.

She in turned touched him and rubbed his neck and back. Suddenly she put her hands on his hips and pulled them to meet hers. She felt him engorge and harden. She liked the feeling of being so close to him. Then he gently picked her up and placed her on the sleeper and kissed her lips.

Next he showered her body with kisses. Then he added a touch of tongue going round and round the areola surrounding the nipple. She reacted to his stimulation and her nipples went harder. Glady moaned and sought to reach down to touch him but he moved beside her. He trailed his left hand from her neck, down her cleavage. Then he stopped to kiss her navel and slowly slid his hand down between her legs. Once more Glady felt a craving and desire to possess and be possessed by him. She pulled his head up to her breast and offered it to him. He took it and stimulated her further by flipping her hard nibble with his tongue. She moaned and ached for it all. He held back and then he lay down and pulled her on top of him. She tried to slide down onto him but his knees were up. Instead he played with her breasts and she kissed him and melted. Slowly he lowered his legs and allowed her to seek him out. The blood rushed through her body. She could hear her own heartbeat. She felt an explosion of pleasure and love she'd never known before. Then he rolled her over and started in again and she wanted him even more. Once more they felt the touch and the feel of a mutual orgasm and she melted into his arms.

"Corthain, you don't need a crown, except to show you're a Lord. No doubt this was the most wonderful experience of my life. I'm glad the first man I love has taught me about love."

"Thank you, Gladriel. I will always remember how I taught you what real love is without a crown. I remember this so much clearer and wonderfully. Will you make love to me again?"

"Corthain, I am satisfied with the love we shared. If you want more you'll have to ask Lori. I will ask her to make love to you until you are satisfied. Lori and I have important work to do tomorrow. I need my rest. She doesn't require the sleep I do. She will share my love with you as my gift to you."

"Why would you do such a thing, Gladriel?"

"Because I love you and I may not be able to satisfy you as you need. I want you to be as happy as I am."

Corthain kissed her and ran his hands over her body. He now knew what Lori meant. He didn't want to hurt Glady either.

"Lori," called Glady.

"Yes, Glady."

"Lori, would you make love to Corthain for me? I must have rest and I can do no more. Honestly it would make me happy to have you share my love with him."

205

"I don't know how you'll feel about this in the morning, Glady. You need to rethink this decision. Remember how you were feeling the other day."

"I now know what real love is and I am not jealous or worried. Besides that I need my rest and Corthain has a bigger sexual appetite than I or almost any woman can fill. I am satisfied. Corthain, go to her and please her as you have me."

He got up and went to Lori. "Gladriel wants me to share my love for her with you without a crown. Will you make love to me? Don't be shy, she asked me to share her love for you." He took her hand and she picked up the sleeper and they went outside. The sapling plants stood guard all around as they slowly removed their garments and laid these to one side.

Lori ran her hands all over his body to see it better in the pale moonlight. She flicked his earlobes and nuzzled his neck. She took out a cleansing pack and washed his body slowly and gently. She cleansed him and threw the pads in a pile and then ran her hands over the cleansed area feeling and searching for the magic spot. He began to harden she stroked him slowly and rhythmically. He got fuller and more rigid. Then she reached her lips to his and kissed him gently then harder and harder and her tongue slipped in and played on the roof of his mouth. She felt him stiffen even more. She kissed and stroked him once more. She pulled him down to the sleeper. As they sat down she sat on his lap and they were one. Afterwards she lay down and waited for him to come to her. Shortly he sidled up beside her. "You have given me pleasure I never knew existed. Can you show me more?"

"I can. You should realize most women cannot accommodate all of your desire. Learn to be satisfied with one grand pleasure and one woman."

"I will. But not tonight I want you more than ever."

"Then don't blame me if you're tired tomorrow." She reached over and pulled him closer. "Now you are the pupil and I am the teacher. Don't complain about the lessons." She kissed him and teased him until he couldn't control himself and then they made love for most of the night. Finally Lori kissed him and sent him inside to rest beside Gladriel. She picked up her sleeper and went inside by the prism to think and finally fall asleep.

Chapter 26

Lori woke and began to gather her supplies to search the village. She fixed herself some tea and half of the last of the biscuits with a fruit. Having eaten she ran a scan on the village and called Redford. She hefted her work bag and went off to explore the other empty roofless ruins.

Corthain rolled over and kissed Gladriel. "Good morning, my love. How did you sleep?"

"Wonderfully." She kissed him and held him tight. "I have never known such happiness or pleasure as last night. I love you, Corthain. I truly do."

"On the raft yesterday, Lori and I visited. We talked of many things. I wish to know where your village is. I do not intend to tell Lord Ameral. I only wish to see your village and your women to know if they are as Lori says."

"Did Lori tell you we are not of this world?"

"She said you both are. I cannot believe this. Will you tell me the truth?"

"She told you the truth, Corthain. We came across the skies between the stars to this place for a purpose."

"Did you and Lori come to fulfill the women's prophecy?"

"What prophecy?"

"The mothers tell their children an old story. It gives women hope. It will encourage them to do good as they are taught, other women will come from the skies and set them free. It is a silly prophecy which the women tell to one another. At times even I cannot help but think of the tales when I hear you or Lori talking into empty air or into those bands on your wrist.

Could you be those women? Have you come to fulfill the prophecy?"

"We did not come here for the people. We came to save the people from a great danger. We are women from the stars. We did not want to contact you. In fact, we didn't know humans would be on the world we were sent to save. If Lori hadn't gotten poisoned by the spear grass we would never have met. We cannot help your people in any way, it is against our law."

"I would like your power and weapons."

"We came in secret and were sent by our Council. Fortunately or unfortunately our meeting may change your life and culture. Accidently we may have fulfilled your prophecy. All individuals want to be free. Since we came in secret we would have left in secret and you'd never have known of our worlds. Corthain, your people have dreams and now you have the power in you to do great things with or without the crown."

"Who are you, Gladriel?"

"I am a woman who has completed her training and has been sent out to be tested, much like your young men in the Villages."

"Are men tested in this way too?"

"Yes, it doesn't matter if you be male or female to our Council. Many of the people who pass the test go on to be leaders in other worlds. We came here to find to find a piece of equipment which is dangerous to your world. Once we find it, we will remove it from here and leave. To leave before we find it would be to leave your world in jeopardy. Do you understand what I am telling you?"

He pulled her to him and faced her. "I understand two things. One, you and Lori are not members of any Lord's village of which I know. Two, you and Lori are strong strange women who are capable of great things. Where are your men?"

"They are in many places, Corthain. We women do not always travel with men. Sometimes it is women only. Sometimes it is with one woman and one man, or two men. Our men and women are scattered through the stars. Some men are leaders like you. Others are artists, teachers, doctors and agriculturists. Some men raise their family while their wife works. Men, as well as women, can do anything they choose, as long as they are skilled at what they do."

"This is difficult for me to understand, yet I see proof in you. Who in your world are stronger, men or women?"

"Generally men are stronger physically. Different occupations require different strengths and skills. Lori is much stronger than I am. On her world the women are almost always strong. On my world the men are strong and women are smaller yet more adept and agile. We have one man and one woman to a marriage. Lori's world is different from yours or mine."

"It is difficult for me to understand and believe. I have seen the things you and Lori have done. No woman I know can do these things. I was attracted to you and greatly annoyed with you. You seemed docile and then you turned against me. I must accept what you tell me as true, because your actions say you have been telling the truth."

"Gladriel, did you know Lori threatened to kill me? Would she have killed me?"

"She could have, but only if she thought it necessary. I see you are alive."

"I escaped and almost got killed. To my surprise she saved me."

"That's Lori. Are you attracted to her?"

"Yes, I am attracted to her, yet a bit fearful of her too. Will I ever get back to my village and women?"

"Once we complete this job we will return you safely. I promise. I will get you a crown so you can be a Lord once more. One big piece of advice, don't wear your crown often, you don't need it for making love. When you wear the crown it draws power from the women. This can make them lose a baby or not get pregnant. When you use it, it gives you a strong dose of something which makes you more developed and virile. Women receive pleasure from the crown yet lose their ability to carry a potential child to delivery, particularly males. I have something I want to give you. It is a pill. It will protect you from the THRAX we dismantle here today." She handed it to him. This will make sure you are a potent breeder and keep you strong." She handed him her canteen and he swallowed the pill. She took one too.

"Lori and I want to protect you and Mathina from Lord Ameral who will arrive today with some men. I am doubtful they are your men. We don't want to put you or Mathina in danger."

"If any men arrive today they will be mine. Why would Lord Ameral want to harm you? He is respected by all the villagers. He is honest and fair. In trading he is beyond reproach and he is my cousin. He has always treated me well. I will not believe ill of him."

"Have you ever wondered why so many of your young men fail to return from the trials of the flaggets?"

"There is no mystery. You have seen the harsh land we live in. It has taken many years for my people to establish the village where I live.

"Yes, Corthain, the land is harsh and dangerous. Fortunately the land can be understood here. We saw cultivated patches of flaggets."

"This is impossible. Flaggets are not cultivated. The Law forbids it. My Lord Ameral insists we do not try to domesticate these horrors."

"We told you earlier of Jeames. He was a lovely young man. He claimed Lori and slept with her right there by the patch. I broke them up and destroyed his beautiful crown. I wish I hadn't. It really caused him pain and fear. I didn't know how important to your culture it is. He got two more and took these to the men, including their leader Lord Ameral. At first they treated him well. They ate and drank hearty. Then Lord Ameral ordered him to put on his crown. It was so potent all the men attacked him. Then Ameral killed him by slitting his throat. We looked for his body but never found it. They could have fed him to a flagget or a number of carnivorous plants. I'm glad he had affirmation of his crown when he attracted Lori. He thought she was a golden goddess. When she saw Lord Ameral kill Jeames, she was angry and wanted to kill them all. We had orders not to contact the natives of this planet. So she didn't."

She waited for him to speak. He said nothing.

Glady continued. "Even now, I believe we are all in great danger. Lord Ameral wants all the women outside the villages to die; he could possibly let you live since he'll own you."

"I cannot fear Lord Ameral. He is my cousin and has been like a brother to me.

"Be careful, my love." She got up and hurried to the other room.

Redford began to speak, "Glady, he does not believe you. Do not feel any remorse. You have done your duty and warned him."

"Thank you, Redford. It doesn't help. I still hurt at the thought of him dying."

Chapter 27

Glady contacted Lori, "How are you doing, Lori?"

"I'm in the northern most part of the ruins. I still have to look in the last two. Can you gather our equipment and head this way? On your way here, stop by one of the two first two former homes on row 10 and 11. These have great views of the trail coming up to this village. Then you leave our personal packs and camp equipment there. Also leave Mathina and Corthain there out of sight. By the time you join me we can get started. I'll let you know which building.

"Mathina isn't with us. She's gone. I think she went back to the water for some pretty rocks or is talking to some plant creature. Do I need to go look for her?"

"After you deposit our stuff you need to see me and we'll see who gets the draw on the THRAX unit. Why did she do it?"

"That's who she is, Lori. We cannot protect her from the Tangle."

"It's not the Tangle, it's the men. I'll see you shortly. I'm going in the first one now."

Lori walked in and saw the shuttle chair which had fallen through its platform. "Lori, it's in the tenth row the first house and the readings are high. I'm sending these to Redford. Did you take your pill, Glady? I'm taking mine. See you soon."

Lori took her pill and began to examine the room. In one corner in rubbish which once contained a table or cabinet lay a metal chest. It was a personal locker much like the ones sailors use now for personal privacy items.

She wiped off the dirt and mold and ran her hand across the lid, searching for the release button. There was nothing. She turned it over and held it up and sighted along one edge. A slight indentation caught in the dim light. She set it down and pulled out her scanner. She was aiming carefully when Gladriel and Corthain came into the house.

"Look at the throne, Lord Corthain," said Glady.

"The name I found on the seat is Arvella. I have never heard of a Lord Arvella. Have you, Lori?" he asked her.

"I'm sure neither Gladriel nor I have heard of him. I'll bet this chest is his locker and has a ship's log inside."

"Why would anyone put a piece of plant in a box to protect it?" Corthain rubbed his head in doubt as to the validity of her remark.

"This could be a written record of his journey here and how they survived."

"Then Arvella was a Lord, for only Lords can read and write."

He watched Lori use her knife and to run down the edge until the tip touched the indentation. They heard a faint click. The lid lifted a few inches. Lori forced it open a bit more. Inside lay a small diary sealed in an airless package.

"We've really found something, Glady. Won't the fellows in history be happy when I report this find? This writing is more than 500 years old."

"Send me a sample via scanner and I'll translate it."

"I will do so immediately."

Corthain smiled as he heard her talk to herself.

Lori had Corthain hold the book as she scanned its contents.

It says this is the diary of Captain Arvella, who was in command of *The Triumph*. He thinks meteor damage to the drive of the ship was extensive and the section where the men were held in suspension was hit. The majority of the women were saved, as well as most of the working officers and crew. Some of the children were saved. The ship had very little power, and it could not move between the stars. So they were forced to land in this sector on a habitable planet. A scout ship took readings to insure the quality of the air. The survivors were unloaded after most things had been removed from the ship via the flyer. The second trip brought the passengers, seed and animals. They also removed the seats for more space to strip the ship of all items useable by the survivors. It was while they were unloading and storing they found the THRAX unit. A group took the THRAX and isolated it in this area. A party of officers and two men went to the yellow mountain to set a beacon. They never returned. Slowly over the years the remaining people established a colony and a government in an area where the water was pure. As the years passed we learned of the fate of most of the males born on this planet. They were sterile. There will be no future for the hundred or so people left."

"There is more, Lori. I have summarized most of it. Indeed Professor Brass in ancient history will find this most interesting. Preserve this diary. I shall store the reading I took for later reading and interpretation. This will be a star in your future Spacer Lori."

"Lori, there is no THRAX in this building. I'm checking the other now. We have a problem over here. Come quickly."

"The readings are off the chart. I cannot access the building. The saplings are guarding it. I cannot get to it. Oh, no, the plants are advancing on me and have their leaves spread." When Gladriel touched one it closed around her. In panic she attempted to pull away. A second later she felt a warm glow of assurance.

When Lori saw them she found the four had wrapped Gladriel in their arms. The hummed softly and released her. She stepped back. They dropped their green fronds to their sides. She stepped forward each time they spread their fronds. Glady tried to skirt around between the leaves but they would not allow her to pass.

Lori hurried up and approached her. "I'm sorry I was delayed. I found an old ship's log with information on this colony. They were marooned here over 500 years ago. That is why the THRAX is an older model and might even be one of the first of its kind. It may be quite unstable. We need to get inside." The green saplings would not permit them to enter.

Corthain saw they had difficulties and came closer to them. He would not come nearer to the plants.

Suddenly the walkers moved toward him. Their humming increased in frequency and volume.

Corthain ran in fright. The walkers followed him.

Lori looked at Glady and smiled.

While the walkers harassed Corthain they entered the building. The room was dimly lit. Lori told Glady to stay. She ran for her pack and the prism. In a few minutes she returned. She told Gladriel the walkers were still pursuing Corthain. He seemed to be able to stay away from them.

She set up the prism and they had light. It revealed the THRAX which was resting upside down on a wooden rectangle which normally sat on six stubby legs. Like a dead beast its legs now stuck up into the air. Its smooth sides reflected distorted shadows of the women.

Gladriel reached out and gingerly touched it. She was surprised. It felt cool and slick. Running her hands over it she discovered a series of numbers between the first and third leg. She called them out to Lori. "Those are only serial numbers of the THRAX," explained Lori. Then she looked at Glady who was upset.

Lori knew then Redford had explained what the numbers really meant. It was a much older model than they'd practiced on. "If you want, Glady, I'll give it a try."

"It's similar to one I worked on in the six month course for this mission. I will do it alone. You see to the safety of Mathina and Corthain. Mathina has wandered off. You may want to round her up before they get here. See you later. "I'm setting up the shoot with a wide angle so Redford can assist me if necessary. Next I'll set up the scanner."

"Glady, I will set up the perimeter when I leave and I'll have you turn on the switch. So if we fail you have a chance to succeed. I have a small ground cloth too. Do you want it?"

"Sounds good, Lori."

"I put a canteen with water within your reach and arranged the tools. Be careful, you are special to me and I love you."

"I love you too, Lori. Thanks for everything, including keeping Corthain away so I could sleep. I couldn't have done as good a job as I need to do. Thanks, I really mean it and I know you didn't want to interfere in my life. Now get out of here and save us all."

Lori tossed her the switch and Glady turned it on. "There is no going back now."

"Glady, Corthain loves you, you know, don't you?"

"Yes, I do. I love him too. He loves you too; still he's a bit afraid of you. It's a thought provoking relationship, eh?

"We are friends only," She turned and walked from the room. "How long do you think this will take?"

"Give me a couple of hours if I'm lucky, longer yet if I'm not or even longer if it falls apart. Will you promise me to look after Corthain, if necessary?"

"I promise. You can see to him yourself. Love you and see you later." Lori caught her heart rate increasing. She meditated briefly and then walked away.

Lori scouted the area more closely. If they were to fight she wanted her back to a protected space. She wanted to see the men as she confronted them. A house on row twelve seemed perfect. She wanted to see them yet wanted some foliage and rocks between them which could impede an outright attack.

Corthain snuck out from behind a house further in on row twelve. Glady saw him. "Over here, Corthain. My spy in the sky says the men are almost here and Mathina is playing in the water. We don't have time to get her. I hope they don't harm her. I see you eluded the walkers."

"They would have harmed me. I have heard of them; they do not like men. The women tell of them standing on the edge of the fields humming to them. Several times I have ordered my men to run them away with firebrands. They are known to lure the women into the Tangle and kill them."

Lori looked at Corthain as he babbled nonsense. "That's silly superstition, Corthain." She laughed as she patted him on the shoulder. "You saw Glady and me with them. Did they try to kill us?"

"The plants didn't because I was with you."

Lori laughed again. "Corthain, they were more interested in you than in us. It was you they chased. You didn't have to worry as long as you ran fast and stayed ahead of them. They are not bad."

Approaching voices made Lori forget the walkers. Mingled in with men's voices was a woman's. Lori knew it was Mathina's voice.

"Let's move back into the clearing. I'll feel safer," she said as she handed him her cutter and drew her disruptor. Then she decided against appearing hostile and holstered it. "I wished I had thought to get Gladriel's disruptor. Two would be better than one," she said to Corthain. "It's a bigger party than I thought. Lord Corthain, stand away from me. I don't want you harmed." It was quite possible Lord's Ameral and his men would start something.

Corthain did not move aside as she had ordered. Instead he moved to stand slightly in front of her. He spoke over his shoulder, "Do you intend to kill Lord Ameral and his men?"

"I do not intend to harm them. I shall wait and see what they intend. I think it is wise to be prepared. If you continue to stand there I will not be responsible for your safety."

He stepped back to stand beside her. "You do not attack first, do you?"

She smiled at him. "I do not. If Lord Ameral is the good fellow you've been insisting he is, I won't have to harm him. But, if he's not and he attacks then . . ." She let the sentence fade as Ameral's party entered the clearing. They drug a protesting Mathina with them.

Corthain, who still believed in Ameral's honesty, called a cheerful greeting.

Ameral did not respond.

Corthain would have advanced toward the group, which had stopped when they saw them, had Lori not touched his arm. He now did not move. Corthain noticed Drupel, Ameral's handpicked lieutenant, had Mathina by the arm and was dragging her like a rag doll.

"Release the old woman, Lord Ameral! She cannot be of any threat to you," called out Corthain.

Ameral walked to within fifty feet of Lori and Corthain. He had been studying them as he approached. The beautiful woman, whom Jeames called a golden goddess, looked the part. Her sheer size made him curious and jealous. He could see Corthain stood at ease with her. Corthain had known her and had claimed her. A streak of searing jealousy ran through him as he realized this.

In the short time he'd seen Lori; he felt an overwhelming desire to possess her. With her in his household he could father more sons, sons who would rival Corthain's. When he spoke his voice was pleasant and cheerful.

The old woman is my woman, Corthain. She met us at the landing and obligingly brought us to meet you. Who is the woman with you?"

Mathina became aware of Lori and Corthain. She struggled to break free of Drupel's grip. He slapped her. She screamed in rage and attacked him with her fists, delivering a flurry of inadequate blows. Drupel was shocked and didn't try to stop her. Another man stepped forward and delivered a sharp blow across her face. Mathina stopped her struggle, crumpled to her knees and began crying again.

The action of Ameral's men disgusted him and served as a warning to not approach Lord Ameral. At first he had thought to greet his brother Lord and cousin. Now he stepped back in contempt. No Lord would allow his men to mistreat a woman in this manner.

Ameral repeated his question, "Who is this woman?"

"A friend," Corthain replied.

Lori looked at him in surprise. What was Corthain doing? "You may release Mathina, Lord Ameral. We will see to her. She is old and forgetful. Thank you for finding her."

Ameral did not order his man to release Mathina. "My cousin, Corthain, we have followed your trail for many days and we are tired. Could we rest and talk about what has happened?"

"How were you able to find us, Lord Ameral? I left no real trail after I left the road."

"It was simple after we knew where you were headed once we met your men on the road. They believed you died when they showed me pieces of your tunic. There were no bones, I knew you still lived."

"Where are my men now?" He was more suspicious of Ameral's intentions once he saw all the men wore Ameral's color.

"They returned home once they thought you were dead. I told them I'd check further. They are not waiting for you. They went home to their families. The rain slowed us, as did several walkers. We were delayed by devastating rains, as were you."

The women tell me the walkers don't harm humans," Corthain said and watched Ameral's reactions carefully.

"Merely women talk. What can they know of the Tangle?" Ameral snorted. "I see you have the woman in control. I have the old one. We would be commended by the Rex except for the fact he is dead." Ameral began to walk closer.

"Stop where you are and take two steps back!" yelled Lori.

"Shock registered on his face. It turned from shock to dark anger. "No woman orders me," he thundered. "Corthain, if you have claimed this woman then you should have taught her manners."

"I cannot teach her anything, Lord Ameral. She is not my woman."

Ameral smiled and thought, 'this is my chance. I shall show Corthain how women should be subdued. I will claim her as mine.' "I have come to escort you home, Corthain. We will see you get there safely. We saw many wild creatures. Your message about two women from the Tangle brought me to you. Where is the other one? Surely you do not mean this old woman?"

Drupel jerked Mathina to a standing position. She pried at his hand. He slapped her when she hurt his finger. She cried out. From out of the jungle to the right of the group came the little doeg as it ran straight for Drupel and Mathina. When it reached Mathina it reared up on its hind legs to lick her hand. Drupel kicked at it. Mathina tried to push Drupel off balance and she hit him in the stomach. A friend of Drupel's grabbed Mathina by her hair and jerked her. She cried out again.

The doeg snapped at Drupel's heels. He kicked at it again. The doeg rushed in and bit at Drupel's foot as it came toward him. The man's booted foot caught the doeg in the stomach and knocked it to the ground. Mathina cried out and reached toward the doeg. Another man stepped forward and crushed the doeg beneath his foot.

Lori started to move forward and stopped.

Ameral had been watching Corthain's reactions to his men's performance. He hoped Corthain would intervene and a scuffle would ensue. In the struggle Corthain might be badly wounded. "What is this? Why would a woman defy a Lord's order? Do you wish your training to begin now?"

"Corthain, I don't understand why you select women who need so much disciplining. How do you control her?"

"I have no control over her."

"What kind of Lord are you, Corthain? Lords always control their woman."

"She is not my woman," insisted Corthain.

Lori had taken two steps toward Mathina when she caught the slight move of Ameral's hand and saw the men spread themselves in a semi-circle around her and Corthain.

Mathina stood quietly beside Drupel and cried. Each time she reached out to the doeg Drupel would jerk her back.

Lori halted her advance and retreated until she was beside Corthain. All the time the two Lords had been talking she had been watching the men behind Ameral. When they began moving off to either side she guessed they intended to surround her and Corthain and force their surrender. Once she thought of calling to Gladriel via Redford, but dismissed the thought. By now Gladriel was into the dismantling and it could not be stopped short of an implosion. Redford might have helped. However it might mean starting a jungle fire. She and Gladriel could be caught in the inferno. Instead she decided to take care of the situation on her own.

Ameral who had watched her closely saw she had reached toward her belt when Mathina had screamed.

"Corthain, does the woman carry a weapon?"

"I have no idea if it is a weapon or not. Why have you allowed your men to abuse and old woman and kill a harmless doeg? You are not the man I thought you were. You disappoint me. What has happened to you?"

"If she has a weapon then we should relieve her of it. She is not of any of our villages. I would know. I've seen what a weapon like the one she has can do in my flagget patch. I think she is the one who butchered the plants."

"What patch?" asked Corthain as a cold fear rose in his stomach. The women had told of such a patch.

"It's not important now. A woman should not carry a weapon. Only men, we Lords, are granted the privilege."

"I think the old woman would not ask for the privilege, Lord Ameral. Tell your man to release Mathina. She is old and will not harm anyone. You are in no danger from her."

"I cannot take your assurance on this matter. The old woman ran from us at the river. When Drupel caught her she bit him. I suppose you do not care how she came to be alive? Didn't you know she has been cast out?" Ameral wanted to keep Corthain distracted while his men surrounded him and the woman. Although Ameral had been talking to Corthain he had been watching the woman. There were many interesting things attached to her belt. Curiosity and power beckoned Ameral. He wanted what she had.

"My men and I are tired, Lord Corthain." It was the first time he'd used Corthain's title and shown any respect for him. "We would appreciate it if you have your woman fix us something to eat. Then we can talk."

"I do not order her to do anything. It would do no good. Now the old woman will fix you something to eat. Release her to me and give her your food. She will fix it for you."

"Take the old woman to Corthain, Drupel."

Drupel advanced with his hand on his blade and dragged her toward Lori and Corthain. He thought he could dispatch Lori easier than Corthain. So he advanced carefully while looking at Corthain. Ameral thought of Lori. Sudden he threw the woman at Corthain who caught her.

Drupel attacked and Lori felled him with one shot. He lay at her feet. She took his knife and handed it to Corthain.

"Mathina, would you get behind us. Who has the food bag? Bring it closer and set it down. Then walk away. Now, you on the sides, get over with your fearless leader. I'm turning this weapon on to kill. Move it now!" ordered Lori. She flicked the settings. She smiled sweetly. Always do what you say you'll do, was one of her first lessons as a child.

"I think it is time to talk right here and now, Ameral."

"Corthain, where are your manners? I am Lord Ameral."

"No longer to me. You are a disappointment. My name to you is Lord Corthain; I have not sullied my name."

"Corthain, women are foolish things. They do not understand men. If you cannot control her, than I shall."

"That may not be wise. The woman has a powerful weapon. She does not need our protection. She is not like our women. She has trusted me. I do not believe she will harm any of your men or you, unless you threaten us."

"She is not important. The weapon is," he screamed and his face flushed red.

"She is no danger to any of us. These women are peaceful."

"How dare you talk to me in this manner? I will be the next Rex, once you are dead. She's a woman and I shall do with her as I choose. I do with anyone what I choose."

"Even Jeames? I was told Jeames was murdered. Is what I heard correct?" asked Corthain

"No, a flagget caught him and killed him."

"That's a lie," Lori yelled at Ameral.

He flushed again. "What kind of stories has she been telling you?"

"She told me you killed Jeames at the camp after he returned with two crowns. Is this true?"

"He knows, father," blurted a pale young man standing a pace or two behind Ameral.

"Shut up!" Ameral shouted to his son yet kept his eyes on Corthain. "It was necessary. He was not fit to serve as a Lord. I had to make the decision when I learned about him."

"What was his difficulty?"

"He was tainted. Someone had to decide and I was the one. He claimed he'd finalized his test with a conquest of a golden goddess. There is no such thing as a golden goddess, unless . . . he meant her."

"Why not let the Rex determine his condition?"

"The old Rex was old and there was no one else fit to rule, except me. You are only fit for frolicking with your women and taking parts in our games. You're not a man, Corthain; you never really went into the Tangle as you should. You should be dead now and this little drama here would not be happening."

Corthain looked away, rested his eyes on the cool green of the Tangle and then back again at Ameral. "All this time I thought you were an honorable man. I defended you when others said you had grown greedy. How many sons and daughters have you killed, Ameral?"

"I killed enough to place me in command. I started with your father Kameal. He was growing powerful in the Council. When he sought to limit my household after the last famine, I appealed to the Rex, who eventually came to understand my need. He granted me refuge in the northern settlement. When Kameal came north to inspect the fields, I killed him. I nurtured my power. Today I declare I am the only fit Lord. Once I finish with you, I will be the Rex and I'll appoint my Lords to serve me faithfully. Then I will take all the women I want. No one can stop me."

"You killed my Lord Kameal! You murderer, you killed him!" screamed Mathina as she ran straight at Ameral and began pounding him with her fists and screaming, "Killer! Killer!"

He put his hand on the top of her head and threw her back from him enough to strike her firmly.

She fell to the ground as Ameral signaled his men to attack.

Lori drew her disruptor and shot the nearest two men in their thighs.

They screamed and the onward rush slowed as the men looked at their comrades and stopped to pull them back to Ameral.

"I told you to attack." He picked up Mathina by her hair. "Give us your weapon and you can have the old woman back."

"I cannot give you my weapon it is against my directive. Let her go and I'll let you live."

"There are more of us than of you. Give me your weapon now." He forced Mathina to her knees facing them and drew his knife.

"Is this the same weapon you used to kill Jeames?" asked Lori.

"As a matter of fact, it is. I will kill you all with this same knife." He raised the knife and Lori shot him through the heart.

"Anyone else want to join him?"

The men retreated into a group discussion. They no longer had a leader.

His son Garth stepped forward. "It is my duty to arrest you for killing Lord Ameral, my father." His voice almost trembled, no doubt from seeing his father killed and the task which awaited him. "You deserve a horrible death for what you have done. No woman has ever killed a Lord. It is against our Law."

"How about all the deaths your father carried out on both men and women. He is the killer," yelled Corthain. "She carried out my order and protected the old women and us. You may join me or face similar judgment by the Rex, which I now am according to Lord Ameral."

"You have a valid point, Lord Corthain. I must tell you why my father felt you were flawed. He said, 'Corthain always thinks the best of everyone, even women. He is not the ruler this world needs.' Lord Ameral explained this to the Rex before he killed him. When the will of the Rex was read he found out you are to be the new Rex. It upset him and he raged for some time, He knew under the code of the Law he must inform you of this news. He was on his way to your village when he ran into your Uncle Cleese who sought him out to help you get two women out of the Tangle. He told Cleese he would help you and bring back the women if they were still alive. He told us you were not to return and whoever killed you would get a woman, even if he was not a Lord. My father was going to give me your women. Then he announces today he's awarding your women to my brother, who never even went into the tangle during the time you, Lord Corthain, was assigned to lead the committee. My father got my brother his crowns and you didn't even notice because you were in a rush to get back to your comforts and women. Look at my brother he's frail even with the use of a crown. He's weak and my father gives him the women. It was wrong. He has never treated his women or his sons with any kindness or love, except Pall. He only wanted power. I will not kill you for him. You are a worthy man, Lord Corthain. You have my loyalty. My father's women should be given to you or to the Lords you wish to whom you think will treat them well. My mother has suffered because she only gave him one son, me. She is due to be released into the Tangle, even though she can still bare children. Throwing her out is wrong. I ask you to take her into your household."

"That is a fine speech, Lord Garth; I will accept you as my son, if your mother comes to me. Now if all you other men lay down your weapons, we have things to do." Corthain watched and waited. Only Garth gave up his weapon and walked to Mathina. He picked her up and walked toward Lori.

Suddenly one of the men rushed him and grabbed Mathina. Garth held on to her while the man sought to take her from him.

"Stop!" yelled Lori, "or I will shoot."

The man backed off.

At this moment the walkers advanced humming loudly and vibrating the earth as they encircled the men. The men hacked at the walkers but the plants kept coming. Quickly each walker selected a man and each wrapped its fronds around a man. All the men collapsed onto the ground. The plants guarded them and waited.

"Thank you, Lord Garth, for your help in bringing Mathina to us." Lori took Mathina to the rock and gave her some water. "Stay here, mother. You must stay here."

"I will daughter. Is Lord Ameral dead?"

"Yes, he is."

"Good. I'm happy now." She got up and started dancing around the rock.

"Is she all right?" asked Corthain.

"Much better than she would be if he'd gotten to her." Lori looked around her.

Garth was not there. He had returned to his father's side. They watched as he took his father's head in his hands and wept. His half-brother joined him. They mourned together.

Corthain spoke to Lori. "I could honor Lord Ameral with a grand funeral, at least for his children's sake. Sadly I do not feel it is appropriate, since he has slain so many and brought disaster to many more. I will order him a private family funeral with the Lords present. Then I will hold a dinner for the Lords at my current home. I will have to move, Lori. Would you consider coming with me to my new settlement as my number one woman and advisor. I would like Gladriel as my official wife. You two can help me build a great country and life for my people. Will you come with me?"

"Thank you, Lord Corthain, for your gracious offer. A woman would be good to speak out for women's rights and give you good advice. I would like to work with you. However, I have a duty to my world and I must leave this planet. I leave not because of anything done against me or Glady. We both love and respect you. You will be a great Rex. I speak for both of us, "Thank you, for all you've done for us."

"I need some information from you, Corthain. How do you treat your dead?" asked Lori.

Before Corthain could answer the walkers began their humming again.

Lori spun around to see who or what was approaching. "Hi, Gladriel, are you finished?

"What happened here?" she asked Lori.

"We had a small skirmish, Glady. Blood was shed," Lori told her as she took her hand.

"Who are these men? Ameral's?"

"Yes, Lord Ameral's men and his body." Lori paused and asked, "The THRAX?"

"It's in a thousand or so pieces. It wasn't hard at all. Where is Mathina?"

She looked toward the rock and saw a crumpled figure. She ran to her. "I told her to stay by the rock." Lori ran to her and took vital signs. She was living but sleeping most soundly.

Glady ran to them, "I think she is exhausted and worn out? She has some bruising too. What happened to her?"

"Ameral and a couple of men caught her when she was down by the water playing with the colorful stones. Right in front of us a couple of the men slapped her and flung her about by her hair. He had everyone afraid of him. He wanted to kill Lord Corthain."

"I hope you killed him for abusing Mathina and planning to kill Corthain," she said and hurried to Corthain's side.

"Glady, Lord Corthain, is no longer a Lord. He is Rex of the villages. It is a great job and opportunity for him and his people."

"Dearest, Glady, will you be my first wife and come be with me? I've asked Lori to come as an advisor for the Rex. She will not be my wife. I ask you because I love you and would like to have you in my family."

"I appreciate your offer, Rex Corthain. I have an obligation to my Council. Once I am free from my contract, and if we are both living, I will be your wife."

"Thank you, Glady, I accept your answer and will wait for your return. I know it won't be soon. I will wait until someday."

Gladriel reached up with her hands and tilted his head down. Then she really kissed him and he fully and lovingly kissed her waiting lips.

"How are we going to get all these men back to the villages? It will be difficult explaining how they all died." Rex Corthain shook his head and realized they could not return them all for burial.

"Only Lord Ameral is dead. The others were put to sleep by the walkers. They are not dead. They will awaken in about four hours. Once we get our shuttle we can load them aboard and return you to a location not far from your home. Would this please you?" asked Lori?

"First, let's bury the doeg with all honors due a heroic stand. Mathina, will you bring doeg up here so we can bury it with honor?" asked Gladriel as she began digging a shallow grave for the small doeg.

When Mathina laid the little doeg down, it looked so lonesome. Mathina borrowed Lori's knife to cut off a coil of her braided hair and laid it across the little ball of fluff. Glady covered the doeg with the small blanket she'd used in fixing the THRAX. Lori buried a small piece of Corthain's crown she'd kept and Corthain spread fresh leaves over the small green ball. Then they all praised the doeg's life and his loyalty. Garth shoveled in the soil and put the shovel in as a head stone.

"Corthain what will you do with Mathina and the older women in the villages?" asked Glady.

"I've been thinking on this problem. It is against the Law as handed down to us generations ago. I will proclaim amnesty for the older women who no longer can bear children and set up a home for them. Mathina, I ask you to teach both boys and girls of the things they need to know to survive in the Tangle. I ask you to instruct both boys and girls of the power of the herbs and healing of patients. You will be an instructor, a teacher. Would you like this, little mother?

"Yes, my son, I will. I have daughters who can help me and in time they may teach the classes or my grandchildren may. Whoever comes will be taught."

"Corthain, the embroidery on your gown on our first night was made of the most intricate gold and silver threads with the bright green must have been Mathina's work too. She once worked as the official keeper of the wardrobe for you father. She was one of his wives."

"Mathina, is this your real name?" asked Corthain.

"No, my son, my name was Marilee."

"I remember when you were removed from Kameal's family. Her youngest grandson walked her part way. He was worried because no one waited for her outside our gate. He gave her food and water and she thanked him and kissed him goodbye. Then she walked into the Tangle. He was sick for three days and now he refuses to apply to be a Lord. I have long wondered what caused this in him."

"It is the Law, my son. I live by and accept the Law and I have lived in the Tangle since then. One day I found Lori and on another day you two. Now I have a family. What will happen now?"

"You will come to live with me and my family, until we can build you your own home. It will house all the older women who wish to live there and help the Village. You are welcome to my home and I will call you by the name you choose."

"I choose Mathina. I have been her since I left my Lord's house and set out for the Tangle. It has served me well. It has brought us together and I brought you two possible wives. Both are beautiful, loving and kind."

Garth ran up to Corthain and got down on the ground and extended his arm, palm side up, "I pledge my support to you, Lord Corthain, Rex."

"Thank you," Garth. "There will be much work to do to correct the sins of murder by your father. You will work with the families. Then you are to reimburse them for the harm done to their families. Your brother will no longer be a Lord, since he has not truly achieved this title. His women will be distributed to the other Lords and new Lords in the future. The men who traveled and caroused with Lord Ameral will stand trial and lose their women if they have any. There is much to be done. I can use your help, Garth."

Redford informed the women *The Flynn* would touch down in five minutes.

"All right, everyone. We need to pull the men to the left side and our bags over there too. Garth will you help Rex Corthain. Lori, Mathina and I will bring our supplies over there," explained Lori.

As they ran to the safe house Lori spoke with Glady. "Soon we will have an arrival. Glady, can get out a sedative to relax and disorient Lord Garth. He does not need to know about our shuttle."

"Sure thing," she yelled as she speeded up her pace. She opened the first aid kit. She loaded a syringe and grabbed the log. Lori and Mathina carried the three bags.

Lori reached him first. When Glady and Mathina returned to the landing sight they saw a sleeping Garth. "Maybe we should have left him awake to help us load the shuttle," said Glady.

"You load up our materials and Corthain and I will load up these men and their bags."

Soon everyone was on board and they took to the air.

When they landed a short distance from the village, Lori, Glady and Corthain unloaded the men and their items and confiscated all weapons.

"I have a request. May I see my world from up there? Is it possible? I think my world is much larger than I ever thought possible. I will need to know more about this world and its possibilities. I must change laws to help my people. I would like to know more."

"I don't see any reason we should not take you up, do you, Lori?" Glady asked and ignored Redford's voice in her ear. She ignored Redford's ranting and ravings about protocol.

The three boarded the shuttle. Corthain was shown his planet from the air and his saw all three of his villages. They flew across the expanse of ocean which separated the continent where his people lived for another large continent which lay to the south.

All the time they flew, Corthain did not speak. Only after they returned a short distance to where the unconscious men waited did he speak. "You judged me fairly, Lori. I was nothing. I was ignorant of life and its value. Ignorant too of the size of the land on which I live. I see my world in a different view. My people have much to do to live in harmony with nature. This new world will need a strong people who know how to work, and I mean both the men and women. They will have to work together. Women need help at home with the young children and working in the fields. They must not always be tending the fields and bearing children or serving their Lords. They have rights, feelings, hopes and dreams. I want to help make those dreams come true for all my people."

Gladriel walked over to Corthain and looked up into his eyes. "Corthain, I have thought about your offer to live with you. I love you so much it hurts however, I must leave with Lori. I really want to stay. I feel I need to learn more things before I settle down. I am truly glad we met."

"I am truly glad we met. Then why not spend the night with me in my home. I won't use a crown," he said teasingly

"You don't have a crown," Lori laughed.

"If I had one I would not use it against either of you. Soon I will have a crown again. I will need one to show the people.

While Lori and Corthain continued talking Gladriel returned to *The Flynn*. Set the coordinates and took off.

Lori was surprised to see Gladriel disappear. She tried both means of communication; Glady did not answer. Shortly she returned in the shuttle and sat it down. She came out carrying Corthain's wooden box chest.

"I promised you I would do this for you, Corthain," she said as she handed him the box.

"Would you share the evening and night with me, Glady? I would appreciate your company. You know I love you."

"I know you love me and this is all I need to know. You are now a Rex and should live honorably as such. Your wives deserve your love and attention. We had our time."

"Do you want to stay the evening with Corthain, Lori?" asked Glady.

"No, I don't, Glady. Rex Corthain, I thank you for all you've done for us. We'll remember you, and hope this adventure is enough for your life time."

Corthain smiled at Glady and set the bag aside. He turned to Lori put his arms around her and kissed her with a long lingering kiss. Then he released her and turned to Glady who reached up her hands to pull his face to her as she stood on tiptoes to kiss him. He hugged her tightly and picked her up.

His kiss was warm and tender and filled with desire. Openly she returned it and sought to make it linger and never end, eventually they let go and he set her down.

Corthain spread wide his arms and drew them close to him. He kissed them on their foreheads and said, "Go with the blessing of the Rex."

They moved away from him toward the shuttle. Before they sealed the door they turned for one last look. Corthain had moved to where Ameral's men still lay in sleep. Garth was stirring but not yet totally awake. Corthain looked at the ship and waved goodbye.

Lori sealed the vessel. "See, Glady, I told you it would be easy."

"If it had been any easier, we'd both be dead. I never imagined the danger."

"Neither did I. We're almost home." Lori said while checking the instruments. Swiftly they arrived at *The EmPolo*.

"Redford, does this planet have a name?" asked Lori.

"No, it doesn't, only a location. Why do you ask Lori?"

"I'd like to claim it for Gladriel and me. This will protect this world and keep it a bit insulated as it develops. I want to name it in honor of Mathina. She is a remarkable woman and in her choice to save me she changed a system which had outgrown its present form of governance into a more equal balanced world with the potential for freedom and equal rights. I will never forget her."

"I'll do that right away, Lori. That is a wonderful idea. You have a whole world of potential for yourselves as well."

"How so, Redford?" asked Gladriel.

"Since you own it others cannot claim it, nor legally mine it or develop it. This is a good move for the planet of Mathina. It also gives you the right to return when you want to return."

"Glad you like the idea, Redford. Say, are you drawing that soaking tub yet?"

"It is filling as we speak. Dinner is ready in twenty minutes. First you need to stop by the health booth. Then it's a shower and a relaxing soak in the tub."

They stopped to be checked out by the health booth. Accumulatively they had lost forty-five pounds. Lori lost twenty-five and Glady twenty. They both were fit, hearty and hungry.

They sat in the tub relaxed and reminisced for about ten minutes; it wasn't enough time before Redford sent in their dinner. They got up and wrapped their towels around them. This was living.

"You have lost a few unnecessary pounds, Glady. Have an extra dessert," said Lori as she handed Glady a bowl of fruit from cold storage. "I don't want you to suffer. So I have a dried food bar for you."

Gladriel laughed and caught it. "I hope I never have to eat these again."

"We really need to work on that recipe for the food bars. How do you think we did, Glady, in terms of meeting the assignment?"

"I believe every new cadet must complete a real assignment to win his or her bars. Ours was more difficult than it first seemed, still we learned and we became closer. Some may say our test was trivial and less dangerous than theirs. I have found it doesn't matter the degree of hardness. It does matter as to the qualities of each of the cadets. It's what they achieve and how they do it. At least we didn't get an abort the first time," said Gladriel, as she swallowed her last sip of tea.

"Besides, I think this was easy." Lori laughed.

"To easy indeed, we were lied to by Corthain, set down and deserted at the wrong coordinates on the wrong planet, attacked by alien creatures, ran out of provisions, I almost lost you to a blade of poisonous grass, I fell in love, I left love, we were seduced and faced death. What more do you want to make something difficult?"

"All right, it was difficult, but we're alive and we've learned. Oh, how we have learned? You discovered there is more to life than work and the Academy, I've discovered I care more about another person than myself and I do not want to hurt my friend in any way, and we watched someone be murdered all for the sake of greed and power."

"I made a most difficult choice," Gladriel said, staring into the empty tea cup. "I really wanted to stay with Corthain. I know in time I would become another woman to him. I would no longer be special. I could have given myself freely to him without the power of the crown initially. After all, I'm not sure if there are still some residual effects."

"Glady, you slept with him out of true love the last time for sure. He had gone through a cleansing and near death to get out from under its power. So he loves you as you love him. It was good for both of you."

"We are from different worlds however the agriculture was like our own. Sadly his world is not my world. Someday he may welcome people from the stars who will help him develop the planet as it prepares to become part of Glather."

"I don't know if they should be a part of Glather and all those politics. Advisors will only come if we request their help. Maybe it isn't Mathina's time to join Glather. They need unfettered time. Gladriel, you made the right decision. I cannot imagine you tending a Lord, not even Corthain. For the last few days, I wasn't sure if you would leave."

"On my world I learned never to get involved in a relationship. Love means marriage, home, fidelity to one person, and being a slave to a man for life. I chose to give it up when I was accepted into the Academy. Still, right now I ache for him."

"Sometimes we have to let go to understand what we have left behind," Lori said and added, "The price was high and too soon in your life."

"I think Corthain learned from us as much as we learned from him. He must wear his crown if he wishes to continue being a Lord. He need not wear it when he is with his wives. I hope he'll wear it with care for his people's sake. I would like to return someday and see what changed because of us. I would like to return to Mathina," said Gladriel. "Let's go back there someday. Promise?"

"I promise. We will go back someday. After all, we own the place technically."

Chapter 28

Lori smiled and took her last sip of tea. It was time to check in with Sheffield.

As if on cue, the console sounded its chime. Lori hurried over, "Lori here."

"Lori, we've taken care of things. Thanks for the report you had Gladriel bring with her. We arrested twelve more crew members. Soon Lt. Colonel Jord will get his team to work and we'll have most of the others apprehended within two weeks. Good work, Lori. Say, what made you have your ship's computer check all those files? You didn't even tell me you were doing this."

"I thought it might save time and bigger problems. I had Fergus take Corporal Brighton to the brig. Someone also took the two stunned young men to the brig too. They all had weapons set on kill. They were planning a rather a chilling future for me."

"Fergus told me this. He also found evidence in Captain Kidwell's quarters and plenty of proof as to their sabotage and mutiny."

"I'll be with you within the hour. Glady's heading back and Fergus will leave with us in the morning. I love you."

"I love you too. See you soon."

Lori changed into a gown of teal lingerie and lay down on the bed waiting for the man she loved. She was not disappointed. He was there within ten minutes.

"Who is this divine creature I find on my bed?" His face was flushed from hurrying to be with her and he was feeling as if he was finally on leave.

"You'll have to make me talk or you'll never know."

"Do we really need to talk?"

"Someday we might, not tonight, unless you want to tell me about it."

He began taking off his clothes. He started with his jacket, and then his shoes and socks. He walked over to the bed. "I need a little help here, if you don't mind, lady in blue."

"Oh, I can never be blue when I'm with you," she said as she stood up and slowly unbuttoned his shirt while she fought the urge to rip it off his body. "I need to note your physical condition."

"Hurry up with those buttons."

"Impatient aren't we?" She continued to take her time. Then she unbuckled his pants and unfastened his zipper. She could feel the heat of his lower body on her hands as she slowly pulled his slacks down and looked down at him with her deep blue eyes.

He pulled her up to him. "I've wanted to be with you all evening. Now it is past the witching hour and I want you even more." He pulled her to him and kissed her. His lips began to caress her neck and shoulders as his hands slid under the gowns straps and shoved them off her shoulder and down her arm. The gown slipped further down exposing her full breasts. His hands cupped them from the outside and his thumbs pressed the nipples against his opposing fingers. Her nipples hardened and so did he. He bent over her as he pulled her breast to meet his lips and teeth, and then he nibbled gently and firmly. She quivered. He continued. He didn't stop licking and sucking the fullness of her. Then he went to the other side and did the same. She meantime was kissing and sucking his neck and shoulders while her hands careened down his back and slid to the front as she sought his hardness. She slowly caressed him. He leaned her back over the bed and lowered her onto the bed. She tugged him to follow her and he did. She regained her hold and stroked him propelling him toward full contact. He pulled her hand away and kissed her until she arched toward him for the next kiss and then he sought her breasts once more. Now he had even more control and drew in as much as he could and nibbled. She almost screamed when his mouth left her breast and his hand sought her lower regions. She reached for his erection as he lay to one side and slowly circled it with her fingers. Then she encircled it with her hand and led him to the entrance of her joy and they went to the next level. They made love for most of the night.

At 06:00 the console began to chime. Lori got up.

"Is this Colonel Lori?"

"Yes, Redford, this is Colonel Lori. How may I help you?"

"You can get over to your ship. We're ready to leave in one hour."

"We're in bed. It was a long night. We haven't eaten or anything. Give us two hours and we'll be over."

"Impossible. We are ready to go once you get here. Make it within the hour. We have schedules to keep, things to do."

"Redford, it is Sheffield and my union we are going to. So take it easy. You fix us a grand breakfast and we'll be over within the hour. Okay?"

Lori went back to the bed and nuzzled Sheffield's neck. "We need to get up and go to our ship. They are ready to leave within the hour. Breakfast will be ready for us when we arrive."

"Then we'd better get back to what we started last night." He kissed her and ran his hand down the contour of her body.

She knew the only way she'd get him up was to get him moving. She jumped out of bed and sprinted into the shower.

"Wait for me. I'll be right there," he yelled as he bolted for the shower.